He squinted at the newspaper ad in his hand, then at Maggie Tyrell again.

"I'm still settling in, as you can see," she said brightly. "But I'm open and ready for business. Please have a seat...." She belatedly realized that the only chair in the room was the one jammed in behind her desk.

A good detective knew better than to act like a ninny in front of her clients. Maggie darted down the hall to grab a folding metal chair from her brother's office. She wished her very first client had seen her dressed appropriately, wished her office had a window, wished her client had been a seventy-eight-year-old war veteran. But none of these things were true.

Noah Davis was just about the sexiest-looking man she'd ever seen, and now she was going to have to persuade him that, regardless of his first impression of her, Finders, Keepers could provide exactly the service he needed.

"I'm searching for a woman," he said as he straddled the chair. He looked at Maggie. Looked hard. Looked at her as if *she* were the woman he was searching for.

And so she was. She was the woman who could find *the* woman. "Let's begin," she said.

Dear Reader,

The one that got away.

So many of us have such a person in our pasts: the first crush, the first love, the boy we dreamed about in high school, the woman who wasn't ready to settle down. Most of us move on, find new loves and build happy lives for ourselves. But a tiny voice inside us may occasionally whisper, *I wonder where he is now. I wonder what she's doing. I wonder if that old flame still smolders, just a little.*

The novelist's job is to ask, What if? When I sat down to write this book, I posed some questions—what if someone created a detective agency devoted exclusively to finding "the one that got away"? What if a private investigator who believed in true love and happy endings decided to make it her job to bring separated sweethearts back together again? Maggie Tyrell appeared before me—smart, stubborn and oh, so romantic—willing to dedicate herself to finding lost lovers. She named her agency Finders, Keepers.

Found: One Wife describes her very first case, in which businessman Noah Davis hires her to track down his missing fiancée. Along the way he discovers that what we think we're looking for may not be what we hope to find, and that sometimes the opposite of losing isn't finding; it's winning.

Judith Arnold

FOUND:
ONE WIFE
Judith Arnold

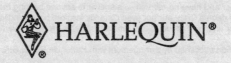

TORONTO • NEW YORK • LONDON
AMSTERDAM • PARIS • SYDNEY • HAMBURG
STOCKHOLM • ATHENS • TOKYO • MILAN • MADRID
PRAGUE • WARSAW • BUDAPEST • AUCKLAND

ISBN 0-373-70809-2

FOUND: ONE WIFE

Printed in U.S.A.

For Carolyn,
who will always be with me

PROLOGUE

BY THE THIRD DAY, Noah knew she wasn't coming.

He sat at his table—*their* table—near the corner window of Romeo's. If he were occupying the other chair, he would be able to glimpse a narrow sliver of San Francisco Bay between the taller buildings flanking Grant Avenue. But he took the seat facing the door, just in case.

Just in case what? Just in case Sisela decided to show up seventy-two hours late?

She had promised to come, as he had. One year after they'd bidden each other farewell—one too-long, too-short, too-surprising year during which they'd gone their own separate ways, chased their own dreams, wrung from their lives the last of drops of selfish solitude—they had promised each other that they would meet at Romeo's. Exactly three hundred and sixty-five days after they'd parted. At exactly five o'clock in the afternoon. At *their* table.

That was the promise.

Noah had kept it. Sisela had not.

The café was atmospherically dark and intimate. Noah and Sisela used to meet at the corner table after work several times a week. Sisela would usually be waiting for him. He would stroll the few blocks to Romeo's from his office on Montgomery Street, and there she would be at the corner table, blond and willowy, the dusk light filtering through the window and playing over her delicate features. She would turn toward the door the instant he stepped inside, as if she were tuned in to a secret radar that alerted her to his arrival. A cool smile would whisper across her lips, and Noah would be momentarily stunned by her austere beauty. He would weave among the tables to reach her and kiss her cheek, and by the time he was seated, Maurice would be bringing their regular order—espresso with a curl of lemon rind for him, frothy cappuccino dusted with unsweetened cocoa for her.

Noah glanced down at the empty demitasse cup, the forlorn sliver of rind perched on the saucer, the newspaper unfolded next to it. He'd brought the paper so he would have something to do while he waited. He'd known, without having to think about it, that he would be waiting for a long time.

Maurice approached the table. Dark-eyed and solicitous, he had served Noah and Sisela at their table for the past two years. He'd been a hovering presence as they'd caught up on their days, as they'd exchanged simmering gazes, as Noah had lifted his hand from his cup to Sisela's wrist, tracing her skin with his fingertips. When they'd decided to get married, Maurice had been the first person they'd told, because he'd been there the moment Sisela had said yes.

He'd witnessed their joy, and today, one year later, he was present to witness Noah's dawning comprehension that Sisela wasn't going to be his wife, after all. If she'd intended to marry him, she would have come to Romeo's. If she hadn't been able to come, she would have let him know, somehow.

But she hadn't come, hadn't let him know, hadn't contacted him in any way. The private school where she'd taught music had no idea where she was. Her landlord hadn't heard from her since her lease expired, months ago.

She was gone.

"Would you like a refill?" Maurice asked gently, motioning toward the empty cup.

"No, thanks." Noah managed a grim smile for the waiter. "Do you need the table?" Romeo's started filling up with diners at about 6:00 p.m., but at five-thirty, half the tables were still empty.

"No rush. You can linger as long as you'd like."

"She's not coming," Noah said, mostly because he had to hear the words. As strongly as he felt them in his heart, he had to hear them spoken aloud before they became real.

"Don't give up," Maurice urged him. "Maybe she got detained somewhere. Maybe she's on her way—"

His smile expanding, Noah shook his head. He appreciated Maurice's kind concern, but false hope wasn't going to do him any good. The irony was, he didn't exactly feel despair at Sisela's failure to meet him. Curiosity, yes. Disappointment flavored with resentment. And a strange, gnawing bewilderment that the woman with whom he'd chosen to spend the rest of his life—the woman to whom he'd been planning to give the diamond ring he'd tucked into his pocket every day for the past three days—could disappear without so much as a goodbye.

"On second thought, I think I will have another espresso," he said quietly. Maurice seemed pleased.

Apparently he wanted to do something for Noah, to make things better for him.

Noah didn't want Maurice to fuss. He felt restless, a touch anxious, a bit irritated. Not heartbroken, but more than a little concerned that something might have happened to Sisela. Something—the possibility sent a chill down his spine—bad.

To distract himself, Noah flipped open the paper. He had already read most of it, but he skimmed the editorials again, and the business section. Having resumed his career in solar-power architectural design, he needed to stay informed on the health of the construction industry. But the business pages didn't grab him. Nor did the sports section. After the past year, he no longer cared about the contracts of millionaire quarterbacks and relief pitchers, the strategies of coaches and the standings of teams. His time abroad had altered his perspective on a lot of things—not just sports, but business, and priorities, and marriage.

Maurice returned to the table with a fresh cup of espresso. "On the house," he said.

"Thanks, but I'd rather pay." Noah didn't want or need sympathy. He was tempted to hold up a sign reading, She's Gone and I'm Okay about It. He knew Maurice only meant well, though, so he smiled, accepted the cup, and returned his gaze to the newspaper.

A small, boxed ad tucked into the bottom corner of the back page caught his eye.

Finders, Keepers
Private Investigations
Lost Lovers Found

A Van Ness Avenue address and a phone number followed.

Noah's first reaction was a laugh. His second was a snort.

He sipped his espresso and contemplated his third reaction.

Sisela wasn't really his lost love. If she'd ever loved him, she would have met him at the appointed hour. Or she would have gotten word to him, somehow. She would have sent a message to Maurice.

Unless something had gone terribly wrong.

Lost Lovers Found. He drained his cup, let the supercharged caffeine sting his nerves and reread the print in the tiny box at the bottom of the page. *"Lost Lovers Found."*

It was stupid, the idea of hiring a private investigator to track Sisela down.

But he was curious. And worried. If he could be adventurous enough a year ago to leave San Francisco to discover the world and himself, he could be adventurous enough today to visit a private investigator who specialized in finding lost lovers.

CHAPTER ONE

IF THE OFFICE WERE ANY smaller, Maggie could have worn it as a dress.

Calling it an "office" was too generous, actually. It was a storage closet—part of the suite her brothers leased for Tyrell Investigative Services—and Maggie considered the fact that both she and her desk could occupy the tiny room at the same time nothing short of a miracle. She and the desk might fit into the cramped space more easily if she lost ten pounds. But she'd been trying to lose those ten pounds since she'd gained them in a final flourish of puberty when she was fifteen, and a decade later they were still with her, a built-in seat cushion clinging loyally to her rear end.

Even if she never managed to lose weight, she might not mind her figure so much if her office had about five hundred more square feet of floor space, a window, and a nook for an easy chair and a reading lamp. However, commercial rentals in downtown San Francisco were outrageously expensive. She ought to count her blessings that her brothers had offered her the closet for free.

One year. That was the deal. She had one year to make Finders, Keepers a going proposition. If she couldn't at least break even by then, her brothers were going to evict her from the closet, and then she would have to resume her employment in the family firm, yawning her way through the tedious chores that fell to her as office manager of Tyrell Investigative Services: processing contracts, billing clients, reordering supplies and keeping the coffeepot full. She had one year to prove to her brothers not only that she could handle investigations herself, but that investigations could be put in the service of happy endings.

"You're gonna crash, sweetie," Jack commented.

She turned—not an easy thing to do, since she was standing on the only corner of her desk not occupied by computer and phone equipment and boxes of supplies, and she was cradling a heavy carton of printer paper in her hands. Her oldest brother observed her from the doorway, his arms folded across his chest and his handsome mouth spread in a smirk.

"I'm perfectly balanced," she argued, praying that the swirls of dust drifting down from the built-in shelves behind her wouldn't make her sneeze. One violent sneeze and her balance would become imperfect really fast.

"I meant, this whole thing is going to crash—this enterprise of yours. It's stupid, Maggie."

"Thanks for the vote of confidence." Turning from him, she hoisted the box onto a shelf. She was used to not being taken seriously by her brothers. It had never mattered to Jack, Sandy and Neil that their little sister could throw like a boy, that she could climb trees and drive a five-speed, that she wasn't afraid of spiders or dark alleys or thugs built like NFL linebackers—that in truth she wasn't afraid of anything, not even of starting a new business in a storage closet.

Her brothers loved her and they doted on her. But they didn't have much faith in her.

"Could you pass me that box of pens?" she asked, offering Jack a phony smile as she gestured toward a carton of fine-point markers.

Jack edged into the room, careful not to smack his knee against the corner of the desk, and lifted the box of pens up to her. "I don't know why you're laying in all these supplies, Maggie. You can walk down the hall and borrow a pen from us if you need one."

"Yeah, sure." She took the pens and turned from him. "Then, when I show my first million in profit, you guys are all going to say I couldn't have done it without your pens. No, thanks."

"You couldn't do it without our largesse on the rent," Jack reminded her. "You can't even do it *with* our largesse."

"Why don't you go lie down on the cable-car tracks?" Maggie suggested sweetly. "Maybe you'll get run over. Better yet, just stand exactly where you are. You'll get run over by the hordes of clients stampeding in to hire me."

"What hordes?"

"I ran my first newspaper ad. Sentimental lovers are going to be lining up any minute now, begging me to find their old flames."

"Sentimental crackpots and lunatics, probably." Jack extended his hand to help her down from the desk.

Alighting, she wiped her dusty hands on the seat of her denim overalls and shoved back the stray curls that had flopped onto her forehead. If San Francisco were more humid in June, her hair would be frizzing like a fright wig. As it was, she looked like a poodle in desperate need of grooming. The barrettes she'd used to hold her mop back from her face were literally losing their grip. One of these days she was going to hack her hair off.

Right after she lost ten pounds.

"Tyrell Investigative has been serving crackpots and lunatics for thirty years," she reminded Jack. "Crackpots and lunatics put all four of us through college. It's thanks to crackpots and lunatics that Mom and Dad are enjoying retirement in Hilo. The only difference between your crackpots and lunatics and mine is that yours are looking for scandal and sleaze and mine are going to be looking for love."

"They're all looking for love, Maggie." Jack wiped her chin with his thumb; she must have had a smudge of grime there. "Our clients are just a bit more realistic than yours."

"A bit more vindictive, you mean."

"And that's assuming you'll even have clients. Listen, Maggie, I don't want you climbing on the desk unless one of us is around to catch you when you fall."

"*When* I fall? I keep telling you, Jack, I'm not going to fall." Edging past him—not an easy feat in the cramped space—she headed out the door and down the short hall to the suite of offices where her brothers ran the family business.

Jack was right: She could always take a quick detour down the hall if she needed supplies. But just on principle, she wanted her own supplies. She wanted to prove to her brothers that she could make Finders, Keepers fly.

Or at least not crash.

"We're out of coffee, Maggie," Sandy hollered from his post behind his favorite computer. The offices that housed Tyrell Investigative were well equipped with high-tech hardware; nowadays, a great deal of investigative work was done seated in front of a computer monitor, culling data banks in search of credit reports, employment records and auto registrations. The information a detective with a mastery of the cyber-universe could reap was daunting.

Sandy, the middle Tyrell brother, was the agency cyber-wizard. Neil, the youngest brother, was the gregarious Tyrell, responsible for working one-on-one with clients. As the eldest, Jack was the boss man, happy to give orders, oversee budgets and hand out praise or admonishment.

Until yesterday, Maggie had worked for all three. She'd majored in art history in college, but there were only so many museum jobs in the Bay Area, and the year she graduated, no one had been hiring. It didn't bother her much; she'd more or less assumed from an early age that she would eventually join the family firm.

Maggie would have liked Finders, Keepers to be a part of the family firm. She had originally envisioned it as a satellite, orbiting the larger Tyrell Investigative. "There was an article this morning in the *Chronicle*," she'd explained to her brothers over lunch a few months ago, when she'd first explored the idea with them. "A seventy-eight-year-old widower from Daly City got to thinking about the woman he'd fallen in love with in London, England, when he was stationed there in World War II. It took him five years to track her down, but he finally found her. She was widowed, too. He flew to London, they fell in love all over again and got married.'' Maggie had wept as she'd read the story—and after drying her eyes, she'd wondered whether the war veteran and his London love might have found each other years sooner with the help of a skilled detective. Someone like her, she'd thought—a detective with a romantic streak as wide and as deep as the ocean.

Her brothers had responded with skepticism to her concept of an adjunct agency dedicated to locating lost lovers. ''How often do we get a client who wants to find his old prom date?'' Neil had scoffed. ''Once in a decade? I think we can handle that without wiring in a separate phone line.''

''We get a lot more clients looking to dig up dirt on their old prom dates,'' Jack had said. ''All those folks who married their prom dates and lived to regret it.'' Tyrell Investigative did a lot of work for divorce attorneys.

''If you start doing this lost-lovers stuff, who's going to make the coffee?'' Sandy had asked.

Well, Maggie wasn't going to make the coffee anymore. She was twenty-five, and she'd been doing scut work for her brothers for three years. Now she wanted to do something for herself. Something romantic. Something that might lead not to a more favorable divorce settlement or a stronger criminal indictment or a more reliable security clearance, but to true, lasting love.

She lifted the framed poster she'd brought from her apartment—an enlarged photograph of Rudolf Nureyev and Margot Fonteyn dancing a pas de deux from

Swan Lake—and lugged it down the hall to her minuscule cubicle. Jack flattened himself against the wall so she could pass, then retreated toward his own office, shouting over his shoulder, "I'm going to the deli to pick up some sandwiches. You want anything?"

"No, thanks." Her hunger to set up her office was greater than her hunger for food. And once the poster was in place on the wall facing her desk, the office would be pretty well set up. Then she could sit at her desk, stare at the graceful, passionate clinch of the dancers and wait for the hordes to begin their stampede.

She eased the picture onto the nail in the wall that used to hold a small mirror. Stepping back, she assessed the poster, decided it was too low and grabbed one of the loose nails she'd swept from a corner of the office. She doubted her brothers had a hammer handy, but her weighted metal stapler might work.

She positioned the nail half a foot above the mirror nail and whacked it with the stapler. Her fingers stung from the impact, and she cursed under her breath.

Jack was watching her—she knew it without having to turn. She felt his presence filling the doorway. She could almost hear him cackling with snide amusement.

"Go away," she snapped without looking toward the door. She didn't want her big brother snickering at her while she tried to hammer a nail with a stapler. Slamming the stapler against the nail a second time, she drove the nail into the plaster perfectly. "Just back off, Jack, okay?" she said as she hung the poster.

''I'm not Jack.'' The voice was low, shimmering with laughter.

She flinched and turned with difficulty. When she saw the man standing in her doorway, she flinched again.

She had never before seen eyes like his. They were blue—not the color of the sky, not the color of the bay, but a shade in between—a light turquoise, intense and electrifying and outlandishly beautiful.

''And that's not a hammer,'' he added, gesturing toward the stapler.

His hair was black, his smile enigmatic, his body lean and lanky in a gray suit that looked too stylish to have come off a rack. He had dimples and a sharply carved jaw, a nondescript nose, and…oh, those eyes.

She must have been gaping at him, because he held up his hand. Pinched between his index and middle fingers was a small, rectangular piece of paper. Maggie recognized it as her Finders, Keepers ad, neatly clipped from the newspaper.

A client! The stampede had begun.

Why had she thought her clients would all be bald, stoop-shouldered World War II veterans searching for the girl they'd smooched with during the Blitz? Why hadn't it occurred to her that her clients were as likely to be gorgeous young men?

Because, she answered herself silently, any man who looked like this guy wasn't likely to lose his lover. How could a woman run away from a man like him?

Maggie allowed that there were several possibilities: He could be incredibly obnoxious, or perhaps he

smelled bad. Or he could be pathologically dangerous.

Detectives were used to pathologically dangerous
people. Even the office managers of detective agencies were used to them. In the three years she'd
worked for Tyrell Investigative, Maggie had exchanged pleasantries with and served coffee to sub-
stance abusers, reckless drivers and convicts hoping
to gather enough evidence to clear their names. She'd
directed cross-dressers to the men's room, the ladies'
room and sometimes both. Nothing frightened her.

Except, maybe, eyes as seductive as this man's.

He was still standing in her doorway, kind enough
not to comment on her pitiful office. Pretending she
hadn't noticed that he was just about the sexiest-
looking man she'd ever seen—screen idols and rock
stars included—she smiled. "I'm Maggie Tyrell. If
you're looking for Finders, Keepers, you've come to
the right place."

He circled the puny room with his gaze, his smile
growing dubious. He squinted at the newspaper ad in
his hand, then back at Maggie.

She couldn't just stand there ogling him. "I'm still
settling in, as you can see," she said brightly. "But
I'm open and ready for business. Please have a
seat...." She belatedly realized the only chair in the
room was the one jammed in behind her desk. "Uh,
just let me get you something to sit on," she
amended.

"There's no space for an extra chair," the man
replied.

She surveyed her office as if she didn't already
know how tiny it was.

"I can stand," he volunteered.

No, he couldn't—not if she was sitting.

"I'd suggest that we use one of the desks out there—" she gestured toward her brothers' offices "—except that I'm not really part of Tyrell Investigative Services. But don't worry, it's not a problem. I can fit a chair in here. Just sit tight. I mean, stand tight." She flashed him another smile, then struggled to squeeze past him without brushing against him.

The two seconds it took her to get around him convinced her that he hadn't lost his lover because he smelled bad. He smelled like mint—velvet-green leaves freshly pinched from their stems. It was an absurd thing to notice, but she couldn't help herself. A good detective learned to pick up on all the details, no matter how trivial.

A good detective also knew better than to act like a ninny in front of her clients, Maggie reminded herself as she darted down the hall to grab a folding metal chair from Neil's office. She wished she were dressed appropriately, wished her office had a window, wished her very first client hadn't seen her grungy and flustered and hauling furniture. She wished her very first client had been a seventy-eight-year-old war veteran.

But none of those wishes was going to come true. Which meant she was going to have to persuade the client that, regardless of his ghastly first impression of her, Finders, Keepers could provide exactly the service he needed.

As she neared the "closet" at the end of the hall, he lifted the chair out of her hands. She didn't have a chance to stop him. He deftly opened the chair and

wedged it into place under the ballet poster. He had
to swing his leg over the metal seat as if he were
mounting a horse.

Maggie suppressed the urge to apologize. Acting
humble wouldn't convince him that she was the detective he needed. From here on in, despite her overalls and her disheveled hair, despite her inferior work-
space, she was going to present herself as a
consummate professional.

"Now," she said, projecting what she hoped he
would interpret as abundant self-assurance, "what can
I do for you, Mr....?"

He ought to have looked uncomfortable straddling
the chair, but he appeared remarkably at home. His
suit flattered his physique, and his tie was loosened
at his collar but still neat. He ought to wear blue
shirts, she thought, studying the rust-hued cotton of
the one he had on. Blue would heighten the color of
his eyes.

On second thought, his eyes were quite blue
enough without help from his apparel.

"Davis," he introduced himself. "Noah Davis. I'm
looking for a woman." He looked at Maggie. Looked
hard. Looked at her as if she were the woman he was
looking for.

And so she was. She was the woman who could
find *the* woman. "Why don't you tell me about her,
Mr. Davis?"

"Her name is Sisela Hansen," he said. Maggie noticed the taut angles of his knees shaping the wool of
his trousers. Then she noticed his thighs. Wisely, she
lifted her gaze to his chin. "Sisela is my fiancée. Or
she *was*. I guess she's not anymore. She disappeared

before I could give her this." He pulled from his pocket a delicate ring set with a diamond solitaire as dazzling as his eyes.

Maggie avoided looking directly at the ring. "Have you reported her disappearance to the authorities?" she asked, both disappointed and relieved. Relieved that she wouldn't have to endure the torture of reconnecting this gorgeous specimen of masculinity with his beloved fiancée, but disappointed that her first client wasn't going to be a client, after all. Missing persons were a matter for the police to handle.

"It's not like that," he said, then smiled. He didn't seem particularly alarmed by his fiancée's disappearance. "Sisela and I went our separate ways a year ago. It was a pact we made. We each had a dream we wanted to fulfill before we settled down. She wanted to see if she could make it as a pop singer. She thought one year would be enough to succeed or fail."

"A pop singer." Maggie pulled a lined pad from the center drawer of her desk—not an easy thing to do, given that she had no room to inch the drawer open—and started taking notes. She wrote down "Noah Davis, Sisela Hansen," and "pop singer." After ruminating for a moment, she added "ring." "What exactly did she do in pursuit of this dream?"

"I don't know," he replied. "I was pursuing a dream of my own."

Maggie almost didn't want to hear his dream. It might be too intimate. Or too mundane. What if he told her his dream had been to build a kit car? Or to write a novel? Or to set a record for sexual conquests before he had to pledge fidelity to one woman?

"I wanted to travel around the world," he said. "Sisela had done a lot of traveling as a child—her father lives in Denmark and her mother lives in Saint Martin. She has no interest in traveling. So I thought I'd take the year and travel while she tried to break into the music business."

Traveling around the world wasn't mundane. It was adventurous and romantic.

Maggie cleared her throat and poised her pen above the pad. "So you and—" she glanced at her notes "—Sisela Hansen became engaged, and then...?"

"It wasn't a formal engagement," he corrected her. "We agreed that we would get married after the year was up, but it wasn't as if we'd made an announcement."

"Okay. So you agreed to get married, and then you went off and traveled around the world?"

"Actually, no. I only got as far as India. I wound up spending the rest of the year there. It doesn't matter," he said, dismissing her questioning glance. "What matters is, we had agreed that at the end of our year apart we would meet at Romeo's, in North Beach. I don't know if you know it—"

Maggie nodded. She'd walked past the café a few times. She'd never gone in, though. It seemed like the kind of place patronized by couples.

"We promised to meet there exactly one year after we parted, at five in the evening. We both knew the time and date." His gaze was so intense, Maggie felt as if it were burning her skin. If she ever saw this man again, she would have to wear sunblock. "I was there at the appointed time. She wasn't."

Maggie scribbled "Romeo's, one year—stood up" on her pad, then lifted her gaze to him again.

"I went back the next day, and the day after that," he said. "Just in case she'd gotten confused about the date. She isn't the sort of person to get confused about that sort of thing, though. But I went back anyway. She never came."

"Did she call or write to you during the year you were apart?"

He shook his head. "That was part of the deal—that we wouldn't be in touch for the entire year. It was to be our last year of freedom. Our last year of complete independence."

Maggie stared at her notepad and mulled over what he'd told her. His story was odd, to say the least. If he'd truly loved Sisela—loved her enough to want to marry her—why would he want a year of independence from her?

"Well," Maggie said, smiling to soften her words, "I'm sure it's occurred to you that she might have changed her mind about the marriage."

"I'm hoping that's the case," he said, then explained, "That would be better than the alternative."

"Which is...?"

"That something bad happened to her."

Maggie nodded solemnly. "That isn't too likely, Mr. Davis. If something bad had happened to her, I'm sure you would have heard about it. Family or mutual friends would have gotten word to you or you would have found out when you got home."

"You're right." He appeared mollified.

"It's possible that she forgot, that she got mixed up—or delayed or detained," Maggie suggested.

"Maybe she lost track of the time." That seemed like a frivolous excuse for breaking such an important date, but Maggie wouldn't be surprised if that was the case. Her brother Sandy was a terrific fellow, but he was forever deleting dates and appointments from his memory. It drove his wife crazy. Karen often telephoned the office to ask Maggie to remind him about a doctor's appointment or a dinner engagement. "Tell him it's my mother's birthday and we're taking her to the Top of the Mark," Karen would say. "Remind him to pick up the silver candy dish we're having engraved for her at Gump's. Tell him to be there at six o'clock. Tell him if he forgets, I'll slit his throat."

"I'll tell him," Maggie would promise. And she would tell him, and he would stare at her blankly, as if she were speaking a foreign tongue. He would swear this was the first he'd heard of his mother-in-law's birthday and an engraved dish at Gump's, but sure, if Karen wanted him to, he would meet her and his in-laws at the Top of the Mark. So far, Karen hadn't slit his throat.

"Sisela wasn't the sort to let anything this important slip her mind," Noah Davis said.

Of course not. No sane woman would let a man like him slip her mind. "I'm sure I can find her," Maggie said with a touch more conviction than she felt. "I'll need some background information on her—last known address, last employer and so on. A photo of her if you have one."

He reached into an inner pocket of his blazer, pulled out a photo and passed it across the desk to Maggie. If anyone deserved a man of Noah Davis's heart-stopping handsomeness, it would have to be Sisela Hansen. She was blond, with pale, long-lashed eyes, the cheekbones of a *Vogue* cover girl, and a mouth so perfectly formed the world's classiest lipstick makers couldn't hope to improve on it. Of course this woman could be found. All Maggie had to do was search for a swarm of drooling, sighing men, and Sisela Hansen was sure to be at its center.

"I can find her," Maggie said.

"Fine."

"Before I write up a contract, we should discuss my rates." Cripes. Maggie hadn't even gotten her computer up and running, let alone worked out her fee schedule. She decided the rates her brothers charged would have to do. "I charge five hundred dollars a day, plus expenses," she said.

The change in Noah Davis's expression was subtle, but its meaning was clear: He was not going to pay her five hundred dollars a day.

She needed his business, though—not just to earn money, but to validate Finders, Keepers. She couldn't let him walk out the door without contracting for her services. "However," she said, as if she'd been planning to say this all along, "because you're my very first client, I'd like to give you a discount."

"How much?" he asked tersely.

"Three hundred."

"A three-hundred-dollar discount?" he asked. "I think we can work with that."

Damn. That meant she was going to get only two hundred a day. "Plus expenses," she reminded him.

"Reasonable expenses, subject to my approval."

Double damn. Where were the sweet, romance-addled World War II veterans she'd been hoping for?

She should have guessed from Noah Davis's fancy
suit that he was no fool. Probably he was a hard-
headed executive at a high-powered corporation, used
to negotiating multimillion-dollar deals.

And come to think of it, he didn't exactly seem
torn in two about his missing fiancée. If he were that
devastated by her vanishing act, would he have dick-
ered with Maggie over her fee with such cool equanimity?

All right. Whatever his mood and his motive, she
could take him on. Two hundred dollars a day was
better than nothing. She'd find his gorgeous sweetheart, collect her earnings and gain enough experience
to be able to raise her fee for the next client who
stampeded through the closet door.

She only hoped that client wouldn't have blue eyes
like Noah Davis's.

CHAPTER TWO

IT HADN'T BEEN WHAT he'd expected. But then, Noah wasn't quite sure what he'd expected.

A real office with real chairs, for starters. A secretary, a waiting room, a sofa within reach of a table piled high with month-old magazines, a reception desk, a phone console with flashing buttons. And beyond the frosted glass that separated the waiting room from the office—a detective. Someone poised, prepared and professional.

But if he'd learned nothing else in the past year, he'd learned to forget about expectations, to be open to chance, to take risks, to explore possibilities. When he thought about Maggie Tyrell and her hole-in-the-wall operation, he had to admit he saw possibilities. He saw a chance.

He definitely saw risks.

At least he'd limited his financial risk by bargaining her price down by sixty percent. But two hundred dollars a day was still significantly more than pocket change, and as he strolled down Van Ness to California, where he would catch the bus back to his office, he couldn't help wondering whether locating Sisela was really worth that much money.

Entertaining such a doubt was unforgivable. He'd

made a commitment to Sisela. He'd planned to marry her.

Yet he couldn't deny the truth—that he'd signed a one-week, subject-to-renewal contract with Maggie Tyrell not because he was looking for Sisela but because he was looking for...adventure.

This lust for adventure was a relatively new thing for him. He'd grown up cautious, impoverished and humble, and always fearful of making his mother's life more difficult than it already had been. They'd lived on the outskirts of a dust-caked village in the north-central Valley. His mother had worked odd jobs: operating the cash register at the convenience store, delivering newspapers before dawn, letting out the seams and raising the hems of hand-me-down dresses for short, chubby girls. Noah's father had been, as his mother used to say with forced dignity, "itinerant." The old man had roamed the West Coast looking for work, every now and then doing Noah's mother the enormous favor of sending her a little money.

Noah had kept his head down and his nose clean. He'd studied, he'd finished his chores before his mother had had to ask him to and he'd earned a full scholarship to the University of California. From there he'd gone to Stanford for a business degree and then to his current position as a marketing executive with a solar-power products company in San Francisco.

But about two years ago, he'd heard a frightened, frightening whisper inside him: *Take a chance.*

At the time, he was going to work each morning, to his pleasant office in a pleasant building, where he would hustle marvelously lucrative contracts for his company with developers whom he'd convinced to incorporate solar panels into their new construction. After work he'd go to Romeo's, where he would see Sisela and be dazzled by her cool Nordic beauty. He would drink espresso and then have dinner with her. Afterward they would make love, and that, too, would be pleasant.

But the whisper inside him had kept growing louder: *Take a chance. Have an adventure. Stick your neck out. Do something impulsive and illogical.*

The first illogical, impulsive thing he'd done in his entire life was to request a year's sabbatical from his job so he could travel around the world. The second illogical, impulsive thing was to take his round-the-world journey alone after Sisela had told him she didn't want to go with him. The third was to arrive in a small hillside village near Midnapore, less than two hours from Calcutta, during a wicked monsoon. He'd been there when houses flooded, roads washed away, the clinic's roof caved in and the village school was destroyed.

Do something compassionate, the whisper had urged him. *Take a chance. Do something humane.*

Nine months later, the village had a new school building and a new clinic, and Noah had new muscles, new calluses and new friends. Living in Halore had not been his plan, but listening to that whisper, obeying it and opening himself to the unexpected had made him a different, better man.

The whisper filled his head now, as he rode the bus back to his office. It told him that whether or not she could find Sisela, Maggie Tyrell could bring him a new adventure—and when the adventure was done, he would be a different man yet again. Maybe a better one still.

He wasn't sure what it was that gave him that impression. Ms. Tyrell was hardly a destitute Indian peasant whose neighborhood was ravaged by storms and floods. She was, rather, a frazzled, disheveled Californian. He couldn't name exactly what about her he found so compelling. Her smile promised more than she could ever deliver; her eyes were too full of hope. Her hair was a mess, her attire inappropriate. She was creative enough to attempt to hammer a nail into the wall with a stapler.

There was no good reason Noah should have signed that contract with her. But if he'd learned anything in the past year, it was that doing things for no good reason sometimes brought interesting results.

He got off the bus at Montgomery, stopped at a street vendor's canopied cart to purchase an apple, then entered the building that housed Solar Systems, Incorporated. By the time the elevator reached his floor, he'd devoured half the apple and was feeling inexplicably chipper. He swept through the reception area and down the carpeted hall to his office, a bounce in his step and a laugh tickling his throat. He didn't for a minute believe in Maggie Tyrell's smile and her dancing hazel eyes. But he was curious to see what she was going to come up with for him.

"You got three calls while you were out," Violet told him as he swept past her desk. "Two of them are in your voice mail, but the third one asked me to have you call her back right away. Said her name was—" Violet peered through her heavily mascaraed lashes at the message slip in her hand "—Maggie Tyrell, and she said it was business. She didn't sound like business to me, Noah." Violet was forty years old, on her fifth husband and convinced that she understood male-female interaction better than anyone else. She was an excellent secretary, but Noah thought it best not to discuss his personal life with her. Anyone who'd been married five times couldn't possibly understand male-female interaction as well as she thought.

"Ms. Tyrell *is* business," he said, hiding his surprise that she had gotten back to him so soon. Probably to cancel his contract, to tell him she didn't think she was up to the task.

"We don't have any accounts with her name on them."

"She's business," Noah said laconically, then silenced Violet with a bland smile.

He took the message slip from Violet and shut himself inside his office. Not until he was seated in his ergonomic leather chair behind his spacious, uncluttered desk adjacent to a window that afforded him a water view did he allow himself to look at the paper in his hands.

"Maggie Tyrell—Says it's business. Call back ASAP."

For the briefest, oddest moment, Noah wished the word *business* was *personal.*

No. He didn't want anything personal with her. She wasn't his type—not even close. And anyway, he'd hired her to find Sisela. Who was definitely his type, wasn't she?

He felt another odd twinge. He shook it off, then

lifted the phone receiver and punched in the number Violet had jotted down. Before the second ring, the phone was answered. By Maggie herself, of course. She didn't have a secretary.

"Finders, Keepers," she said crisply.

"Noah Davis, here."

"Oh. Mr. Davis." Her voice took on a brisk quality that he sensed wasn't genuine. Maggie Tyrell might or might not be a talented detective—he'd just wagered a thousand dollars for a week of her time in the hope that she was. But briskness wasn't a trait he associated with her. He couldn't imagine her carrying a leather briefcase or wearing snappy medium-heeled pumps. He couldn't even imagine her with her hair tamed into a normal-looking arrangement.

"I've tracked Sisela Hansen as far as Los Angeles. I need to fly down there. You said you would want to approve all my travel expenses, so—"

He frowned, then realized he was chuckling. Maggie had already accomplished so much? The ditzy woman who used a stapler to hammer a nail into a wall had already found Sisela? "That was fast," he blurted out.

"It's what I do," she said, the barest hint of pride in her tone. "Do I have your go-ahead to fly to L.A.?"

He took a few seconds to collect himself. Yes, he wanted her to fly to Los Angeles and bring back Sisela—or at least bring back the reassurance he needed that Sisela was all right and that breaking her promise to meet him at Romeo's had been a deliberate choice. Yes, he wanted the mystery solved. And the fewer days it took Maggie to solve it, the less it would cost Noah.

But then his adventure would end—before it had even begun. Maggie would accept her fee and vanish from his life, and he...

Noah would be exactly where he already was. He was ready to risk so much, but if Maggie figured everything out, he would emerge from this mess and wind up back in his pleasant, predictable life, where every expectation was met and no surprises lurked around the bend.

"Meet me at Romeo's," he said.

"What?"

"After work this evening. I'll be there at five-thirty. We need to discuss this."

Maggie said nothing for a minute. Then: "Romeo's? The place where you used to meet Sisela?"

"If you'd rather we got together somewhere else—"

"No, that's all right. I can be there by five-thirty."

"I'll see you then." He hung up before he could change his mind, before he could even contemplate why he'd suggested that. Romeo's was *their* place, his and Sisela's. Why, of all the cafés in San Francisco's North Beach, would he ask Maggie to join him there?

He didn't know why—and as he considered it, he decided he didn't care. The prospect of meeting Maggie Tyrell in just a few hours, sipping espresso with her at a quiet, cozy table for two and plotting the next chapter of this adventure made him smile.

ENTERING THE COZY bistro, Maggie blinked until her eyes adjusted to the dim light, then surveyed the room until she spotted Noah Davis. He was seated at a corner table near a window, the knot of his tie loosened, his collar button undone and his piercing blue eyes focused on the door. When he spotted her, he rose and nodded.

She let out a breath. She'd debated long and hard about whether to be prompt, on the chance that she would arrive at Romeo's before he did. Years of drilling by her mother had brainwashed her to believe that a lady should never be waiting for her escort, but should arrive just late enough to suggest that she was very, very busy and was doing him an enormous favor by allowing him the pleasure of her company.

But at the moment, she wasn't a lady and Noah wasn't her escort. She was a detective and he was a client.

That was why she'd raced home to change her clothing, she told herself: not to look more appealing, but to look more professional. If she'd wanted to look appealing, she would have chosen something a little more daring than the plain white silk blouse she wore tucked into a pair of tailored linen slacks that she hoped made her butt look marginally smaller. If this were a date rather than a business meeting, she would have piled her curly hair onto the top of her head, pinned it and sprayed it and prayed for it to behave, and she would have looped dangling, flirty earrings through her earlobes. She would have darkened her cheeks with blusher and her eyelids with shadow and tinted her lips with a nice coral lipstick.

That she'd tried on and discarded three different outfits before settling on the jewel-neck blouse and navy slacks had nothing to do with wanting to look fetching for Mr. Davis, the lovesick swain willing to pay a small fortune for the return of his wayward wife-to-be. All Maggie wanted to look was reliable and reasonably intelligent.

A wiry dark-haired waiter intercepted her halfway to Noah Davis's table and ushered her the rest of the way, as if he knew whom she was there to meet. Once Maggie had lowered herself into the chair facing Noah, he resumed his seat, as well. The waiter gave him a quizzical gaze, then turned to Maggie and asked, "Would the lady care to order?"

She assumed the place offered food as well as coffee, but she wasn't going to eat in front of Noah. She wasn't going to order any of the exotic coffees, either. She had a feeling Noah and his fiancée were exotic coffee drinkers, and she wanted to distance herself from them as much as she could.

"Just a cup of coffee," she said.

"Today we have Kona, from Hawaii, a very nice Kenyan and an Indonesian blend," the waiter recited.

"I'll have the Kona," Maggie said, as if she could tell the difference between one coffee bean and another.

"The usual for you?" the waiter asked Noah.

"Please."

Only after the waiter was gone did Noah smile at Maggie. It was such a charismatic smile. A knowing smile. A dimpled smile. A smile as full of uncanny power as his eyes.

"Thank you for meeting me here," he said. "Your office was a little uncomfortable."

Given that he'd finagled a three-hundred-dollar-a-day discount, he hardly had the right to complain about her office. But Maggie only returned his smile and did her best to resist the magnetic pull of his gaze. "I'm not really sure why we needed to get together. We could have worked everything out over the phone, and..." *And I wouldn't have to be sitting at this tiny table staring at the best-looking heterosexual male in San Francisco.*

"I couldn't spare the time to talk this afternoon," he said, "but I wanted to hear how you managed to locate Sisela."

She gave him a measuring look. She might not be able to distinguish Hawaiian coffee from Kenyan, but she had an extremely discerning mental palate, and she could taste even the faintest trace of dishonesty in a person. Noah Davis wasn't a flagrant liar, but she knew he could have found a few minutes for her in his busy, busy afternoon.

He'd asked her to come to Romeo's not because he'd been pressed for time earlier, but for some other reason. Maybe to size her up the way she was sizing him up. Maybe to see if she was really up to snuff, given how "snuffless" she must have seemed at their first meeting.

"First of all," she said calmly, pausing as the waiter delivered their steaming drinks, "I haven't *found* Sisela yet. I've tracked her to Los Angeles, but I have no idea if she's still there."

"How did you do that?" he asked, then shook his head. "It took you all of—what?—twenty minutes to track her to L.A. How?"

"It's my job," she said.

"Yes, but twenty minutes?"

She decided she liked the touch of awe in his smile. She wanted him to be amazed by her skill. "Would you ask a magician how he got the bunny out of the hat?"

"You're going to tell me you found Sisela through magic?" He laughed—a deep, surprisingly musical sound.

She wished he would stop laughing. Better yet, she wished *she* would stop responding so viscerally to him—to his eyes, his smile, the intriguing hint of beard darkening his jaw. And his sexy laughter. "I hate to disillusion you, Mr. Davis, but even magicians don't use magic to get the bunny out of the hat."

"They use tricks," he said. "Are you going to tell me you use tricks, too?"

"Something like that, yes."

"But you're not going to tell me what your tricks are," he guessed.

There would be no great harm in telling him that she'd contacted a friend of her brother Neil's who worked for the postal service and asked him to check whether one Sisela Hansen, formerly of Pacific Avenue, had filled out a change-of-address form a year ago so her mail would be forwarded after she'd left town. Not exactly magic.

But she chose to let Noah Davis think she was capable of miracles. "I'm not going to tell you," she said, then lifted her mug and sipped. Whatever country it had come from, the coffee was good.

She observed Noah as he tossed the curl of lemon rind into his demitasse cup and lifted it, not bothering to maneuver his large fingers around the tiny handle.

His eyes remained on her as he drank. Maybe he thought she wasn't being totally honest, either.

So what? She was under no obligation to be one-hundred-percent honest with him. Most detectives, in the course of their work, had to indulge in occasional deceptions, misleading statements and misrepresentations. She'd done nothing to deceive him, at least. All she'd done was to refuse to share her trade secrets.

Still scrutinizing her, he lowered the miniature cup to the saucer. In another context—in another life—Maggie could have pretended he was truly fascinated by her. The way he studied her in the bronze light of the café, the way his gaze wandered over her face, taking her in, "learning" her as if she really, really mattered to him...

Damn, but he was something. Not merely too hand-some, but too intriguing, as well. Too intense. Too adept at undermining a woman's defenses.

Why in heaven's name had Sisela Hansen left him? Even if he weren't paying Maggie to find Sisela, Maggie would want to find Sisela for herself—just to ask how she could have walked away from a man like Noah Davis.

He rested his elbows on the table, linked his fingers and rested his chin on them. "What I was wondering," he said, "was whether I could come to Los Angeles with you."

"No," she answered without thinking—without having to think. No way was she going to fly to another city with him.

She tried to convince herself that her immediate reaction was professional. Just as she didn't choose to reveal how she'd tracked Sisela to L.A., so she

didn't choose to let him see her in action. She didn't
want him to realize that the vast majority of detective
work entailed plodding and slogging along, calling
people, asking questions, taking notes and using the
computer to run through databases. Detectives needed
to preserve the mystique of their work.

But her real reason for saying no was more complex. She didn't like the effect Noah had on her. She
didn't like the way she felt when she was near him.
Or, more accurately, she liked it too much.

He seemed to be waiting for her to elaborate on
her answer. He leaned forward slightly, his face too
close to hers, his eyes too bright. "Mr. Davis," she
began.

"Noah."

He wasn't coming on to her. She was positive
about that. No man searching desperately for his ab-
sent lover would be toying with the woman he'd hired
to find her. And no man who'd known love with a
Scandinavian blond goddess would waste his energies
on a sort-of-cute, sort-of-chunky, run-of-the-mill lady
like Maggie. He'd invited her to use his first name
only to put her at ease, to insinuate a level of familiarity that might make her more willing to let him
accompany her to Los Angeles.

"Noah," she said, then had to swallow and begin
again, because calling him Noah seemed way too intimate. "I don't know what's going on in L.A. Neither do you. Sisela moved there, and if she's still
there, she could be..." Sighing, Maggie sought a discreet way of phrasing it. "Let's just say she might
not want to be found."

"For instance, she might be involved with another man?"

So much for discretion. "For instance," Maggie confirmed with a grudging smile, "she might be doing something she doesn't want you to know about—a new relationship or something else."

"Sisela has no interest in drugs," he said.

"I didn't say she—"

"Or anything else illegal or nefarious," he continued, still too close to Maggie, still gazing at her too intently. "I'm well aware she might be in a new relationship. Whenever I consider all the possible reasons she didn't make our reunion, I have a hard time coming up with any that are going to flatter my ego. This isn't about my pride."

"What is it about?" she asked, wondering why her voice sounded so husky.

"Two things," he explained. "One, I want to put my mind at rest that Sisela's safe and sound. Two, I want to satisfy my curiosity."

"You're paying a lot of money just to satisfy your curiosity."

"I'm paying a lot less than you asked for."

"And I don't believe this is just about satisfying your curiosity," she added, testing him. She needed a clearer idea of what he was doing with her, what he was after. "I think you'd be heartbroken if I went to Los Angeles and found Sisela madly in love with a new boyfriend."

Noah smiled—a cool, enigmatic smile. "Don't worry about the state of my heart," he said. "When are we leaving for L.A.?"

"You're not coming with me," she argued, wondering if he was going to refuse to pay her expenses if she insisted on traveling alone. If he did refuse to pay, her investigation would grind to a halt and he would still owe her a thousand dollars. It was how she'd drawn up the contract, to protect her against the client's quitting on her. "I don't see how you can come, anyway. Didn't you just take a year off from work? I'll bet you've used up all your vacation days for the next hundred years or so."

His smile relaxed. "I took a sabbatical," he told her. "I've made a lot of money for the company. I earned my bonuses, and I decided to use them. The company was willing to give me my year, and they were happy to take me back when the year was up. They wouldn't mind if I took a day off."

He must be quite the go-getter. She sipped her coffee, regarding him warily. "I'd suggest you spend tomorrow making more money for the company. It could take me more than one day down south to figure out what's going on. I'll be flying on the cheapest fare I can get, and if I have to spend a night, I'll stay in a motel, not the Beverly Wilshire. The expenses shouldn't be too high. Do I have your go-ahead?"

He nodded and pulled back, settling in his chair. He looked on the verge of sighing, but he only smiled; the same cryptic smile she had so much trouble reading—and so much trouble resisting. "You have my go-ahead," he agreed. "And I won't come with you."

"Fine." Why did she feel a little let down?

"You'll keep me informed by phone, though."

"If you'd like. I have your work and home numbers. You're paying for the calls."

"I'm beginning to learn that finding out the truth can be a costly venture," he said mildly, as if the cost was really no great concern.

"And for all that, you might not like the truth once you find it out," she warned. No "might" about it. She didn't know what she was going to uncover in L.A., but she couldn't shake the conviction that it wasn't going to be what Noah Davis wanted to hear.

"Believe me," he said, his eyes locked on hers, "whatever you find out, I can handle it."

Maybe he could. Maggie returned his gaze, because letting him outstare her would give him some sort of victory over her. She was the detective, the expert, the pro. And she knew, she just *knew,* that to look away from Noah Davis would be an act of surrender.

Maggie wasn't about to surrender to him—in a staring contest or anything else. Nothing frightened her—not thugs, not bugs, not secrets swept under rugs. And certainly, not Noah Davis.

CHAPTER THREE

ACCORDING TO HIS secretary, he was in a meeting. Maggie asked the secretary to tell him she'd called and would try him again later. Then she hung up and tried to convince herself she was relieved.

Of course she was relieved. She'd telephoned him only because he was the client, footing the bill for her excursion to the City of Angels, and he'd requested that she keep him posted. She hadn't called because she lived for the sound of his voice.

She stepped away from the phone booth at the back of the sandwich shop, leaving the phone available for anyone else who might need it. Apparently, no one did. In a world of cell phones, nobody relied on public pay phones anymore—except people like her, whose cell phone had a way of going on the fritz at inconvenient times. Once lovesick hordes started stampeding her office—at her full five-hundred-dollar-a-day fee—she was going to invest in a top-of-the-line portable phone.

She'd reserved a room at a chain motel in a fringe neighborhood, but she probably wasn't going to have to use it. Her trip to Los Angeles was proceeding smoothly, and the motel clerk had assured her that if she canceled her reservation by 6:00 p.m., her deposit wouldn't be charged to her credit card. She didn't want to have to spend the night in town if she could avoid it. Los Angeles was too hot and dry and dirty. The smog parched her throat and made her eyes sting.

Finishing her business in town by six was definitely doable. She'd been managing her brothers' professional affairs long enough to know how to be a detective. She knew the right questions to ask and the right way to ask them. She knew how to streamline her efforts, how to simplify the search, how to stay focused and organize the information she gathered. Sisela Hansen hadn't covered her tracks. Maggie was able to see her footprints without squinting.

The superintendent of the building where Sisela had rented a small one-bedroom apartment last July had only negative things to say about her. "She was so full of herself, so sure she was gonna hit the big time," he'd muttered, sweeping the tiled lobby as he spoke. "Then, one day she just disappeared. Stuck me with the unit and walked out on the lease. All I got was her security to tide me over until I could find another tenant. She acted so high-and-mighty, she didn't even have the courtesy to sublet the place. Just stuck me with it. Selfish bitch."

But the genteel old man renting the apartment across the hall from Sisela's was much more forthcoming. He went on for several minutes about what a vision of beauty Sisela was. "You'd see her carrying her recyclables down the hall to the compactor room, and it was like a vision from a dream. She was so tall and willowy and blond. *Real* blond, too. Not bleached. The real thing. I used to just stare at her hair and dream." Once he'd completed his rhapsody on Sisela's shimmering tresses, Maggie learned from him that Sisela had found an agent within a few days of moving to Los Angeles. "Not one of the top agents, mind you—but he was an honest fellow. An unbesmirched reputation. I was the one who recommended him to her."

From the "unbesmirched" agent, Maggie learned that Sisela was no longer in town or looking for work. "I got her one gig," he said when Maggie telephoned him from the luncheonette pay phone. "It was a start, you know? She was happy to do it, too. A commercial jingle. They need voices for that, you know? Pay's not bad, either. Plus I negotiated her residuals for every time the ad goes out on the radio. She could be earning a few bucks on that thing for years to come. It was for Cosmic Candy's new chocolate bar. Cosmic Star Crunch. Yeah, that was it."

When Maggie looked at the photograph Noah Davis had given her of his ice-queen fiancée, she had trouble associating the beautiful blonde with a candy bar called Cosmic Star Crunch. She imagined that Sisela's voice would be an erotic whisper, not something sweet and sugary. But the agent insisted. "Yeah, Cosmic Star Crunch. She taped it in—wait a second, I'll look it up—August of last year. I had a few other auditions lined up for her, but she told me she was taking off. She said if she wanted any more jobs, she'd call me, but she never did. I could've done things for her. Too bad she quit. She showed promise."

She also broke promises, Maggie thought as she rechecked the name and address of the studio where the Cosmic Star Crunch commercial had been recorded. She stopped on her way out of the luncheonette to buy a jumbo chocolate-chip cookie, pocketed the receipt for reimbursement and headed back outside into the sour, desert-dry afternoon.

The studio was a ten-minute drive in her rented car. The fellow who had produced the radio ad for Cosmic Star Crunch remembered Sisela, too. Apparently she was unforgettable to everyone who had ever had the opportunity to gaze upon her. Maggie decided that of all the people she'd met since Noah Davis had entered her office yesterday, her favorite was the grouchy landlord—the one who'd called Sisela a "selfish bitch."

Indeed, Sisela didn't seem terribly smart or savvy to Maggie. Not only had she given up Noah, but she'd given up her chance for a singing career. Few women attracted good luck more than once—and fewer yet were foolish enough to turn their back on that good luck.

Maggie reminded herself again that Noah might not be what he appeared. He might be temperamental or selfish. He might belch. He might snore. He might leave the seat up and neglect to cut his toenails.

In other words, he might be like ninety-nine percent of the world's men.

Why had Sisela quit on him? And why, after she'd taken the first positive step toward realizing a singing career, had she quit on that, too?

"Oh, yeah, I remember her," the producer murmured as he ogled the photograph of Sisela that Maggie held in front of him. He was a slightly paunchy fellow, bald on top, but his fringe of hair was long enough to gather into a skinny ponytail at the nape of his neck. "I wouldn't forget her."

"Why wouldn't you forget her?"

"Because Cosmo Delaney himself was here when we laid it down."

"'Laid it down'?"

"Taped the track," he explained, lighting a cigarette and then taking a chug from a bottle of mineral water.

"Am I supposed to know who Cosmo Delaney is?" Maggie asked. She prided herself on being on top of new fads, new singers, new hit records. She could distinguish one grunge growler from another, and she guessed the right rapper three times out of four. She'd never heard of Cosmo Delaney, though.

"The owner of Cosmic Candy Company. He sat right next to me while I mixed the tracks. He couldn't take his eyes off her. He would just stare and stare. The guy was infatuated. He told me that as soon as we were done recording, he was going to take her away."

"Take her where?"

"How should I know? Away. To wherever it is millionaire candy-bar executives go."

A half-hour later, Maggie was at the airport. She turned in her rental car, phoned the motel to cancel her reservation, then took a seat in a lounge and waited for the next flight back to San Francisco.

And thought.

And moped.

She hadn't envisioned her new detective agency as a service that would shatter already-broken hearts. She'd conceived the agency with grand, sentimental notions about elderly veterans and their wartime girlfriends. Or high-school sweethearts torn asunder by their tyrannical parents but brought back together by none other than Maggie Tyrell. Or once-nerdy swains, now strong and virile, seeking the cheerleaders who'd snubbed them—and the cheerleaders, now wise and mature, taking one glance at the new, improved nerds and swooning in ecstasy.

Maggie had hoped to facilitate joyous, loving reunions. Not searches that led to the discovery that a former lover had run off with a millionaire candy-bar executive.

A bank of public phones lined the wall on one side of the lounge, but Maggie avoided them. She couldn't tell Noah over the phone that his beautiful Nordic princess had hooked up with someone else. She needed to be with him when she broke the news, if only to comfort him when he dissolved in tears.

A shudder skidded along Maggie's spine. She didn't want to witness Noah Davis's tears. As for comforting him... *No.* Nothing in the contract they'd drawn up had guaranteed him a happy ending. Nothing had insured that she would bring his fiancée back to him. Nothing had stipulated that Noah would be delighted by her results.

All she'd sold him was her skill at tracking down a wayward lover. She would phone him when she got back to her office and ask him to come in. Then she would tell him Sisela had tied her fate to a candy man named Cosmo. She would hand Noah a box of tissues and wish him well.

And she would probably spend far too much time afterward trying to imagine what it would have been like to take him in her arms and comfort him.

AT EIGHT-FIFTEEN NOAH'S telephone rang. He had just finished dinner, poured himself a Scotch on ice and gotten comfortable in the easy chair in his living room, with Elvis Costello on the CD player and a folder of notes concerning a high-tech research firm in his lap. It was a small project compared to what Noah usually oversaw, but he'd worked with the same architect on a huge mall in Texas two years ago, and he wasn't going to toss this project to anyone else.

The light of dusk shimmered through the window. Night took a long time coming in June. But then, everything took a long time coming when you were waiting for the phone to ring.

Maggie had phoned him at his office earlier that day, but he'd been in a meeting. The message Violet had handed him after the meeting indicated that she would call again later.

Much later, apparently. From the moment he'd received that message until now, six hours later, she hadn't called. And he'd been far too aware of his phone's silence.

He told himself his eagerness for Maggie Tyrell's call was based on his need to know what she was finding out about Sisela. But it was more than that, he knew. As soon as Maggie called, he would be back in the game, not reviewing the specs for a building in San Jose but charging into new territory, taking chances, courting risks.

He sipped the Scotch, listened to the ice clinking in his glass, and acknowledged that wanting Maggie to call had to do with something more, even, than his desire for adventure. He wasn't sure what he was waiting for, hoping for. He wasn't sure what he expected, other than the unexpected.

He swore to himself that he wasn't dying to hear the sound of her voice. His edginess had nothing to do with her personally. Yet the instant the phone rang, his breath caught in his throat and his mind sang out: *It's her. It's Maggie.*

He smothered his anticipation beneath a scornful laugh, closed the folder and set it aside. He was on his feet as the phone rang a second time, and lifting the receiver before it rang a third. "Noah Davis," he said, annoyed that his heart was pounding so fast.

"Noah, it's Maggie Tyrell."

Damn. He did *not* want to be this excited—or at least, if he had to be excited, he didn't want it to be because of her. He wanted to be excited only about whatever news she had for him.

"I'm back from L.A.," she reported.

"You are?" He'd thought she would be spending days down there, racking up expenses. That she was back so soon probably meant she had no news for him at all. The trip must have proved fruitless.

"I need to talk to you. Can you stop by my office tomorrow?"

He pictured her "office"—that windowless cell at the end of a hall, so cramped he'd had to contort himself to fit into a chair. He pictured her on the other side of the desk, garrulous and wild-haired, her hazel eyes incandescent. And then he pictured her as she'd appeared at Romeo's—a bit more composed, a bit more controlled, but still incandescent, as if she were so full of energy, some of it had to escape from her in the form of light.

He erased that image and forced himself to concentrate on her words. She was requesting that he stop by her office tomorrow. "If you have something to discuss with me," he said, "I'd rather not wait until tomorrow."

"Well..." She hesitated, then said, "I'd rather not talk about it on the phone."

That sounded ominous. He wondered why he wasn't filled with dread. "Can we meet tonight, then?" he asked. "I could come to your office now, or—maybe it would be nicer if we met at Romeo's." Romeo's was a bit of a trek from his Marina-neighborhood apartment, but no more of an inconvenience than her office was.

"I'm not at my office," she told him. "I came straight home from the airport. Romeo's is all the way in North Beach."

She sounded fatigued. "I'd be willing to come to your house if that would be easier for you," he offered. When she didn't respond right away, he added, "Or you could come here if you'd prefer."

There was another, longer pause. He must have breached the bounds of propriety. Detectives and clients weren't supposed to meet in each other's homes, apparently. But he hadn't invited her to his apartment to do anything improper. He wanted only to hear what she'd learned in Los Angeles, what portentous news she couldn't reveal over the phone.

"All right. I'll stop by your place," she finally said. "I've got your address." She'd made note of it as well as his home phone number when she'd written up his contract. "I'll be over in a half hour." She said goodbye and hung up.

Noah stared at the disconnected receiver, then replaced it in its cradle. A sense of foreboding crept over him. The news Maggie had for him was obviously ghastly. Something terrible must have happened to Sisela. Something so horrific, Maggie refused to discuss it over the phone. Something so appalling, she was willing to come to his apartment to tell him, even after her hectic day.

She was on her way over. He would have to brace himself for her disastrous news—but before he did that, he would have to tidy up the place.

He wasn't a slob, so there wasn't too much to tidy. His dinner dishes had to be moved from the sink to the dishwasher. His Scotch would keep in the freezer; that would prevent the ice cubes from melting and diluting the liquor. If Maggie's message was as bad as he feared, he was going to need that drink eventually.

He tucked the folder back into his briefcase, turned off the CD player, detoured to the bedroom to brush his hair and pop a breath mint, then checked his reflection in the mirror on the back of the closet door. He used to be particular about his clothing—having spent his childhood clad in hand-me-downs and rummage-sale bargains, he enjoyed being able to dress well now. But after spending nine months immersed in manual labor in India, he couldn't bring himself to care about his wardrobe quite as much as he used to.

If Sisela were around, she would see to it that his apparel was fashionable and impeccable. But she wasn't around, and instead of lounging in a pair of neat khakis and a pressed polo shirt, he was wearing comfortably faded blue jeans and one of his old UC

T-shirts. Sisela would die if she ever saw him dressed this way.

The thought that she might be dead seared through him. He closed his eyes, inhaled sharply and offered a silent prayer that whatever Maggie had to tell him wouldn't be as bad as that.

The intercom buzzed. Sending a final, silent prayer heavenward, he strode out of the bedroom and down the hall to the foyer. When he pressed the intercom button to respond, Maggie's voice crackled through the speaker. "Noah? It's Maggie."

"Come on up." He activated the lock release, allowing her into the building. His apartment occupied the third floor of a charming stucco walk-up in the Marina; his living-room windows overlooked Fisherman's Wharf and the bay. The apartment wasn't large, but he would rather have a bay view than a lot of square footage.

From the foyer's arched doorway, he surveyed the living room, marveling for a moment that he, Noah Davis of Butte City, descendent of Okies, actually owned an apartment with a view of San Francisco Bay. Even after three years, he still loved it. Sisela had had a much larger flat in the exclusive Pacific Heights neighborhood—her parents were wealthy enough to supplement her modest income as a private-school teacher—but one without a view. Noah had always preferred his place to hers, and he'd been anticipating some friction over where they would live once they got married.

They weren't going to get married, though—not with Maggie on her way upstairs bearing grim tidings. Yanking his gaze from the window, Noah inspected the living room to make sure the sofa cushions were in place, the lamp shades level, the sparse furnishings clean and correctly positioned. Having had nothing as a child, he had learned to appreciate quality and the absence of clutter. The surfaces of his tables were clear, the rugs plain, the walls adorned with austere modern prints.

The doorbell sounded. He wanted to pray again, but if Maggie was already at his threshold, it was probably too late. Returning to the foyer, he opened the door.

She looked more tired than tragic. Her shoulders slumped inside the utilitarian gray blazer she wore over a rose-hued T-shirt and new black jeans. Most of her hair was restrained by a silver barrette, but strands had come loose at the edges of her face, giving her a soft-focus appearance. Her smile was weary and wistful. Only her eyes looked fully engaged, as luminous as he had remembered them.

"Please, come in." He stepped aside and gestured her into the foyer.

As soon as she was inside his apartment, he felt a subtle shift in the atmosphere. He'd had female guests often enough, yet Maggie Tyrell's presence was different.

Maybe because she was here on business. Maybe because she was here to convey gruesome news about Sisela.

"Come in," he said again, moving toward the living room. "Sit down. I'll get you something to drink."

"No, thanks." She stood where she was, quiet and still, observing his home and then him. She was shorter than he'd realized. The top of her head barely reached his chin. His gaze snagged on the rippling waves of her hair. He could see the varying hues, brown with glints of copper and gold where the curls caught the light.

He had always preferred sleek hair on a woman. For that matter, he'd always preferred sleek women. Maggie Tyrell wasn't fat, but there was a lushness about her, an overabundance of curves to match the overabundance of her hair. And her eyes were too bright, too eager. She definitely wasn't his type.

He wasn't even supposed to have a type. He was supposed to be devastated about Sisela.

But Sisela had never entered a room with as much purpose as Maggie did. Sisela's movements had never seemed so full of commitment. He wasn't sure what it was about Maggie, but she radiated an aura of...excitement. Determination. Pleasure in being where she was, doing what she was doing. Even if all she was doing was standing in his foyer, staring up at him with a vaguely apprehensive, vaguely pity-ing smile.

"How bad is it?" he asked, knowing damned well that it was very bad. Bad enough that she'd traveled all this way less than an hour after she'd gotten off a plane just to break the news to him in person. "Is Sisela all right?"

"I don't know," she admitted, then her smile grew contrite. "I didn't exactly find her."

"Oh." He could forget about mourning Sisela for the time being.

"The thing is..." Maggie refused to look away. "I think you might want to call off the search. I know you signed a one-week contract, but I really hadn't expected that things would end this way."

"What do you mean, 'end'? If you haven't found her yet—"

"She left Los Angeles with another man," Maggie said softly.

"Another man?" He wanted to laugh with relief. He'd been expecting Maggie to present him with a coroner's report.

"I'm so sorry, Noah. She was hired to sing an advertising jingle for Cosmic Candy Company's new chocolate bar. The head honcho of Cosmic Candy was in town to observe the production of the ad campaign, and he fell hard for Sisela. I gather..." She sighed, then forced out the words. "I gather Sisela fell hard for him, too. Or for his wealth and power. As soon as the ad was in the can, she severed her relation with the agent who'd gotten her the job, broke the lease on her apartment and skipped town with Cosmo Delaney."

"I see." Noah exerted himself to look morose, but he wasn't good at pretending. The truth was, Maggie's news cheered him enormously. For one thing, Sisela was all right. For another, his adventure didn't have to end yet.

"I figured you'd want me to quit at this point," she continued. "I know you contracted me for a week, but I won't hold you to that—not now that we know Sisela's with another man." Her eyes shimmered, filling with tears.

He wouldn't renege on the contract. She probably needed the money; he was her first client, after all. If what had her worried was the possibility that he would fire her, she could relax. "Let's keep going," he said. "I hired you to find her, and you haven't found her yet."

"But she—" Maggie let out a long, shaky breath "—she's involved with someone else."

"That's all right," he said with a shrug. Her frown of bewilderment demanded an explanation. "I'd still like to see her, to find out why things turned out this way. It wasn't what either of us had planned."

"I know, Noah, but..." Maggie seemed to be struggling not to weep. "I set up Finders, Keepers to reunite lovers. I wanted to bring love and joy into their lives, And instead, here I am, bringing pain into your life, and I..." She lost the fight. A tear spilled through her eyelashes and slid down her cheek. "This isn't the way it was supposed to go." Another tear skidded down her other cheek. She glanced away and swiped furtively at her eyes.

It was a reflexive thing, drawing her into his arms, closing them around her. Weeping women needed to be held, even if their tears made no sense.

She stiffened, but before he could relax his embrace, her resistance vanished and she melted against him. She didn't bawl or blubber—just rested her head on his shoulder and sighed damply. He felt her tears through his shirt, felt a tiny shudder inside her as she leaned into him. Her hair smelled of wildflowers. Her breasts, full and round, pressed into his chest.

He suppressed the impulse to stroke his hands up and down her back. She might find such caresses comforting, but it was just as likely that she would be offended by such a presumption of intimacy. It was just that she was a woman, and she was crying, and he wanted to make her feel better.

His hands ached from the effort of not touching her.

She let him hold her for less than a minute, then eased back. She'd been so warm in his arms; he resented the chill of her withdrawal. "I'm really sorry," she said again, this time apparently referring to her behavior rather than her news. "This is so unprofessional. I just— I wanted—"

"You wanted to bring good news," he prompted, oddly touched. Most people took a perverse joy in spreading bad news, being the first to tell their acquaintances something awful.

"I just—" She sniffled and dabbed at her cheeks with her fingertips. One final sigh, so deep it seemed to originate in her toes. "I wanted to make you happy."

It dawned on him that he would be a whole lot happier if she would let him console her—and—damn it—hug her. Even if he harbored no romantic feelings for her, he wanted to hold her tight.

"I'm sorry, Noah—coming here and telling you you've been betrayed by the woman you wanted for your wife. Maybe it would have been better if you'd never come to me in the first place."

"No." This much he knew for a fact. "No, it wouldn't have been better. I'm glad I came to you."

Maggie hadn't failed him. Far from it. She was competent and amazingly vulnerable. He was definitely getting his money's worth. He couldn't recall the last time a woman had cried in his arms. He'd seen women cry in India as they'd surveyed their storm-related losses—but they hadn't cried in his arms. They hadn't turned to him for comfort.

And they hadn't cried because they felt like failures.

"I think you're doing fine," he told Maggie.

She closed her eyes and shook her head. "Noah, I blew it, okay? I—"

"Maybe the way to make me happy is to keep going," he argued. "I'm paying you good money. There's no need to get upset about this, okay? Cheer up and get back to work."

"You want me to keep going because you pity me," she groaned.

"No. I don't pity you. I want you to keep going, because—" *Because if you stop, the adventure ends, and I'll never find out why Sisela did what she did, and I may never have the chance to put my arms around you again.*

That last thought startled him so much he fell back a step. He did *not* want to put his arms around Maggie again. Definitely not—the tears threatened to extinguish the blinding glow in her eyes.

"I want to know what happened to Sisela," he said. He couldn't express what he was actually thinking; he couldn't even begin to make sense of it. Maggie's eyes were irrelevant to him. The plump curves of her body pressing against him caused no response within him. That she was a woman, that her hair smelled sweet, that her head nestled so nicely into the hollow of his shoulder... Meaningless.

He opted for the only explanation that seemed reasonable. "I want to know why Sisela did what she did," he reiterated. "Please stick with this until you

track her down.'' At Maggie's dubious frown, he
added, ''Whatever you find out, I can handle it.''

''Are you sure?''

He wasn't sure of anything right now. Not of how
he felt about the woman standing before him with her
tearstained cheeks and her mussed hair. Not of how
he felt about the woman who'd betrayed him while
he'd been rebuilding a village in India. Not about his
own need to know, his own crazy need to stay on this
adventure until Maggie could uncover the truth for
him.

''I'm sure,'' he said.

CHAPTER FOUR

WELL, SHE'D CERTAINLY botched things. Crying in front of a client. Even worse, crying *in the arms of* a client! So much for her career as a tough-as-nails detective.

The amazing thing, she thought as she stared at the phone in her office, was that after her disgusting display of emotion, Noah Davis hadn't fired her on the spot. He'd had sufficient reason to give her the ax: not just her utterly unprofessional display of waterworks, but her inability to deliver good news about his fiancée. Surely he hadn't hired Maggie to spend her time uncovering the painful truth that his fiancée had betrayed him. A person didn't pay two hundred bucks a day for the privilege of having his heart broken.

It should have occurred to her that she wasn't always going to bring joy to her clients. Her brothers often brought misery to clients in the course of their work—but that had to be expected in a detective agency that specialized in digging up dirt, not diamonds. In fact most of the time, their clients were pleased to get dirt. The divorce lawyers who kept Tyrell Investigative Services on retainer salivated at the prospect that Maggie's brothers would be able to unearth something truly scandalous—the estranged husband's extracurricular affairs, the duplicitous wife's siphoning-off of funds from the joint bank account. To them, bad news meant big settlements.

But all of Maggie's high hopes for Finders, Keepers had fallen flat on her first case. She was a disaster.

All right. She'd given Noah the chance to sever the contract and he'd refused. If that was his choice, she'd have to respect it.

A computer search had located Cosmo Delaney. The corporate headquarters of his candy empire was in New York City, and he resided north of the city, in the tiny Westchester County community of Bellewood. Whether or not Sisela was still with him, Maggie hadn't yet ascertained. She'd phoned Delaney's office, posing as an insurance broker, and asked Delaney's secretary to confirm the names he'd listed as beneficiaries and their relationship to him. His secretary was no fool, though. Refusing to take the bait, she'd suggested that Maggie send her questions in writing.

Nor would she put Maggie through to Delaney. Just Maggie's luck. Delaney had a guard dog answering his office phone, and his number in Bellewood was unlisted.

The only way Maggie was going to reach Cosmo Delaney was to get on a plane and fly east. And to do that, she was going to have to ask Noah Davis to fund another airline ticket. If he was wise, he'd decide to cut his losses and ask her to end the search.

For some reason, Maggie suspected he wasn't wise. Smart, yes, but not wise enough to fire her.

She needed to find the courage to call him. Memories of last night mortified her. She'd been held by men before: not just her father and her brothers, but a boyfriend here and there. However, she'd never been held by a man who looked—or felt—like Noah Davis. And no man's hug had ever left her feeling quite so...*warm.*

This was a big problem. He was her client, for crying out loud, and all she could think of was the inappropriate pleasure she'd felt in his arms.

All right. She hadn't been professional last night, but she could be professional today. It was time to share her information with her client. Gritting her teeth, she reached for her phone. As her hand settled on the receiver, the phone rang shrilly.

She gasped and sprang back, then caught her breath. Noah couldn't possibly be on the other end of the line. Just because he'd let her blubber on his shoulder last night didn't mean there was some sort of psychic bond between them.

She inhaled, then lifted the receiver and braced herself just in case. "Finders, Keepers—can I help you?" she said briskly.

"Maggie? It's Karen." Sandy's wife.

Maggie slumped in her chair, relief mixed with a measure of disappointment. "Hi, Karen. What did Sandy forget?" She knew her brother too well.

"Everything." Karen issued an anguished sigh. "I got your anniversary card, Maggie—and it was really sweet, thank you. I didn't get anything from him."

"No anniversary present?"

"No present, no card, no 'Happy Anniversary, honey—I'm so glad you married me.' Nothing."

Maggie swore under her breath. Sandy was a great

guy, but he was also a jerk. "Well, you know he can be a little absentminded—"

"A little? We've been married three years, Maggie. Is it too much to ask that he bring me a flower? It doesn't have to be a dozen long-stemmed roses. One daisy would be enough. I mean, is that too much to ask?"

Maggie wanted to point out that Karen had dated Sandy for two years before they got married. She had to have learned how absentminded he was during their courtship. But she'd married him because she loved him, even knowing that he was intense about the things that interested him—like computers, and woodworking, and the Forty-Niners—but inexcusably casual about everything else. He loved Karen. He just didn't love remembering significant dates. "What can I do to make it better?" she asked Karen.

"I don't know." Karen sighed again, tremulously. "I really can't talk right now. It's a zoo here—all these summer interns storming around the studio thinking they're Edward R. Murrow." Karen was on the staff of one of the local television station's nightly news broadcasts. "But I was so angry last night and I just couldn't see the point of venting to Sandy. I don't want apologies—I don't want him to feel guilty. What I want is for him to do the things he has to do so he won't have to apologize for anything. You know what I mean?"

"You want him to change his personality," Maggie suggested.

"Something like that." One final sigh, and Karen made a sound that might have been a laugh. "I guess it doesn't matter. I feel better talking to you. Your brothers are for the birds, but you understand.''

"Unfortunately I understand all too well." Maggie understood that Sandy needed a good, hard smack upside the head—which, she imagined, was very much in tune with what Karen had in mind.

"I'd better go," Karen said. "Talk to you later."

Maggie said goodbye and hung up. If her office had had a window, she would have gazed through it until she'd sorted out her thoughts. Instead, she stared at the ballet poster hanging on the opposite wall, barely eight feet away. Nureyev had his hands on Fonteyn's petite waist. She was balanced on one pointed toe, with her other leg extended behind her and her hands arched gracefully above her head. Maggie had taken ballet lessons for two years as a child, but the teacher had advised her to quit because she didn't have the right body type.

If Noah had put his hands on her waist, the terms "graceful" and "petite" would not have leaped into his mind.

And if she didn't stop thinking of the fact that last night Noah *had* put his hands on her, however chastely, her fledgling detective agency was going to go down the tubes.

She had to call him—and she would, just as soon as she chewed Sandy out for forgetting his anniversary. Cursing at her own cowardice, she shoved away from the desk, her chair colliding with the wall behind her, and stormed out of the office to pick a fight with her brother.

"I'M SORRY TO INTERRUPT," Violet told Noah through the phone, "but you told me to put through calls from that woman.''

Noah shot a quick smile at the team of architects seated around a conference table down the hall from his office. They were reviewing the designs for the San Jose project. Easels held large drawings of the complex—two views of the exterior, a diagram of the heating system, a chart outlining the seasonal sun exposure at that site. Noah was excited about the project—but he was even more excited to learn that Maggie Tyrell was on the phone.

Because she'd found Sisela, he told himself. Or because she'd found information that would lead him to Sisela. Not at all because he was intrigued by her contradictory behavior—tough and poised one minute, weepy and emotional the next; sometimes cool and efficient and sometimes scattered and tender; frumpy, yet disarmingly soft and feminine.

"Excuse me," he said to the architects, then turned his back to them and tucked the phone closer to his face. "Thanks, Violet, I'll take the call."

He could picture Violet's scowl as she connected him. Then he heard Maggie's voice and he could picture her, as well. But not scowling. Not weeping. Not with her lower lip quivering and her eyes shadowed. No, he pictured her standing in her ridiculous excuse for an office, armed with a stapler and a truckload of determination. Maggie was a woman who could improvise, be creative, and get the job done one way or another.

"If you want me to pursue this case, I'm going to have to go to New York," she said.

"Okay."

She hesitated, but when he didn't speak, she did. "I can't get through to Cosmo Delaney long-distance. The only way I can communicate with him is in person. And even if I go to New York and confront him, he might not be able to tell me where Sisela is. They might not be together anymore."

"I know."

"So if I fly to New York, I might come back empty-handed. It's just that Delaney is all I've got right now."

"Okay."

There was another pause. "Noah, do you realize what this is going to cost you? I mean, we may be talking wild-goose chase here, and the airfare alone—"

"I said okay," he repeated. "The airfare is not a problem. We'd have to wait till tomorrow, though. I can't get away today. I'm in the middle of a meeting."

"We?"

"Well, of course, I'm coming with you."

"Don't start that again," she scolded. "You are *not* coming with me. I work better alone."

"You and Sam Spade?" He stifled a laugh, this time at a mental picture of Maggie in a beige trench coat and a fedora, skulking around dark alleys and exchanging secret messages with assorted lowlifes in guttural murmurs. The image squelched his amusement. Sam Spade usually wound up stumbling onto corpses, and Noah didn't want this project to include bloodshed or pain—anything that would require 100-proof anesthesia.

He had to accompany Maggie, if only to make sure she was safe.

"Listen to me, Noah. I can take the red-eye to La Guardia tonight, work all day tomorrow and maybe fly back the day after. One round-trip ticket, one night in a motel, a couple of subway tokens and a few deli bagels and coffees. I'm trying to make this quick and simple. Bringing you along would only complicate things."

He didn't like the way she said "bringing you along" as if he were a suitcase. "We could get more done if we were there together," he said, although he had no idea what he could contribute to the process. All he knew was that going to New York City in search of a candy-company executive would be one hell of an adventure.

"No." Her voice held none of the soft sentiment he'd heard in it last night. Today she was the embodiment of granite-hard resolution. "Either I go alone or I don't go at all. If you come with me, Noah, I'm not going to be able to do the job."

He wondered about all the possible implications of her statement. Would his presence hamper her, hinder her, distract her? Was she annoyed with him or afraid of him? Or did she really just prefer to work alone?

Behind him, one of the architects coughed. Noah relented with a wry smile. "Okay," he said one final time. "Book your flight and go."

"You approve the expenses?"

"I'll pay for everything," he promised.

DETECTIVES HAD TO TRUST their intuition. They had to listen to the whispers of their subconscious, the subtexts of their dreams. Maggie spent the six-hour overnight flight to New York hunched in her seat, developing a stiff neck as she drifted in and out of slumber. The subtext of her dreams was that Noah Davis was looking for something other than his wayward fiancée.

That was as far as the subtext went, unfortunately. Asleep or awake or floating in that vague state of semiconsciousness between the two, she couldn't figure out what Noah was looking for.

Except that it wasn't her. His desire to accompany her to New York didn't mean anything personal. If he had any specific feelings for her—or against her, for that matter—he would have expressed them the evening she'd gone to his apartment. If he'd wanted her, he would have let his brief, awkward hug of comfort evolve into a longer, less awkward hug of seduction.

That it hadn't was *good,* she told herself. She wanted nothing personal with Noah Davis.

But it didn't help her to figure out what, precisely, he was after. Until she did, she could only plow ahead in her pursuit of Sisela Hansen.

The plane landed at 6:30 a.m. East Coast time. In a groggy stupor, she slid the strap of her duffel onto her shoulder and plotted her strategy. Delaney would be easy enough to find, assuming he was at his desk in his midtown Manhattan office—but that was a big assumption. He could be out of town on business or on an African photo safari with his gorgeous blond mistress. Or he could be haunting recording studios in search of an entirely new mistress.

Maggie's best bet was not to confront Delaney but

to find out more about his current social situation. She
would travel up to Bellewood and nose around. She'd
spent yesterday afternoon learning what she could,
not just about Delaney's company but about the picturesque village he called home. From what she'd
learned, Bellewood was so wealthy and exclusive, it
probably had town ordinances banning faux pearls
and visible rust spots on cars. It was small enough
that everyone would be likely to know everyone else.
All Maggie had to do was find the town gossip.

Outside the airline terminal, she located a cabdriver
thrilled to take her to Bellewood once she assured him
that she would pay double the metered fare to cover
his trip back to the city. With her duffel and laptop
next to her on the back seat, she closed her eyes and
dozed while he cruised north through Westchester
County to the bucolic town overlooking the Hudson
River.

He dropped her off at a coffee shop on what passed
for a commercial strip in Bellewood. Besides the coffee shop, the block included a gas station, a bookstore
and a small supermarket with green-and-white striped
awnings and signs in the window proclaiming that
Belgian endive and Beluga caviar were on sale. The
waitress who served Maggie coffee and a corn muffin
didn't appear to be the busybody Maggie was looking
for, but she did mention that there was a reasonably
inexpensive motel a few blocks south. "Not in the
town center," she clarified. "It would be an eyesore.
Here in the heart of town you'll find the Holliwell
Inn, but that costs much more than the motel."

Maggie was spending Noah's money, but given the
exorbitant bill for her modest breakfast, she could

only imagine what the Holliwell Inn would cost. "I'll stop by the motel," she said, then took a desperately needed hit of caffeine.

Fueled by three more cups of coffee, she hiked the few blocks to the motel and checked in. She unpacked her laptop and the folder of notes she'd already amassed on Delaney and the Cosmic Candy Company, left a message with her brother Jack to let him know she'd arrived safely in Bellewood, left another message on Noah's voice mail at work informing him that she was hot on Sisela's trail, and headed out in search of a loose-lipped town resident.

Three hours later, she'd learned a few things about Bellewood, the most relevant being that it was full of tight-lipped folks.

She'd learned from the postmistress that the town celebrated Independence Day by holding a carnival on the elementary school's athletic field, and the carnival raised thousands of dollars for the homeless. From this, Maggie deduced that Bellewood's residents were eager to raise whatever fortune it took to keep the homeless out of their pristine town.

She'd learned from the proprietress of a candle shop that clove had remained the most popular fragrance for candles in Bellewood for several decades. "Other scents come and go," she'd said. "But clove is classic."

She'd learned from the salesclerk at a dress shop that the majority of Bellewood's female population wore size eight or smaller. "Oh, we don't have that in *your* size," she'd clucked when Maggie had eyed a blue silk suit as a pretext for getting the clerk to talk.

From the gas-station owner—clad in the cleanest apparel Maggie had ever seen on an auto mechanic— she'd learned that the most popular cars in Bellewood were Mercedes, Infinitis and Range Rovers. From the clerk at town hall she'd learned that the property tax rate in Bellewood was stratospherically high to support the excellent public schools, though nearly half the town's parents sent their children to private schools. And from her own exploration of the walled perimeter of Cosmo Delaney's estate, situated on a winding, pastoral road that afforded views of the river, she'd learned that uninvited visitors weren't welcome. The fieldstone wall was six feet high, the intricate wrought-iron gate locked.

At three in the afternoon, still suffering from the residual effects of jet lag, she trudged back to the coffee shop, slumped onto one of the quaint ladder-back chairs at a table covered with a checkered cloth, and ordered a glass of iced tea. The waitress who'd served her breakfast was gone; this new waitress was a bit older, with a sweet, grandmotherly air about her. "You look done in," she clucked as she delivered a tall, frosted glass garnished with a thick wedge of lemon. "Can I get you anything else?"

"Information," Maggie blurted out. If she weren't still locked in to West Coast time, if she hadn't put a good eight miles of wear and tear on her loafers, if she'd received even one tidbit worth writing down in her notebook, she would have been a bit more cautious. But she'd been exercising tact all day and getting nowhere. She'd been subtle, probing gently, fishing in calm waters—and she hadn't even caught a waterlogged boot.

"Information?" the waitress asked, lowering herself into the chair across from Maggie. The coffee shop was nearly empty. A couple of police officers sat at a table in the corner drinking coffee and eating doughnuts as if on a quest to prove that the cliché about cops was true, but the waitress could see them from where she sat, so if they needed anything she'd know. "I believe you have to dial 555-1212 for Information."

"I'm not looking for a phone number," Maggie clarified. "I'm looking for a person."

"Here in Bellewood? A *person?*"

Maggie wondered whether people were so rare in Bellewood that no one ever looked for them there. Maybe all the well-bred, well-spoken folks she'd talked to were really animatronic robots and the town was actually a perverse amusement park, designed so tourists could see what a rich, ritzy town might look like.

The waitress looked authentically human, though. And Maggie had little to lose by questioning her directly. "I'm looking for a woman named Sisela Hansen."

"Never heard of her," the waitress said.

"Have you ever heard of Cosmo Delaney?"

The waitress looked startled. "Of course I have. He lives here in Bellewood."

"Well, Sisela might be a woman with him. Or she might not be. I'm trying to find out."

"A woman? You mean...like a girlfriend?"

Hope tingled inside Maggie—a sparkly pins-and-needles sensation in her solar plexus. Where had this wonderful waitress been when Maggie had begun her search? No matter; she'd found her now, and the woman was talking about something other than the annoying fact that Maggie couldn't fit into a size-eight blue silk suit. "Yes. Like a girlfriend," she said in an even voice.

"But...Cosmo's married!"

"He is?" Maggie's first thought should have been that this waitress was offering all sorts of useful stuff. But the idea that slashed through her mind was that if Sisela Hansen had run off with a married man, she wasn't worthy of Noah Davis and he was much better off without her.

Maggie had to remind herself that Noah might be a sleazeball, that he might be exactly the kind of guy who deserved the kind of woman who ran off with a married man. But she didn't want to believe that about him. She *couldn't* believe it.

"Took us all by surprise. Nobody ever thought he'd get married. He'd been single for so long, some people were actually whispering about him." The waitress flickered her eyebrows up and down significantly. "But no, he met a woman last year and all of a sudden they got married. Nobody saw it coming."

"Is her name Sisela?"

"I don't know. She keeps to herself, mostly. She isn't from around here."

Maggie reached into her purse and pulled out the photo of Sisela that Noah had provided. "Is this her?"

The waitress studied the woman in the photo for a minute, then shrugged and shook her head. "I couldn't say. Really. She doesn't come into town much. Or if she does, she sure doesn't come in here. I suppose maybe she goes to the supermarket sometimes, but I don't do my food shopping there.'' She leaned forward as if about to confide a deep, dark secret. ''You can't buy iceberg lettuce at that supermarket up the block. Romaine, arugula, Bibb, Boston red lettuce, endive... But try to find some plain, old, ordinary iceberg lettuce. You won't find it here in Bellewood, I'll tell you that.''

Maggie smiled sympathetically, but her mind was racing after its own concerns. Cosmo Delaney was married, and his wife might or might not be Sisela. He'd gotten married recently—probably after he'd met her in Los Angeles. But still, if he could have met her, he could have met someone else, as well.

''Do you know anyone who might know Cosmo's wife?'' she asked, figuring that if the waitress could comfortably refer to Delaney by his first name, she must at least be friendly with him.

''I suppose some folks around here may know her,'' the woman said. ''But she isn't on any of the committees or in the social clubs. The garden-club ladies come in here every Tuesday for lunch. Tuesday's the day they check the potted impatiens in those planters on the sidewalk around the town buildings, and after they do that they always come in here for lunch. But I've never seen her with them. And I've never seen *this* woman at all.'' She eyed the photograph one last time, then handed it back to Maggie.

''Well.'' Maggie sucked her iced tea through the straw. It invigorated her, almost as much as talking to the waitress. She'd gotten somewhere—not where she'd hoped, but *somewhere*. Delaney existed. He had

a new wife, someone from out of town. His wife was
giving Bellewood society the cold shoulder—or perhaps the town was cold-shouldering her.

The cops signaled that they were ready for their
bill. The waitress smiled and rose to her feet. "You
know," she said thoughtfully, "maybe you ought to
ask the police if they've seen that woman. They're
supposed to find missing persons. That's their job."

Maggie smiled. The last thing she wanted to do was
ask the police anything. They would only complicate
matters. Sisela was an adult; she was allowed to disappear if she chose, without having the police after
her.

While the waitress was busy with the policemen,
Maggie left a five-dollar bill on the table, took another
long slurp of iced tea and left the diner. As helpful
as the waitress had been, Maggie didn't want to pro-
long the discussion. The woman obviously couldn't
help her any further.

Her muscles ached from too much walking and too
little sleep as she headed back to the motel. The brief
jolt of energy from the iced tea didn't linger; she was
bone-tired, her feet sore, her head throbbing. She was
going to go back to her room, call San Francisco for
her messages, kick off her shoes and close her eyes
for a minute. Or two minutes. Or maybe a couple of
hundred minutes. She doubted Bellewood had anything new to tell her. Tomorrow she would travel
down to the Cosmic Candy Company's headquarters.
She would try to wheedle her way into Delaney's
office, where she'd be able to see whether he had any
photographs of his new wife displayed on his desk.

For now, the best thing Bellewood could offer her was a bed to stretch out on.

She trudged across the parking lot, passing the glass-enclosed front office on her way to her room at the far end of the motel. Her peripheral vision caught on someone at the check-in desk, but she ordered herself to ignore him. Even if he was tall and lanky and had black hair. Even if his jeans emphasized the length of his legs and his shoulders were broad and angular and oddly familiar, reminding her of a shoulder she'd leaned on not long ago. She ordered herself to ignore the sensation in the pit of her stomach—that same pins-and-needles tingle she'd felt at the coffee shop when she'd been sure she was on the verge of a discovery.

She wasn't going to stop and stare at the man loitering near the front desk. She wasn't going to turn around and see why he'd tweaked her fancy. She wasn't going to pay any attention to her prickling nerves. She was going to keep moving toward her room and her bed, and she was going to lie down and close her eyes and sleep until morning.

She stopped anyway. And turned around and stared. She took one step back toward the office, and another, and then the man emerged from the office, gripping a leather valise in one hand and a room key in the other. He saw her and smiled, nearly blinding her with his brilliant blue eyes.

"Hi, Maggie," said Noah Davis.

CHAPTER FIVE

"HOW THE HELL DID YOU get here?" she demanded.

She looked fatigued—and fiery with anger. Her eyes burned with indignation. Her hair was a mess of windswept waves, her shoulders slumped, her trousers were wrinkled and her shoes wore a thin veneer of road dust. But her fisted hands, though planted on her hips, looked fully primed to slug him, and she aimed her chin at him as if it were a weapon.

He hadn't expected her to welcome him with open arms—which was the point, in a way. He was doing the unexpected and nursing an ill-defined but very real hope that the unexpected would be done to him, as well.

Seeking the unexpected was his plan for adventure, and whether or not Maggie wanted him in Bellewood, his journey here was an adventure. As soon as he'd gotten the specs approved and the contracts drawn up for the project in San Jose, he had booked a flight east.

Maggie Tyrell herself wasn't the adventure. At least he didn't think she was. But he was transfixed by the way her eyes flashed and her chin jutted aggressively and the swirls of her hair quivered as if her scalp itself were trembling with emotion at the mere sight of him.

That emotion was obviously rage, he reminded himself. And he wasn't used to inspiring rage in the people around him. He'd spent his entire life trying to keep his nearest and dearest from becoming enraged. If he hadn't pursued a career marketing renewable-energy technology to architects, he probably would have made an excellent diplomat.

"I took a couple of personal-leave days and cashed in some frequent-flyer miles," he explained, knowing damned well that she hadn't been inquiring about the logistics of his trip to Bellewood.

She opened her mouth and then shut it, obviously thinking hard. He could read her effort in the lines in her brow, in the flexing of her fingers, in the ripple of movement in her throat as she swallowed, in that odd quivering of her hair. It made him want to brush his fingers through the curls and settle them down.

After some inner struggle she opened her mouth again. Her voice was restrained, her irritation just beneath the surface. "You hired me to do a job, Noah. I'm doing that job. If you want to do the job yourself, why did you hire me?"

"I *want* you to do the job," he insisted. "I just want to watch you do it. Okay?"

"No. Not okay. I don't like being spied on by a client!"

"I'm not spying on you," he defended himself, a bit surprised by her vehemence. "If I were spying on you, I wouldn't be standing here talking to you. I'd be sneaking around, trying not to let you catch sight of me."

"Swell." She sighed dramatically. "You're not

spying on me. You're just…in my face. And you're in my way. I really don't want you here."

He heard a thread of desperation in her voice. Maybe impulsively following Maggie to New York hadn't been such a good idea. Perhaps he should have stayed home, staring at his phone and waiting for it to ring, waiting for word from her, growing short-tempered and impatient as the silence stretched on. The message she'd left on his voice mail that morning had been terse enough to put him off—if he'd felt like being put off.

He hadn't. Even though all she'd communicated was the name of the motel where she was staying and the rather obvious promise that she would be in touch if she had anything to report, the mere sound of her voice had whetted his hunger for…

Adventure, he told himself. Nothing more than that.

"Look," he muttered, singed by the heat of her wrath. "You've been working all day. I've been fly-ing all day. We're both tired, and I don't know about you, but I'm starving. Let me drop my bag in my room and then we'll get something to eat." If she had a plate of food in front of her, he reasoned, her an-noyance might wane. Food had a way of soothing ruffled nerves. And unlike Sisela, Maggie appeared to be the sort of woman who enjoyed eating.

She pursed her lips, obviously at a loss for a suit-able argument. She didn't look happy. "I'm tired," she conceded. "You've got that part right. I'm going to my room to lie down. If you want to get some food now, go ahead. If you want my company for dinner, you'll have to wait an hour."

He could wait. An hour wouldn't kill him. And he

definitely wanted her company for dinner. He hadn't flown all the way across the country to eat alone.

Her room was a few doors down from his on the first floor. After stalking inside, she closed her door with more force than he considered necessary, but the earsplitting slam only amused him.

He continued along the row of numbered doors to his own room, entered and unpacked. He'd brought along comfortable clothes and a dress suit, not sure what he'd find in Bellewood or what he'd need. Sprawling out on the slate-stiff mattress, he reached for the phone and punched in the number for his office. "Hey, Violet," he greeted his secretary when she answered.

"You're making me crazy," she snapped. "Noah, I really wish you hadn't taken off like this."

"I got everything organized before I left. The new project—"

"I know, I know." She sighed. "It's just that you were this normal guy when you first came to work for Solar Systems. Then you suddenly took off for India, and now you're chasing all over the U.S. I'm worried about you. I've got this nagging fear that you're going through some kind of midlife crisis or something."

"I'm not old enough for a midlife crisis," he reminded her.

"Maybe you're precocious."

He laughed. "India was the best thing that ever happened to me. This trip…" *This trip could be even better than India,* he almost said, but that would have made no sense. "I won't be gone long," he assured her. "If I don't get results by the end of the weekend,

I'll come home and forget about it." *What results?* he wondered. *Forget about what?* Forget about locating Sisela or forget about spending time with Maggie on her wild-goose chase?

Why on earth did the second possibility trouble him more than the first?

"I promise you, Violet," he said, reverting to his usual conciliatory nature, "everything is under control. Here's a number where you can reach me if you have any problems." He recited the motel's telephone number. "I won't be gone long."

"If it was anyone else," she grumbled, "the company would have kicked his butt out the door by now."

"But I make so much money for them they have to accommodate me," he said sweetly. "I'll touch base with you tomorrow." He hung up the phone, stretched out on his bed, stared at the ceiling and pictured Maggie stretched out on *her* bed a few rooms away. Was she lying on her back as he was? Was her head nestled in the pillows? Was she thinking about how uncomfortable the bed was? Was she thinking about how the two of them could have saved some money by sharing a room?

Noah took a deep breath and exhaled slowly. Something was going on with him—something perplexing, something that appealed to him because it was unexpected, but also troubled him: He was having a lot of difficulty remembering that he cared about Sisela and no difficulty at all coming up with utterly unsuitable ideas about Maggie Tyrell.

She really wasn't his type, he reminded himself. She was cute but rather chunky. Too energetic. Too assertive. Too "out there." What he'd loved about Sisela was her refinement, her reticence, her gentility. She'd had class. Maggie...

Well, no. Maggie was not a classy woman. Despite his modest beginnings, Noah had developed an understanding of class—and he'd attained his own measure of that nebulous asset. He'd wanted class badly and he'd worked hard to earn it. And if he hadn't gone to India and discovered that there were more important things in the world than class, he would never have thought twice about someone like Maggie.

But he *was* thinking twice about her. More than twice. He was thinking that a woman with guts and spirit and hair that quivered when she was riled was more exciting than a woman with gentility.

Too wired to fall asleep, he shut his eyes and rested. He kept his mind focused on his project back at work, and on Sisela. He recalled his futile attempts to contact her mother in Saint Martin—her valet had told him that *"madame"* was on a sloop with friends, taking a month-long cruise around the islands, and could not be reached. Noah had also tried to get in touch with Sisela's father in Denmark, but the man had a knack for refusing to understand English when it didn't suit him. Noah had met him once, during a brief visit Mr. Hansen had made to California, and while the man had spoken with reasonable fluency when the subject was politics or music, he suffered a severe language block when Noah questioned him about his work or the family he'd started after divorcing Sisela's mother and taking a new wife. If Sisela had gone off and married a candy magnate, her parents would have felt no obligation to inform Noah.

They certainly would have made a bizarre set of in-laws.

Noah glanced at his watch. Maggie had had her hour, and his stomach was rumbling with hunger. He stretched, hauled himself off the bed and stalked to the bathroom to wash before dinner. Not only would a splash of cold water on his face refresh him, but maybe it would clear his mind so he wouldn't spend all evening ruminating about Maggie.

When he emerged from his room a few minutes later, he found Maggie pacing in the parking lot. Her trousers were still wrinkled, her hair still wild and windblown, her eyes still glinting with anger. That she had the energy to march to and fro on the asphalt implied that she might have managed to nap for a while. But if she had, it apparently hadn't done much to improve her mood.

She was glowering. Glaring. Crackling with negative energy. She looked overcast and ominous. He was almost surprised to smell the mild fragrance of the motel's soap on her, instead of that ominous scent that filled the atmosphere just before a thunderstorm.

"Are you okay?" he asked gently.

She halted midpace and spun around to face him. Her eyelashes were spiky, as if she'd been weeping. To his relief, her expression softened a bit, letting him believe that he wasn't the cause of her sour mood. At least, he wasn't the *only* cause.

"No," she said, her shoulders slumping as if she were a balloon losing air. "No, I'm not all right."

"What happened?"

She searched his face, hoping to find relief in it.

Then she sighed. "Maybe we should go get something to eat. You must be starving."

He must be. In fact, he was. But if she wasn't all right… "Maggie," he murmured. His arms twitched, and he had to exert himself to keep them at his sides. He wanted to hold her. He wanted to let her weep on his shoulder the way she had last night. He wanted to console her. And that was a dangerous thing to want.

"It's nothing, really," she explained. "Just my idiot brother, who should be shot. No, he should be tortured and *then* shot. He should be hung by his toes from the Golden Gate Bridge and tickled. And then shot. Let's go get some food. I don't want to go back to that coffee shop on the main drag in town. I've already spent too much time there today."

"Then we'll go somewhere else." Noah gestured toward the nondescript gray Ford parked near the door to his room. He had no idea what restaurants were in the vicinity, but he figured that if they drove for any distance, they'd find some sort of eatery.

Maggie frowned. "You have a car?"

"I rented it at the airport."

She gaped at him, her frown deepening. Turning back to the car, she sighed, shrugged then stormed across the lot to the sedan he'd indicated.

He followed her, digging the key from his pocket as he approached the rental car. He unlocked her door, and she sent him another distinctly displeased look as she lowered herself onto the seat.

Why was she angry? Because she'd apparently traveled on foot all day while he'd rented a car? Because her life would have been easier if she'd rented

a car, too? He'd never said she *shouldn't* rent a car.
All he'd said was that she should clear her expenses
with him. Just as his frequent-flyer miles had purchased him a free airplane ticket, they'd also paid for
his car rental. He'd amassed a lot of miles en route
to India last year, and before that trip he'd often journeyed to building sites around the country.

He settled into the driver's seat, slid the key into
the ignition and glanced at her. Beside him in the
bucket seat, she faced the windshield and brooded.
He couldn't shake the unhappy thought that her
brother wasn't the only person making her angry.

"Is there a problem with my having rented a car?"
he asked carefully.

She eyed him briefly, then shook her head. "I
just…well, you're spending so much money trying to
find Sisela, and yet…" She drifted off as if unsure
how to continue.

"And yet, what?"

"You don't seem exactly devastated that she's
gone."

He considered his response. No, he wasn't exactly
devastated that Sisela was gone. Yes, he was spending
a lot of money trying to find her. But if he told Maggie that the hunt alone was worth the money he was
spending on it, she wouldn't understand. She would
think he was wasting her time and behaving frivo-
lously.

Maybe he was, but that wasn't her problem, so she
had no reason to complain.

As he'd expected, they came upon a restaurant less
than a mile down the road from the motel. It was one
of those national chains, a hurly-burly plastic-looking

place. Noah assumed they'd crossed the town line; Bellewood would never allow such a tawdry joint within its borders.

But he could hardly search for a fancier, pricier establishment. If he spent a lot of money on an elegant, intimate dinner, she would fret even more that he was being too extravagant. And he would fret that he was framing Maggie in his mind as…well, the sort of woman he wanted to take out for an elegant, intimate dinner.

The restaurant wasn't too crowded, although it was certainly noisy. A perky, uniformed waitress found them a booth as far as possible from the bar, which seemed to be the source of most of the noise. The menu went on for page after laminated page of entrées, every kind of cuisine from ersatz Italian through ersatz Chinese to ersatz Mexican. He ordered a Swiss-and-bacon hamburger, fries and an iced tea.

Maggie requested a spinach salad and water.

Noah wondered whether she was on a diet. He wanted to tell her not to be. So what if she wasn't willowy? So what if she had a bit more insulation than absolutely necessary? She was…voluptuous; her round, rosy cheeks were adorable. She looked robust and healthy. She shouldn't change a thing about her appearance—if she did, she wouldn't be Maggie Tyrell.

"So," he asked, once the waitress had taken their menus and disappeared, "why have you sentenced your brother to death?"

She rolled her eyes. "His wife kicked him out."

"And *he's* the one you want to shoot?"

"He's a jerk. A lovable jerk, but a jerk nonetheless. All my brothers are."

All? How many did she have?

"The motel had a phone message for me from Jack," she continued. "He's the oldest. He thinks that makes him the spokesman and the problem solver. He might be the spokesman, but he sure as hell isn't the problem solver. *I* solve all the problems, which is why he called me.

"Neil is basically useless when it comes to solving problems—except that he let Sandy move in with him when Karen gave him his walking papers. Like it makes any sense for Sandy to move in with Neil. He's a bachelor, and he lives in the quintessential bachelor pad. I've told him a million times that that's a turnoff. No woman is going to venture into his Mr. Slick condo and want to spend the night. He's got these sofas that are so big and soft that if you make the mistake of sitting in one, you need a forklift to hoist you out. He says that's just the way he likes it, and that the women love it. I guess it's because he's cute." She curled her lip.

Noah had no idea what she was talking about. But he didn't mind. Simply hearing her ramble on about her family was surprisingly enjoyable. "You don't think he's cute?" he guessed.

"He's my youngest brother. He's two years older than me—chronologically. Emotionally, he's still in diapers. I love him half to death, but no, I don't think he's cute. Now Jack—my oldest brother—doesn't want to be cute. He wants to be God." She rolled her eyes in disgust. "And then there's Sandy."

"The one whose wife has asked him to leave," Noah ventured.

"Right. He's a space cadet. The family genius. The computer jockey. He can fly through cyberspace faster than the speed of light. He can find the company anything it needs—"

"The company?"

Maggie paused while the waitress delivered their drinks, then answered, "Tyrell Investigative Services. It's a family-owned detective agency. You had to walk through their waiting area to get to my office. I used to work for them."

"Why did you quit?"

"I got tired of being the only mature person in the company. No, that's not true," she confessed, cracking a slight smile that made her eyes glitter like jewels. "I got tired of being the only optimist. I believe detective services can be put to use bringing loved ones back together. My brothers believe there's more money to be made catching cheaters and adulterers. They're probably right. But I... Well, you know." She shrugged and sipped her water.

"You're a romantic," Noah said.

She seemed to flinch; the water shivered in her glass as she lowered it. Then she smiled—a sweet, almost-bashful smile. "I guess that's true. I'm a romantic."

"Even when your own brother has gotten the boot from his wife?"

Maggie's smile vanished so quickly, Noah was sorry he'd spoken. "It's his own fault," she said, then fell silent as the waitress delivered their dinners. She lifted her fork, toyed with a fat green leaf on her plate and shook her head. "He forgot their anniversary. But that's no surprise. He forgets everything. I guess this was the last straw, though. Karen told him to get lost, and now he's camping out in Neil's studly lair."

Noah willed her to stab the spinach leaf, to bring it to her mouth and eat. If she ate, she might feel better. She certainly wouldn't feel any worse.

"Not every relationship is destined to last forever," he commented, thinking of himself and Sisela, as well as Maggie's brother and his wife. At one time Noah might have thought he and Sisela could make a lasting, loving marriage. But although her disappearance had hurt him at first, the pain had faded like an old bruise, not even leaving a scar. He felt a bit guilty about that. Surely if what he'd felt for Sisela had been true love, he would be scarred, wouldn't he?

Was he that shallow? Was one missed rendezvous enough for him to write her off?

"Sandy and Karen belong together," Maggie declared as if delivering an edict. "They've just got to be a little more sensitive to each other, that's all. They've got to remember what it is they love about each other. Karen loves Sandy's intellect. She loves that his mind is always going a thousand miles an hour. And as for Sandy—he would lay down his life for Karen without even stopping to think about it. He's just too much of a butthead to remember flowers on their anniversary."

"So, you think some couples *are* destined to last forever," Noah suggested, still not convinced. His parents hadn't been destined. He and Sisela obviously hadn't been destined. Yet Noah had been sure he wanted to marry Sisela a year ago, and his mother had always insisted that she and his father had loved each other. "He just can't help himself," his mother used to say. "He can't find work here. He can't even find himself. He loves us enough to stay away."

Some destiny.

"Anyway, Jack thinks I should fly home right now and make things right between Sandy and Karen," Maggie continued. "I told him I was working, but he's having a major fit about the whole thing. Apparently I'm the only person in the whole world who can get them back together."

"You're the romantic," Noah reminded her.

"Well, yes. And I *could* get them back together. They've had fights before, and I've helped them to kiss and make up. But honestly, I'm trying to get my own business off the ground right now. I'm trying to make things right between you and Sisela."

"I don't think even you could accomplish such a miracle." He hoped his smile softened the sharp edge of his words.

She studied him over the rim of her water glass. "But you want me to try," she said cautiously. "I know you love her. No man would go to as much effort as you have to find a woman unless he loved her."

Oh, yes, he would, Noah wanted to argue. He'd go to as much effort as he could if he was chasing down something just as important as a runaway sweetheart. Noah had gone to a great effort in India when he'd been chasing down something vitally important— something that had had nothing to do with love but everything to do with who he was and what he valued in the world. And he would expend just as much effort on this current adventure if it would bring him whatever it was he was looking for.

Risk. The feeling of utter alive-ness he'd felt in India when he'd been worrying less about nonrenewable energy resources and more about getting storm-ravaged buildings up to code. In India, his work hadn't been about theories and trends. It had been about people needing roofs over their heads, children needing classrooms to study in. It had been about using his hands as well as his head, his heart as well as his mind.

And his current endeavor with Maggie Tyrell... It was about hanging on to that feeling, that sense of purpose, that need to do things. It was about believing in something bigger than whether he had a meeting scheduled for two o'clock that afternoon or whether a contract had come through.

Maybe Maggie's brothers wanted her to race back to San Francisco and solve their problems. But she was doing something just as essential here in Bellewood. She was trying to get her business off the ground, as she'd said. She was trying to give wings to her dream, to see if it would fly.

And she was working for Noah. He'd hired her, and he had dreams, too—if only he could get a handle on what exactly those dreams might be.

Eventually he would figure out what he was dreaming of, what he needed, what he wanted from Maggie. Or at least he'd figure it all out if she stuck around and did the job he was paying her to do. But if she left, if she raced back to San Francisco to solve her family's problems, Noah might never know what it was he'd been looking for when he'd signed on as her very first client.

The hell with her brothers. Maggie was on Noah's payroll right now, and he had no intention of letting her go.

CHAPTER SIX

WHAT WAS WRONG WITH HER? Why did she keep acting so damned unprofessional around Noah Davis?

He was her client, for heaven's sake! And here she was, monopolizing their dinner conversation with a nonstop whine about her imbecilic brothers. This couldn't be what Noah had flown all the way across the country for. It wasn't what he was paying two hundred dollars a day to listen to.

Yet he seemed so easy to confide in. The way he watched her, nodded, asked questions and willingly soaked up her every word... Though she couldn't guess why, he acted as if he were genuinely interested in what she had to say.

She appreciated that about him even more than she appreciated his crystal-blue eyes and the delectable shape of his mouth, more than she appreciated the length of his fingers wrapped around his bulky hamburger and the way his dimples slyly winked at her when he chewed. She appreciated his attention and his compassion.

She shouldn't be appreciating anything about him other than his financial patronage. The man was obviously so infatuated with Sisela Hansen that he'd spent several fortunes to search for her. He must love Sisela beyond all reason.

Beyond their table, the restaurant's atmosphere churned in a constant din: children fussing, plates clattering, infants squealing, adults laughing or scolding and an undercurrent of vapid music oozing through invisible speakers. The walls were brightly colored, the floor brightly tiled, the ceiling lights as bright as noon. Yet Maggie might as well have been sitting at a candlelit, linen-draped table for two at a romantic bistro, a place where they served "cuisine" instead of limp spinach salads and greasy burgers accompanied by mountains of soggy fries. Whenever Noah gazed at her, she felt as if they were all alone in the universe.

"How long have they been married?" he asked.

She shook her head to clear it of romantic nonsense. "Sandy and Karen? Three years," she said.

"Any kids?"

"Not yet." God, but she was glad she had Noah to talk to, even if she shouldn't be.

"Three years and no kids," he repeated, then munched thoughtfully on a fry. "Maybe they ought to cut their losses and call it quits."

"No!" Maggie retorted, then offered an apologetic smile. "What they ought to do is use their brains. I told you. They love each other. They're perfect for each other." She couldn't bear the thought that their latest spat was for real and forever. When two people belonged together, Maggie would do anything to keep them that way.

"If they were perfect for each other," Noah observed, "they wouldn't be separated right now."

Maggie studied him in the glaring light. Was he speaking from experience? What did he know about marital problems? Had he been married before Sisela or was he thinking of his aborted marriage plans with her? Did he think Sisela's unexplained disappearance meant they weren't perfect for each other? If he did, why was he paying so much money for Maggie to remain on the case?

Maybe she should have investigated him further before she'd accepted his business. But he was her first—her *only*—client. If she'd put him off long enough to run a background check on him, he might have marched out of her tiny office and found a detective agency willing to begin the search immediately, no questions asked.

She assured herself that his background was irrelevant. Her job was to find his current beloved for him, not to learn how many marriages and divorces littered his past. "I believe," she said firmly, "that true love exists, and that when it exists it must be honored. When I see it—when I sense it—I feel it's my duty to protect and preserve it. That's why I'm doing what I do—because I believe in true love."

"You believe you can recognize true love better than the lovers themselves? Maybe your brother and sister-in-law know something you don't know."

"They know they love each other," Maggie argued, recalling all the times she'd seen the two of them arm in arm, wrapped in a palpable aura of mutual adoration. Of course they loved each other. They were just a pair of stupid, stubborn idiots.

The waitress stopped by their table to ask if Maggie and Noah wanted anything else. He glanced at her and she shook her head. She ought to have been famished, but she'd had to force herself to finish half her salad. "Just the check, please," he said to the waitress, then eyed Maggie again. "Are you feeling all right?"

She nudged her plate away. "Just tired. And drained. It's amazing how three brothers can wipe a woman out. Do you have any siblings?" She couldn't come right out and grill him on how many divorces he'd racked up, but asking about his family was innocuous enough.

"None." He dug into his hip pocket for his wallet and pulled out a credit card, then scanned the bustling dining room in search of their waitress.

His laconic reply piqued Maggie's interest. Lots of people were only children—and more than once, after dealing with her brothers, Maggie had found herself envying them. But Noah's answer didn't prompt envy. It was cold and curt, like a dead bolt sliding shut.

"Where did you grow up?" she asked in a casual voice so he wouldn't think she was prying.

"North of Sacramento. You've never heard of the place."

"Try me."

He shot her a swift look, then twisted in his seat to follow the progress of the waitress as she approached their table. She handed him the bill; he skimmed it and handed it back with his credit card.

When he turned back to Maggie, she smiled, hoping to erase his sudden tension. The smile seemed to work; he settled back into the banquette and tossed her a faint grin. "Butte City," he said. "But it isn't a city, and I lived on the outskirts. It's farm country. Orchards and rice fields."

"Were your parents farmers?"

His jaw flexed, and he gazed past her for a moment, as if the question needed to be deconstructed before he could offer an accurate reply. "In a manner of speaking."

Maggie smiled again. "This isn't a police interrogation, Noah. I've just sat here running on and on about my family. I thought maybe you'd want a turn to talk. Sorry I asked."

Apparently chastened, he flashed her another grin, this one less hesitant. His smile was a breathtaking thing, both sweet and taunting, full of dimples and glitter and something more, something oddly fragile, something that reached inside her and made her want to touch him. She buried her hands in her lap.

"My father was a migrant worker," he said. "I saw him, at most, once or twice a year—if he happened to be passing through town. He'd send my mother money sometimes. He'd work down south in the Imperial Valley, then up north in Washington State, picking apples. Then he'd head into the nearest town and harvest whatever liquor he could afford. So, yes, I guess you could say he was a farmer." He drained his glass, then set it down. "He and my mother loved each other, but they sure as hell didn't belong together. I don't think it's always necessary to honor true love."

Maggie struggled to assimilate everything he'd told her. She would never have guessed that he'd come from such humble beginnings. He seemed so polished, so confident, so in control. And his erstwhile fiancée was so beautiful. A private-school teacher, a citizen of the world, her father in Denmark and her mother in the Caribbean. Sisela—what Maggie knew about her, anyway—was cosmopolitan and sophisticated, and Noah seemed her ideal match.

Yet here he was, telling her he was the son of an itinerant farm worker, an absentee father who drank too much. Noah must have worked awfully hard to transform himself so completely.

Despite her residual jet lag and her worry about Sandy and Karen, Maggie forced her brain into overdrive. One of the most important tools for a detective was the ability to psych out a person, to read his emotional strengths and weaknesses and motivations. Working through the puzzle that was Noah Davis, she suspected that his drive to find Sisela, his need to make her his wife, might have something to do with his harsh childhood. He'd grown up poor and now he was a hot-shot executive with a leading-edge technology company. At some point, a refined, cultured, beautiful San Francisco woman—a woman who could make him feel as if he'd truly overcome his past— had been his. No wonder he wanted her back.

Well, Maggie would do what she had to do to make that happen, if that was what it would take to restore Noah's sense of himself. While Maggie believed in true love, she didn't dare to evaluate it, to claim that some reasons for loving a person were better than others. If Noah needed Sisela, if he appreciated the way Sisela completed his life, that was good enough for Maggie. She would do what he'd hired her to do.

The drive back to the motel passed in silence. Noah pulled into a parking space halfway between their rooms. As soon as he opened his car door, she opened hers. She had the feeling he might have been about to assist her out of the car, and she didn't want his help. She wanted to be the professional; the one offering help, not receiving it.

They met on the sidewalk in front of the car. "Thanks for dinner," she said.

He offered another stunning smile. "Next time we'll have to go someplace nicer," he said. "Are you sure you aren't still hungry?"

She didn't want to think of Noah in the context of a next time, let alone hunger. The spinach salad she'd ordered hadn't whetted her appetite, but Noah's smile, his coal-dark hair and lean grace made her ravenous.

She blinked to clear her mind. "I'm fine," she said.

His smile faded slightly. "You're not fine. You're worried about your brother."

She was, but that wasn't Noah's problem. "He'll be fine, too. Everyone will be fine once I get back to San Francisco."

"Maybe you ought to go."

"Go?"

"Now." He sounded serious. "Go back home and help your brother and his wife fix their marriage."

A car cruised by on the road beyond the parking lot, and its headlights flashed across Noah's face. In the brief illumination, his gaze was as brilliant as diamonds, hard and sharp and sparkling. It seemed to pierce her, to slice right through her skin to her soul. He wasn't supposed to be seeing through her, though. Searching, digging for information, learning the truth—that was the detective's job, not the client's.

The car passed and a shadow fell over Noah's face once more. Only then did she realize how unsettled she was. Maggie Tyrell, unafraid of thugs and criminals, lowlifes and bothersome brothers, had been rattled by a man's gaze. She blinked again and again, but her thoughts remained muddled.

"Whether or not you find Sisela this minute isn't going to make a difference," Noah continued when she didn't speak. "But going back to your brother right now might."

Maggie finally regained her voice. "No. Finding Sisela this minute *is* going to make a difference. It's essential that I find her as quickly as possible."

"We can rework the contract. We can do this some other time if—"

"No," she said more forcefully. "I've got to find Sisela, and the sooner the better. You need her in your life, Noah. Whatever mistakes she's made, whatever she's gotten herself into with this Delaney fellow, it's not too late to undo the damage between you. But if too much time passes... The longer you're apart, the harder it will be to make things right."

He chuckled. For a moment she longed to see his face lit up again, so she could read his mood. Was he laughing at her? Did he think she was insane or just foolish?

"Noah," she said sternly, wondering if perhaps *he* was the fool. She would simply have to explain things to him. "If you and Sisela are destined to be together, it's my job to get you together. You need her in your life. You love her enough to want to find her, to marry her, to—"

Before she could finish, before she could catch her breath, he swooped down and touched his mouth to hers. It was less a kiss than a means of shutting her up. Yet his lips were warm. Hot. Erotic.

When he pulled back, she felt chilled. "Noah?" she whispered, a mere breath of sound in the evening stillness.

"I don't think my destiny is Sisela," he murmured, lowering his mouth to hers again, brushing gently this time, sliding his hand around to the back of her head and digging his long fingers into her hair to hold her steady.

As if there were any chance she'd move away. As if he actually needed to hold her in place, as if she would choose to escape his kiss. She felt magnetized to him, unable to draw back, unable to resist the sensual dance of his lips on hers.

This wasn't destiny, she told herself. It wasn't true love. That a handsome, intriguing, surprisingly complex man could kiss her into a state of abject desire meant nothing more than that Noah Davis knew how to use his mouth.

But for just this one sweet moment, she wasn't going to stop him. She was going to ignore the nagging voice inside her, reminding her that she was a professional and he was her client. The hell with professionalism. She was going to let Noah kiss her silly.

He must have sensed her acquiescence, because he brought his other arm around her waist and pulled her closer. She felt the warmth of his body against hers, the sleek surface of his chest through his shirt, his knee nudging her thigh. She felt one of his hands at the small of her back and the other at the nape of her neck, his fingers twining through her hair. She felt his tongue slide along her lower lip, tasting it, savoring it before he probed deeper. She felt his groan before she heard it.

Or maybe she was hearing her own quiet sigh of pleasure. The combination of his mouth on hers and his arms around her eroded her strength so much that she could hardly stand. Her hips sank against his; her breasts pressed flat against his chest. She lifted her hands to his shoulders and hung on, wishing she could simply melt into him like warm, golden butter.

His tongue slid over hers and she heard another groan. Hers. His. It didn't matter. He pulled her intimately against him, letting her feel his arousal. His tongue entered her mouth, filling her mind and soul with yearning.

He withdrew only enough to whisper, "Come to my room." Then he kissed her again—a deep, devastating, won't-take-no-for-an-answer kiss.

All right, she thought, her heart beating crazily, making her breasts ache, making the muscles in her thighs grow taut. All right. She would go to his room and find out if he did everything else as sublimely as he kissed.

No. She wouldn't do that. Much as she wanted to, much as every cell in her body felt swollen with lust for him, she would not go to Noah Davis's room. He was in love with Sisela Hansen, for God's sake. He was paying Maggie to find the woman he loved. And Maggie's job was to make that love possible—not to stand in its way.

She buried her face against his shoulder and tried to catch her breath. He smelled of soap and summer, mint and masculinity. She had to push away and fill her lungs with the evening air, to cleanse her longing for him from her system.

After a few deep breaths, she tried blinking again.

She blinked so hard he must have thought she had something in her eye. "Maggie?" he asked.

One more blink brought him fully into focus. Damn, but he was gorgeous. She studied his beautiful lips—lips that had performed such magic on her mouth—and his beautiful eyes. His hands still rested on her—one at her waist, one on her shoulder—and if she were an idiot she'd believe he couldn't bear to let go of her.

She might be an idiot, but idiocy had its limits. "I'm not going to your room," she said—the six most difficult words she'd ever uttered.

He stared at her for a moment. She regretted that her vision had grown accustomed to the dark, allowing her to make out his expression. He looked nowhere near as overwhelmed as she felt. He didn't seem particularly frustrated or annoyed or disappointed. Probably he'd thought he would give this seduction a whirl and see what happened. That what had happened was no longer happening didn't seem to trouble him terribly.

"Okay," he said after a minute.

As simple as that. *"Okay."*

Maggie congratulated herself on having found the willpower to turn him down, but she didn't feel much like celebrating. She had just said no to the most phenomenal kisser she'd ever met. She'd turned down a man possessing the kind of sex appeal that made lesser creatures dissolve or burn.

Maybe she was an idiot, after all.

No, she wasn't. She had wisely remembered what she was doing in Bellewood, what her goal was: not just to bring Noah back together with Sisela, but to establish her own detective agency. She couldn't afford a misstep with her very first client. She couldn't afford a detour, especially one that led directly to the edge of a precipice—and then over it.

"I'm sorry," she said, thinking Noah couldn't begin to guess how sorry she was.

"No, *I'm* sorry. I…" He shrugged and smiled sheepishly. "I must have lost my head."

Of course. If he hadn't suffered from a sudden, inexplicable spasm of dementia, he would never have kissed Maggie.

"I'm going to bed," she said, then cringed at her unfortunate phrasing. "Alone," she added.

He nodded, remaining where he stood while she inched toward her door and groped in her purse for her room key. "What are we doing tomorrow?" he asked.

We? "Nothing," she told him, jabbing the key into the doorknob and twisting it open. "Nothing at all." With that, she stepped inside and slammed the door.

HE STARED AT HER DOOR for a full minute, as if the forest-green rectangle could offer up an answer.

An answer to what? He wasn't even sure what the question was.

What he *was* sure of was that, for a moment there, he'd been so hot for Maggie Tyrell he'd lost his mind. If she'd said yes, if she'd actually gone with him to his room—to his bed—he believed he would happily have waved his mind goodbye forever and never suffered an instant's regret.

Shaking his head, he forced himself to trudge down the sidewalk to his own door. His feet felt sluggish,

as if they resented having to carry him away from
her. His heart felt sluggish, too, beating lethargically
after the way it had raced when he'd had Maggie
wrapped in his arms. His whole body felt sluggish,
the strain of a transcontinental flight finally catching
up with him.

That, and the discovery that a frizzy-haired lady
with whom he had less than nothing in common could
ignite him like a match tossed into a jug of kerosene.

It was because Maggie embodied the unexpected,
he told himself, wiggling his key into the lock of his
door. It was because her eyes were so animated, her
words so heartfelt, her concern over her brother so
genuine. He wished he had a sister like her, who
could care so much about whether or not he was ru-
ining his life.

He wasn't feeling particularly brotherly toward her,
though.

His room was chilly as he stepped inside, and he
realized it was an empty sterile box filled with sterile,
boxy furnishings; and the only way it would ever feel
warm would be if Maggie were lying on his bed, if
her curls and curves and softness were his to explore,
to learn, to take.

Merely imagining such pleasure caused his jeans to
feel snug and his heart to resume its accelerated beating.

Forget it, he ordered himself. Perhaps there had
been a chance for something with Maggie, but that
chance was gone. Maggie had turned him down—and
a good thing, too. Self-control had gotten him further
in life than he'd ever dared to dream when he was a
dirt-poor kid, and self-control would get him through

the next twenty-four hours, and the twenty-four hours after that. Chasing adventures wasn't what had carried him from poverty to prosperity. Adventures were diverting, they were exciting—but this adventure would soon reach its conclusion and he would return to doing what he always did: striving, improving, increasing the distance between where he'd come from and where he was going.

He would play this adventure out, reassure himself that Sisela was happy in whatever new life she'd created for herself, and then go back to San Francisco and convince developers to design their buildings with solar power in mind. And he would try not to get hung up on the lady detective who was making the adventure possible.

MAGGIE AROSE EARLY. She could blame yesterday's exhaustion on jet lag, but this morning her weariness was the result of a long night of unforgivable dreams. Dreams of Noah in her bed, dreams of his kisses, dreams of him using his mouth on her body the way he'd used it on her lips. Dreams of flying back to San Francisco with him, solving all of Sandy and Karen's marital problems and celebrating by letting Noah do all sorts of wicked things to her.

She had dreams that convinced her he would be fabulous in bed. Dreams that made her believe Sisela Hansen wasn't his true love. Dreams that a woman of her limited physical assets and even more limited experience could make a man like him crazy with pleasure.

Pathetic, embarrassing, ridiculous dreams.

She staggered into the shower, determined to wash

away the residue of her restless night. She shampooed
her hair, blow-dried it and attempted to tame it with
a tortoiseshell barrette. Then she dressed in a summery beige skirt that didn't make her hips look too
huge, a white cotton shell and a navy blue linen
blazer. Inspecting herself in the mirror on the back of
the bathroom door, she decided she looked like a dean
at a starchy prep school.

Not a bad way to present herself to Cosmo Delaney—assuming she was lucky enough to find him at
his company's headquarters in midtown Manhattan.

It was seven-thirty when she stepped outside into
the blinding sunlight that flooded the parking lot.
Noah's rented car was exactly where he'd parked it
last night, and his door was closed. A cautious glance
at the glass-enclosed motel office revealed that the
clerk on duty was alone.

Good. She would grab a cup of coffee from the
machine in the office, then walk the few blocks to the
Bellewood train station and escape on the commuter
train before Noah could catch up with her. He might
think he had something useful to contribute to the
hunt for Sisela, but he was nothing but a distraction.
He slowed her down. He scrambled her brain waves
so she couldn't think straight. He made her breathe
too hard, sigh too deeply—want too much.

One sip of coffee scalded her tongue. Next to the
tower of plastic cups was a box full of lids, and she
snapped one onto her cup. With a brisk smile for the
clerk, she hurried out of the office, anxious to reach
the train station before Noah emerged from his room
and noticed she'd gone. By the time she found a seat
on the train, the coffee would be cool enough to drink.

Yesterday's daylong hike around town made itself felt today. Her calf and thigh muscles were sore, and her loafers seemed a millimeter too narrow. Her shoulder protested under the strap of her purse, which was crammed with her notepad, several pens, her wallet, sunglasses, lipstick, tissues and a roll of breath mints. Ordinarily it wouldn't seem so heavy, but Maggie was running on empty.

Bellewood's train station was as quaint as the rest of the town. A stucco building with Tudor-style beams and brick flourishes, it was more luxurious than a lot of houses she'd been in. Probably much more luxurious than Noah's childhood home. She tried to picture him young and poor, living in a dusty rural village and waiting for his daddy to come home, waiting months at a time. Had he been desperate for affection and security? Had his mother taken her disappointments out on him? Had he lost the ability to believe in true love and destiny?

Maggie would find Sisela, damn it. She'd prove to Noah that true love and destiny existed.

She purchased a round-trip ticket to Manhattan, then took her place among the well-heeled commuters lining the platform. Bellewood apparently banned canvas totes. Everyone, male and female, young and old, carried leather portfolios or briefcases. Two middle-aged men in double-breasted gray suits discussed golf in hushed tones. A woman in a double-breasted gray suit read the *Wall Street Journal*. Maggie tore a wedge-shaped opening into the lid of her cup and sipped her coffee. It was still too hot, but she craved caffeine.

A southbound train pulled into the station. She

scanned the dozen passengers and let out a sigh of relief. Noah hadn't found her. She was safe from him for the day—safe to work, safe to cure herself of her inappropriate attraction to him.

She boarded the train and found an empty seat by the window. Taking delicate sips from her cup, she stared out at the woods beyond the tracks. Even Bellewood's train station was picturesque, she thought wryly. No shopping area, no crowded highway, no low-income housing lined its rails; only the charming platform building on one side and a verdant expanse of forest on the other.

The train hissed and rumbled, idling for a few minutes before creaking slowly away from the station. Maggie let out another deep sigh. *Free at last,* she thought as she drank from her cup. The coffee tasted burned and it had a subtle plastic undertone, but she didn't care. All she cared about was that she was on the train and Noah was at the motel—too far away to interfere with her work or her fantasies.

"Is this seat taken?" came a voice from behind her. An alarmingly familiar voice. An unwelcome, dreaded voice.

She spun from the window so quickly, a bit of her coffee splattered through the cup's opening and landed on her thumb. She didn't feel it, though. She was too busy feeling panic-stricken and queasy as she stared in horror at the man looming before her in the aisle, smiling at her in all his dimpled, blue-eyed, charismatic glory.

"Yes," she retorted.

"Good." He lowered himself into the empty seat.

"Good morning, Maggie. What's the plan for today?"

"My plan is to ignore you. I have no idea what your plan is."

Noah's smile widened, etching his dimples even deeper into his cheeks. "I'm paying you good money. Why do you want to ignore me?"

"I'm trying to do what you're paying me good money to do," she said sharply. "That's not easy when I've got you shadowing me."

"I guess that's what people must feel like when you and your brothers shadow them."

"I don't shadow anyone," she argued, turning back to the window and willing her temper to cool down. How had he managed to get on the train without her seeing him? *Why* had he?

And really, what did it matter? He was here. He must have driven to the station close behind her and boarded another car while she'd been gazing at the forest. And now he was going to dog her all day.

Damn him for looking so refreshed when her energy level rivaled that of a slug's. Damn him for wearing pale khaki slacks that made his legs look absurdly long and a lightweight denim shirt that emphasized the athletic contours of his torso. Of course, Noah Davis didn't need to wear clothing to look wonderful.

Bad thought. She closed her eyes and prayed for the image of Noah without clothes to dissipate.

"I didn't fly all the way to New York to sit in a motel room," he informed her.

She pursed her lips. "I still don't know why you did fly all the way to New York. You really can't

help with any of this, Noah. I wish you'd back off
and let me do my job. If your life isn't exciting
enough in San Francisco, get a hobby."

He lapsed into a contemplative silence. She wondered if she'd spoken too rudely. His only crime was
that he was too appealing, that he stirred feelings in
her that were wrong.

And he'd kissed her. Lord, how he'd kissed her.

When several minutes passed without a single
word, she eyed him warily. He stared straight ahead,
as if the textured back of the seat in front of them
fascinated him. But his smile was gone, his dimples
nowhere in evidence. He propped one leg across his
other knee, rested his hand on his raised ankle and
drummed his fingers against his shoe. He seemed pensive.

"What is it?" she persisted.

He sent her a quick look, then resumed his inspec-
tion of the faded fabric of the seat back. "You're
right. My life in San Francisco isn't exciting
enough."

His statement lay before her like a thrown gauntlet,
daring her to pick it up. If she did, if she questioned
him about what was wrong with his life in San Francisco, she would be inviting a friendship she knew
she ought to avoid. She had asked a few questions
over dinner yesterday, and his answers had softened
her to him, made her want to know him better—but
getting to know him too well struck her as somehow
perilous.

Yet how could she *not* question him? Wasn't it her
job to understand her client's goals and motives?
"You hired me because you want excitement?" she

asked, then laughed at how silly that sounded. "You could have found a much more exciting lady for much less money."

"I'm not looking for a prostitute," he said so blandly she wasn't sure if he was offended or amused.

Don't ask, she warned herself, then went ahead and asked, anyway. "What *are* you looking for?"

He turned to her, and she saw the same brilliance in his eyes that she'd seen last night an instant before he'd kissed her. "I don't know," he said, then gave her an enigmatic smile.

Maggie recalled what he'd told her last night—in particular, about his father, who had supposedly loved Noah's mother but had repeatedly abandoned her. Maybe that was all it was: Noah's need to know, his need to understand what had gone wrong in his mother's marriage and in his own relationship with Sisela. Maybe it was no more complicated than that.

"So you aren't looking for excitement?" she asked.

His smile returned, dangerously warm as he gazed at her. "I think I've already found excitement," he murmured. He turned away, but his smile lingered.

And it was the most damnably exciting smile she'd ever seen.

CHAPTER SEVEN

HE COULDN'T STOP thinking about kissing her.

She sat beside him, a bit stiff, a bit glum, clearly annoyed that he'd imposed himself on her while she was trying to work. He really couldn't blame her for being annoyed. She wanted to do her job. Hell, he wanted her to do her job, too. If he truly hoped she'd find Sisela, he ought to give her some room to work.

But he had become fixated on her. Not exactly on her, but on kissing her the way he'd kissed her last night. He'd kissed women before, made love with women—but never a woman like Maggie Tyrell. She was...different.

He tried to analyze precisely what it was that set her apart from all the other women he'd known. She was smart, but then he wouldn't be interested in a woman who didn't have a generous measure of intelligence. She was headstrong, but that didn't exactly distinguish her from others, either. Sisela, for instance. Only a headstrong woman would have traveled to Los Angeles chasing a dream of stardom and then departed on the arm of a royally rich candy executive who wasn't the man she'd promised to marry just a few months earlier.

Maggie was considerate, congenial and compassionate, without being a wimp. But so was every other woman he'd ever been attracted to.

What was it that distinguished her from the rest?

She was fat.

Well, no—not really fat. She was solid—and soft. He'd felt her curves when he'd held her last night, felt the plump swells of her breasts snuggling into his chest, the generous width of her hips against his. She didn't have the gaunt, sterile appearance of so many fashionable ladies nowadays. Maggie Tyrell was the kind of woman who wasn't afraid to live, to charge through the world with confidence and vigor and not become obsessed with how she looked as she went about her business.

And kissing her... She'd done that with vigor and confidence, too. With heat and power. With a robust appetite for pleasure.

He closed his eyes and leaned back on the rigid bench seat. His libido simmered. He was going to have to deal with his lust for Maggie one way or another—and he knew the best way would be to ignore it until it burned itself out. Noah found little appeal in the idea of bedding women with whom he had no relationship. And he had no relationship with Maggie Tyrell.

Yet he couldn't seem to keep his distance. Maybe he hoped that by remaining nearby, he could build up his resistance to her. Maybe he hoped that familiarity would breed, if not contempt, at least apathy. And in the meantime, maybe he hoped he could enjoy the adventure of searching for Sisela a little while longer.

Through the public-address system, a metallic, muffled voice announced the train's next stop. Beyond Maggie, Noah could see through the window that they had entered a more densely settled area—houses close together, trees and greenery sparse. Traffic sat motionless on the road paralleling the tracks, a long chain of brake lights glowing red as the morning rush-hour clogged the streets with cars. Noah wondered why more people didn't commute to the city on the train—but if more people did that, he might not have found an empty seat next to Maggie.

"When we get to the city," she said crisply, "I would suggest that you either get on the next northbound train and return to Bellewood or that you visit a museum. You're not coming with me."

"You don't think I could help?" he asked.

"More likely you'd just get in my way."

"You'd be surprised how helpful I can be."

She eyed him skeptically. Her eyes were round, too, he noticed. The curls and waves of her hair were round. Everything about Maggie was round. He had never before thought of circles as erotic.

Her words were anything but erotic, however. "You're right," she said. "I would be surprised. I'm sure you could be helpful if we'd come to New York to sell solar panels. But other than that—"

"Selling solar technology isn't the only thing I do," he argued.

Her cheeks darkened with a blush. She must be thinking of one of the other things he did: kissing. Imagining that she was thinking of that made him think of it, too. His body grew warm.

He had to chill out—literally—to keep them both focused on their mission. "I built a school building from scratch," he said to prove his point.

"A school building?"

"In India."

"Really?" She seemed genuinely interested. "Is that why you went there?"

He shook his head. "I went as a tourist. But there was a flood, and half a town got washed away. Entire buildings were destroyed. It was a mess. So I stuck around to help out."

"'A tourist'?" She looked doubtful. "I know you told me you wanted to see the world, but you don't seem like a tourist type to me."

"What's a 'tourist type'?"

She shrugged. "Someone with an expensive camera hanging from a strap around his neck, a baseball cap and a Hawaiian-print shirt with a map stuck in the shirt pocket."

Noah chuckled. "I guess I wasn't a tourist, then." He groped for a better word. "A seeker?" No, *seeker* wasn't quite right. But it wasn't far from the truth. "An explorer," he suggested, then shook his head, still not satisfied. "When I was growing up…" Again he struggled. He wanted to be precise but not pretentious. The fact was, he wasn't sure exactly why he'd yearned to travel around the world. It had been a compulsion, a deep, inchoate need to learn what existed beyond the drab, dusty roads of his childhood, the labs and classrooms of college and the humming, high-pressure corridors of Solar Systems, Inc.

He'd wanted to cross the line, to get adrenaline pumping in his veins—and not to worry about whether his choices would make anyone else's life easier or better. He'd wanted to risk everything, without knowing or caring what the payoff might be.

"I wanted to see things," he said vaguely. "I wanted to taste things. For once in my life, I..." He sighed. Maggie was staring at him, apparently intrigued.

"In India?"

"All over the world. I'd never been outside the country before that trip."

"You're kidding."

He chuckled. "Do you think I'd lie about something like that?"

She shrugged. "You seem so—so urbane."

"I'm not a hick, Maggie. I outgrew my hometown. I went to college. I live in San Francisco. But I wanted to see the world before I settled down and got married. I visited Japan and Thailand, and just when I got to India the storm hit."

"So you just tossed all your plans aside, all your dreams, and built a schoolhouse?"

He thought about that. If his plan and his dream had been to explore, to see and taste things he'd never seen or tasted before, then he'd accomplished his plans magnificently.

"I chose to stay," he explained. "I made friends in the village and in the nearby city of Midnapore. I had contacts back in the States who could help restore some of the buildings in the region. I do know a few people in the construction business, after all."

"So you built a schoolhouse?" She shook her head, apparently astonished. "That's incredible."

He wasn't sure whether or not to take offense. "You don't think I could do something like that?"

"No, it's just..." She smiled sheepishly. "The first time I met you, you were this poised, debonair ex-

ecutive type in a fancy suit. Then I learned that you'd
grown up in rural poverty, and now I'm learning that
you were a one-man Peace Corps just for the hell of
it. Every time I think I've got you nailed down, you
throw something new at me. You're just full of surprises."

He smiled. "I don't live up to your expectations?"

"You exceed them."

"Then will you admit," he asked carefully, "that
it's possible I can help you with whatever you've got
on the agenda for this morning?"

"No, I don't admit that," she said, the shimmer of
awe fading from her eyes. "Just because you can
build a schoolhouse in India doesn't mean you can be
a detective."

"I didn't say I could," he reminded. "All I said
was that I could help."

"And all I'm saying is no." The train glided into
a tunnel, stealing the urban scenery from the windows
and replacing it with a black expanse. The interior
lights couldn't compensate for the sudden absence of
sunlight. A yellowish tinge washed over Maggie's
face, her outfit, her hands folded in her lap. The rattle
of metal wheels on steel rails drowned out the muted
conversations of the others in the car. "I mean it,
Noah," she continued, but he could hardly hear her
voice. He could make out her words only by reading
her lips as she spoke. They were such lovely lips, full
and lush.

He wanted to kiss her. Again.

The train jerked, slowed, jerked again and stuttered
to a halt. Through the window he saw a broad platform swarming with people—some in business attire,

others in jeans or shorts, some carrying briefcases and laptop totes and others lugging bulging backpacks over their shoulders.

Maggie had made her position perfectly clear. She didn't want him tagging along, getting in her way, encroaching on her territory. He understood—but that didn't mean he was going to board the next train back to Bellewood. It was his alleged sweetheart they were chasing. Much as he appreciated Maggie's professional requirements, he had no intention of honoring them.

She eyed him distrustfully, then waited for him to stand and move into the aisle so she could get out. He followed her off the train, sticking close so he wouldn't lose her in the crush of people headed for the stairs. She forged onward, as if pretending she wasn't aware he was just a few steps behind her. Every now and then she'd glance over her shoulder, make eye contact with him, and grimace.

They ascended the stairs with hundreds of other commuters. As they emerged into the cavernous atrium of Grand Central Station, he nearly lost her among the throngs of important-looking men in pale summer suits and tasseled loafers, the self-assured women in crisp pastel dresses with linen blazers. But then he spotted her up ahead, nearing one of the doors. Stray strands of her hair floated above the tamer locks, shimmering in a haze of light brown curls. He recalled the texture of those curls sifting through his fingers last night. Silky-soft and round.

He had to jog and jostle his way through the crowd to reach the door. Outside on the sidewalk, he saw her marching ahead at a brisk clip. She was much more energetic this morning than she'd been when he'd found her yesterday evening. She weaved deftly among the pedestrians, never breaking stride, never bumping into anyone. Her confidence and grace appealed to him.

Damn it. Everything about her appealed to him.

The traffic light forced her to stop at a crowded corner, enabling him to catch up. He worked his way through the impatient hordes lining the curb until he reached her side. She scowled at him. "This is stupid," she muttered.

"It certainly is. You can't outrun me, Maggie, so—" The light turned green and the crowd surged forward, carrying them both through the intersection. On the opposite corner, he resumed speaking. "I'm here anyway, whether you want me here or not."

"I *don't* want you here," she snapped, accelerating her pace and refusing to look at him.

"Well, that's a real surprise," he retorted. "But I'm not leaving. So you might as well make use of me. Maybe we could present ourselves as a team."

"Present ourselves where? Do you have any idea where we're going?"

"No. I wish you'd share that information with me."

"I'm going to try to locate Cosmo Delaney. You're going to Central Park."

"Why? What's in Central Park?" he asked.

"Not me. That's what's in Central Park." She abruptly turned the corner, heading north on one of the avenues. Cars and buses streamed south in a symphony of horns and wheezing brakes and the occasional curse shouted through an open window. Office

buildings—bland, rectangular towers marked with
ruler-straight rows of windows—lined both sides of
the avenue. The skyscrapers were tall enough to block
out the morning sun—solar panels would be wasted
on them. Noah was glad he lived in San Francisco,
where the steep slopes of the roadways staggered the
buildings, exposing more of them to sunlight.

He tore his gaze from the buildings and panicked.
Where was Maggie? She'd been right beside him....

Just when his panic threatened to transform into
frenzied terror, he spotted her veering toward a revolving glass door. He weaved through the mobs of
pedestrians to reach her. She stepped into a quarter
circle and pushed the glass panel; he stepped into the
quarter circle behind her, chasing her inside.

The lobby was cool, its walls and floor paved with
dark brown marble. The aroma of coffee filled the air.

"Noah, I mean it," Maggie said sternly.

"I mean it, too."

Planting her hands on her hips, she glowered up at
him, making him keenly aware of how much taller
than her he was. His superior height didn't daunt her,
however. "I'm not going to let you come upstairs
with me," she declared.

"You can't stop me." He tried not to sound dic-
tatorial. He was hoping to break down her resistance,
not increase it, and if he came at her with aggressive
arguments, she would never feel comfortable with
him tagging along. In a gentler voice, he said, "I'll
keep my mouth shut if you want. You can run the
show. Just let me watch."

"I've told you I don't want you watching. I don't
like to work in front of an audience."

"Then pretend I'm not watching. Pretend I'm—"

"Excuse me?" A perky young woman approached them. She was wearing a brown minidress with a silver star stitched across the front. Inside the star, the words Cosmic Candy Company were embroidered in red thread. In her hands were two insulated paper cups of coffee. "I was wondering if you'd like to taste this new product Cosmic Candy Company has developed. It's mocha coffee, a blend of Cosmic's own rich chocolate processed into a cocoa and mixed with handpicked Colombian coffee beans. We're offering samples, and I was wondering if you two lovely people would be willing to try some." Throughout her entire spiel, she managed not to alter her smile.

Two lovely people? Noah thought, suppressing a snort. Two bickering fools was more like it. But the hot mocha drink smelled good, and he took a cup from the lady in brown. Maggie shot him a disgruntled look, but she took the other cup and sipped. "It's good," she said, her frown easing slightly.

He tasted it. Not too sweet, not too bitter, but seductively rich and flavorful. "It's delicious."

"Better than that horrible burned-tasting coffee I had at the motel this morning," Maggie remarked.

"I didn't even try any of that. It smelled vile. This," he continued, taking another sip, "smells wonderful. And it tastes even better. There's a hint of cinnamon in it."

"Yep, it's got a touch of cinnamon," the woman in the minidress confirmed, beaming proudly. "So, you like it?"

"It's great," Maggie replied, shooting Noah a frown and then smiling at the Cosmic Candy woman.

"It's the best thing that's happened to me so far today."

"Have you got any more?" he asked after draining his cup.

"Sure!" The young woman beckoned them over to a table set up in a corner of the lobby. Hot cups and insulated silver decanters stood on the table, behind which a video camera perched on a pedestal. "I've taped your reactions," she said, circling the table to refill their cups. "Cosmic Candy will be using clips of people's reactions to the mocha drink. I've got to tell you two—" she handed each of them a steaming cup "—that you'd be great in the ads. Would that be okay with you? Because if it is, you have to sign some forms."

"What forms?" Maggie asked, then sipped her coffee, eyeing the young woman over the rim of her cup.

"Release forms. We need to have permission to use you in the ads. If you're interested, and willing to sign them—"

"Yes," Maggie said so quickly, Noah almost objected. He didn't want to be in any tacky videotaped advertisement for the Cosmic Candy Company. Who knew where or when it might be shown? What would his colleagues back in San Francisco think if, one evening while they were watching the evening news, right after a piece on turmoil in the Middle East, Noah popped up on their screens, smirking and saying, "This smells wonderful. And it tastes even better!"

The Cosmic Candy woman produced a clipboard with a printed form on it. Maggie swiped the clipboard before Noah could skim the paper. "We'll need some time to look this over before we sign it," she said, sending Noah a saccharine smile. "Won't we, honey?"

He frowned. He'd had no trouble reading her expression in the train, but now he couldn't make sense of it—except that it was phony.

"Is there someplace where we could sit down for a few minutes and give this a thorough read?" Maggie asked. "We might want to discuss it with someone if we have any questions. Is there an office somewhere, where someone from your company could help us through the paperwork?"

The woman in the brown dress shrugged. "Well, Cosmic Candy's headquarters occupies the top three floors of this building. If you want to go up there... Well, sure, why not? I can get you passes. Because, I mean, I really think you'd be great in the ads."

Noah got it then. He returned Maggie's fake smile, then slipped his arm around her shoulders. "Good idea, darling," he said, giving her a squeeze. "We don't want to sign something we haven't read carefully. Let's take our time and make sure we know what we're committing to."

He detected a battle being waged inside Maggie— the desire to ease out from under his arm warring with the desire to present herself and Noah to the Cosmic Candy lady as an affectionate couple. True, the young woman already had taken them to be a twosome; Noah was only doing his best to cement that impression in her mind.

She removed a videocassette from her camcorder, then steered Noah and Maggie over to the elevator and pressed a button. "It's a standard release form," she babbled cheerfully. "I guess if you've never seen one before, you wouldn't know that. It doesn't ask for anything much from you. Just your permission to use your images and words in our ads."

Noah wondered whether Cosmic Candy Company was willing to pay him and Maggie to use their images and words in their ads. He and Maggie were all but creating the advertisement. They ought to get some reimbursement. A flat fee plus residuals every time the commercial was aired would satisfy him. Some people might want to appear in ads for mere ego gratification, but Noah was a businessman. He'd be willing to bet Maggie would want to negotiate fair compensation, too.

Then he remembered the real reason he and Maggie were riding the elevator upstairs—to find Cosmo Delaney. Noah angled his head to look into Maggie's face, but she was avoiding his gaze, studying the form intently. If the Cosmic Candy lady hadn't been in the elevator with them, he would have told Maggie how impressed he was by her scheme to get them into the corporate offices. Instead, he gave her shoulder a squeeze.

Her jaw flexed as if she were grinding her teeth.

Did she really loathe his touch so much? Last night she hadn't minded it at all. When they'd kissed, she'd been as passionate as he had.

Maybe she just loathed having him with her that morning. As she'd said, she didn't like to work with an audience. She was probably afraid he'd give them away or bungle things so she couldn't insinuate herself into Delaney's office.

Noah silently vowed not to bungle anything. He

would hold his peace and follow her lead. He'd play the role of devoted husband and Cosmic-mocha drinker.

The reception area of the company looked like an interior designer's version of the young lady's dress. The wall was papered in brown velvet adorned with silver hearts and red script reading "Cosmic Candy." The few chairs were upholstered in brown velvet; heart-shaped silver pillows decorated the seating. Framed oil paintings depicting Cosmic Candy's most successful products hung on the walls—Cosmic Crunch Bars, Cosmic Star-Gazers, Cosmic Fudge— all large and realistic enough to appear somehow threatening. Noah enjoyed a piece of chocolate every now and then, but the overblown artistic rendering of a chunk of Cosmic Fudge made him slightly queasy.

"Follow me," the young woman said, beckoning them down a hall. Noah observed her long, slim legs, amply displayed by the abbreviated hem of her dress. Nice legs. Not the legs of a woman who indulged in Cosmic Fudge on a regular basis.

Maggie's legs wouldn't be quite so slender. But then, she would probably devour Cosmic Fudge with gusto. She would savor every bite without giving a moment's thought to calories, and when he kissed her he would taste chocolate on her tongue.

"Here you go," the woman said with another chipper smile as she opened the door to a small conference room containing a large rectangular chocolate-brown table, upholstered chocolate-brown chairs and a glass bowl filled with Cosmic Chocolate Mints serving as a centerpiece. Noah amended his current fantasy. Chocolate, on Maggie or elsewhere, was losing its appeal.

"I've got to go back downstairs," the lady announced, fiddling with the videocassette, "but if you have any questions, just ask the receptionist and she'll help you out."

"What if we have legal questions?" Noah asked, earning himself a reproachful look from Maggie. Yes, he'd made a tacit promise to keep his mouth shut, but it was a legitimate question. What could the receptionist do for them? How was she going to get them into Delaney's lair?

"She'll help you out," the miniskirted woman said blithely. "Thanks again. You did great. I really think chocolate and love go hand in hand, and it's obvious you two love chocolate."

Not a bad advertising slogan, Noah thought wryly. He wondered if the jingle Sisela had recorded in Los Angeles had lyrics that clever.

The young lady pranced out, leaving Maggie and Noah to confront each other, the clipboard and the mints. "What do we do now?" he whispered.

"I'm sure you'll think of something," she whispered back, sarcasm layering each word. "Perhaps you can take this release form and try to find the legal department."

He plucked the clipboard from her hands and skimmed the top page. He'd done enough contract work to recognize the jargon. This form wasn't too bad—only a few "heretofores" and "hereinafters." The language was simple enough for him to comprehend that they would receive no financial benefit from appearing in the ads. "If they use us, we ought to get paid," he commented, flipping the top page and reading the second.

"Noah." Her voice was muted but stern. "Who gives a damn about the stupid release? We've got to find Delaney."

"And how are we going to do that? Let's check out the form first."

She snatched the clipboard from him, perused the top page and handed it back to him. "I tell you what. You check out the form. I'm going to pay a visit to the ladies' room."

She had no interest in the ladies' room, he realized as she stepped out into the hall. She'd left the conference room to search for Delaney. Without him.

Darting out of the room, he spotted her halfway down the corridor and shouted, "Wait a minute! I've got a problem with the second clause!"

She spun around. Exasperation etched her features, made the tumbled curls framing her face quiver, caused her hands to clench into fists. Before she could speak, three doors lining the hallway swung open and three curious office workers peeked out. One, a youngish man in shirtsleeves with about as much wispy hair as a newborn baby, spoke first. "Can I help you?"

"Yes." Avoiding Maggie's stiletto-sharp gaze, Noah smiled at the man. "We've been brought up here to study this release form. We were videotaped downstairs tasting some coffee, and we were asked to sign this."

"Uh-huh." The man glanced down the corridor at Maggie, who stood, arms akimbo, looking supremely impatient. "And you would be Mr.—"

"Davis. Noah Davis. That's my wife, Maggie." He didn't dare look at her; he knew she was angry enough to begin divorce proceedings.

The man extended his hand. "Tom Sliney. I'm one of the marketing managers. Are you the couple on the tape Laura just brought up?"

"Maybe. I don't know. Was Laura the woman downstairs?"

Tom Sliney nodded. "Come into my office. Mrs. Davis?" he called affably. "Come join us. Let's talk about the release. Maybe we can iron this out."

Noah could feel Maggie's seething anger. It rippled in the air of the hallway, invisible but real, like shimmering waves of heat rising from August-hot pavement. She didn't want to go into Tom Sliney's office. She wanted to find Cosmo Delaney.

But Sliney was waiting for her, and she had no choice but to accept his cordial invitation. She stalked down the corridor, her jaw tense, her eyes fierce. Noah cupped his hand over her shoulder and kissed her cheek, partly to present themselves as a happily married couple, partly to mollify her.

As if a kiss from him would soothe her flaring anger.

"I'm sure we can iron this out," Sliney said cheerfully. Everyone at this outfit seemed awfully jolly. Maybe they were all on sugar highs.

Noah ushered Maggie into the office. Sliney gestured toward two chairs facing his desk, then took his own seat behind the desk. "What can I do for you?" he asked pleasantly.

Maggie shot Noah an irritated look, conveying that she would rather be anywhere than in Sliney's office.

Knowing he'd get no help from her, Noah took over the conversation. "Well, for one thing, we'd like to be paid if we're going to appear in the ad."

Sliney shook his head. "These are man-in-the-street interviews. If we pay the people who appear in them, the people become professionals in a way. The ad loses its authenticity."

"Then we'd require some other compensation," Noah said. "Candy, maybe?"

Next to him, Maggie crossed her legs and stared past Sliney. Her posture didn't exactly communicate that she was Noah's loving wife.

Sliney didn't seem aware of any tension between them. "Candy? Oh, I'm sure we could work that out. That would imply that you love Cosmic Candy so much, you consider it worth more than money. We could use that." Sliney's smile bordered on ecstatic. "We could! Cosmic Candy—more valuable than cold cash!"

"Uh—if you're going to use that, we'd require compensation," Noah informed him, wishing he could think of a way to steer the conversation in another direction—a Cosmo Delaney direction.

Still staring straight ahead and looking mildly put out, Maggie said, "I'd like to speak to your company's president."

So much for subtle manipulation.

Noah eyed her curiously. Sliney gaped outright. "Why?"

"To discuss our situation." Succinct and vague. If she'd turned to glance at Noah, she'd have found him brimming with admiration. Why dance around a subject when you can march straight into it? All the straight-ahead march required was courage—which Maggie had in abundance.

Sliney appeared perplexed. He stroked his fingers through the sparse strands of hair covering his scalp, then smiled hesitantly. "Well, I suppose I could ask him if he'd be willing..."

"Please do," Maggie said tersely. She settled back in her chair next to Noah and clasped her hands over one knee.

"Well." Sliney lifted a silver pen from his blotter, twirled it around and then let it fall. "Well, all right. Why not?" His candy-sweet smile returned as he pushed himself to his feet. "I'll go see if the big man is free for a minute. Why don't you wait right here, and—"

"We'll come with you," Maggie declared, rising from her chair and preceding Sliney to the door. Noah had to scramble to keep up.

But wasn't that the way it always was? She was fast, she was sharp, she was determined—and unlike him, she seemed fully able to put out of her mind all memories of a kiss he would have nominated for first in its class. She was focused, she was smart—and her pointed intelligence turned him on as much as his own tenacious memories of that kiss.

It occurred to him, as he followed her and Sliney through the doorway and down the hall, that if he wanted to keep up with Maggie, he was going to wind up doing a *lot* of scrambling.

CHAPTER EIGHT

THIS WOULD HAVE BEEN a whole lot easier if Noah had stayed out of it. Maggie could easily have bypassed the miniskirted Barbie doll in the building's lobby, gotten herself upstairs to Cosmic Candy's offices and figured out a way past the reception area without being dragged into an absurd playacting exercise that required her to pretend she was Mrs. Noah Davis.

The last thing she wanted to be was Noah's wife. Well, maybe not the *last* thing, but certainly it was somewhere in the bottom ten. The man was a liar, a busybody and a very poor listener. He was practically a stalker. Maggie had told him repeatedly to go away—and instead, he'd shadowed her as if he were the detective and she were his prey.

He'd made things unnecessarily complicated. This whole charade about their being married and reviewing the damned release forms... It could have been so simple if only he'd cooled his heels back in Bellewood. She could have cut a straight, tidy path to Delaney's office on her own, without Noah's arm around her, without his paternalistic affection and his phony kisses. Building a schoolhouse in India might be admirable, but it didn't give him the right to get in her way while she was doing her job.

More annoying than his intervention, though, was the fact that she was annoyed. She didn't want Noah to be able to annoy her; she wanted to be immune to him. She resented that she could be at all affected when he put his arm around her or gave a silly peck on the cheek. Surely her brothers would never go all fluttery inside if one of their clients faked a flirtation with *them.* Well, maybe Neil would, but Neil still had a fair amount of growing up to do.

The carpeting in the hall was the color of chocolate. Actually, the entire decor of the Cosmic Candy Company's offices was the color of chocolate: dark chocolate, milk chocolate, white chocolate. The wallpaper resembled chocolate and shredded coconut. The chrome light fixtures built into the walls reminded her of the foil wrapping of Cosmic Star-Gazers.

The overall effect was nauseating. Maggie wondered whether working in a place like this, with bowls of chocolates everywhere and paintings of candy on the walls, would so turn her off chocolate that she'd be able to lose a few pounds.

At the end of the corridor stood an elevator—a private one, Maggie presumed. Tom Sliney, the midlevel hack Noah had dragged into the scenario, pressed a button and the doors slid open. He was skinny, she noted as she and Noah followed him into the car. The cute little coffee hostess downstairs had been thin, too. Was there a weight rule for employees? She supposed a candy company wouldn't want its representatives to offer visual reminders of what happened to people who overindulged in the company's products. Maybe that was why Sisela Hansen had been hired to sing the company's jingle. While her jingle advertised the joys of devouring Cosmic Star Crunches, her slim figure advertised that those joys didn't necessarily result in the woes of gaining weight.

Without ever having met Sisela, Maggie hated her. She hated Sisela's ex-fiancé, too, for being handsome and meddlesome and able to get on her nerves merely by existing.

And she hated Tom Sliney on principle.

The elevator delivered them into a vestibule several floors higher. If the lower floors had been decorated in a chocolate theme, the motif here seemed to be refined sugar. The walls were bright white, with a glittery crystalline texture. The sight caused Maggie's teeth to ache.

Beyond glass doors, an older woman sat in an equally white anteroom. To her credit, she looked as if she indulged in sweets on occasion. Her chin was cushioned by a layer of fat, and her attractive summer-weight suit could not have been purchased in the boutique in Bellewood that carried no dresses larger than a size eight. At last Maggie had found someone she could relate to in this place.

Without waiting for Tom Sliney to lead the way, she pushed through the doors into the anteroom. "Hi," she said. "We're here to see Cosmo Delaney. Can he spare a minute for us?"

The woman lifted her fingers from her computer keyboard and glanced up at Tom Sliney. "They'll only be a minute," he explained bashfully. "It's about those man-in-the-street ads."

"*Person*-in-the-street," the woman corrected him. Maggie's estimation of her rose another few notches.

"Is there a problem?" the woman asked, her gaze traveling from Maggie to Noah.

Noah inhaled, as if about to speak. Maggie jumped in, refusing him the chance to foul things up more than he already had. "Not a problem, really," she said amiably. "We just want to talk to Mr. Delaney." Short and sweet. An elaborate explanation would only raise more questions.

The woman sized Maggie up. Perhaps she felt a kinship, too—a relief that she wasn't the only well-insulated person in Cosmic Candy headquarters—because she returned Maggie's smile. "Ordinarily I wouldn't disturb him. But he's really enthusiastic about the person-in-the-street campaign. Let me see if he can spare you a minute." She swiveled her chair to reach a telephone console, lifted the receiver, pressed a button and spoke quietly into the phone.

Maggie suppressed the urge to send Noah a superior smirk. She hoped he realized that in detective work, the less you said, the less you had to lie—and the less lying you did, the better. He hadn't had to make believe they were a happily married couple. Being assertive and asking for what you wanted was often all it took to achieve your purpose.

Behind the secretary, a door opened in the sugary wall and a man peered out. Maggie saw his sandy-blond hair first, then his high, aristocratic forehead, his pale gray eyes, his chiseled nose, his sculpted mouth. As he leaned farther around the door, she took note of his starched white shirt, his pristine beige slacks, his narrow, slate-gray tie. The man was utterly colorless. Good-looking in an anonymous way, she supposed, but he had the overbred look of a pedigreed show dog—like an Afghan hound, lean and arrogant and pale.

She almost expected him to bark, or at least to sniff a little. But he offered a gleaming smile. "Is this the couple?" he asked his secretary.

"This is Mr. and Mrs. Davis," Tom Sliney said, practically panting like an affection-starved puppy himself. "They made this tape—" he stared at the videocassette in his hand as if uncertain how it had gotten there "—downstairs in the lobby."

"In the lobby?" Best-of-Breed asked.

"Laura's down there, offering samples of the Cosmic Mocha Drink and taping people's reactions. For the ad campaign." He gazed eagerly at his boss.

"Yes, of course," the boss said, smiling hesitantly. "The ad campaign. And you're Mr. and Mrs. Davis."

"*Ms.* Davis," Maggie corrected, just to let Noah know that if she was stuck being married to him for the morning, she was going to be a feminist wife. "Can we borrow a few minutes of your time?"

"Sure. I'm Cosmo Delaney." He crossed the anteroom, his right hand outstretched. "It's a damned good cup of java, isn't it?"

"Excellent," Noah replied as he shook Delaney's hand. "It has a really nice, subtle flavor."

"Nothing obvious or overdone about it," Delaney agreed. "Not like those sweetened flavored coffees. We're aiming for 'understated and mature'—something that will linger pleasantly on the palate without a cloying aftertaste."

Maggie tried not to scowl. The two of them sounded like pretentious oenophiles. If either of them so much as whispered that the mocha drink was playful, with overtones of vanilla and a finish of cloves, she would kick them both in the shins.

Maybe it wasn't so odd that they would think alike when it came to coffee. They thought alike when it came to women, didn't they? Both of them had fallen in love with Sisela Hansen. No doubt Sisela lingered pleasantly on the palate, too. No doubt she was subtle, without a cloying aftertaste. Whereas Maggie was more like grapefruit juice.

"Well, come on in, Mr. Davis, Ms. Davis." Delaney ushered them past his secretary's desk and into his private office. Maggie shouldn't have been surprised that it was as huge as an airplane hangar, given that he was the company's CEO. The room had windows on two sides, which reduced the wall space available for paintings of candy bars. The carpet was a caramel shade, and the coffee table in front of a low-slung leather sofa the color of peanut brittle was decked out in silver bowls filled with assorted candies.

How could anyone work in this place without gagging? Maggie used to love chocolate. Perhaps someday she'd love it again. But after fifteen minutes in the corporate offices of Cosmic Candy, she found herself fantasizing about broccoli.

Across from the sofa and the buffet of candies stood a conference table, its polished surface a mosaic of inlaid woods. Probably walnut and pecan, she thought wryly.

It was to the conference table that Delaney steered them. "Shall we watch the video?" he asked, sliding open the door of a credenza to reveal a VCR and a television.

Maggie didn't want to see herself on the tape. She spent enough time in front of a mirror every morning to know what she looked like, and she didn't want to waste Delaney's time or her own on an assessment of her and Noah's performance downstairs. What she wanted was to learn if Sisela Hansen was Cosmo Delaney's wife.

His office didn't provide any information about his private life, however. No framed family photographs stood on any of the shelves or on his massive desk at the far end of the room. No personal knickknacks, no golf clubs or paperback novels.

"We had some questions about the release form," Noah piped up.

All right. Maggie would let him run with that subject for a while. Maybe a conversation could evolve— one that would allow for some discreet probing about Delaney's marital status.

She smiled adoringly at Noah. "Yes, dear. Why don't you ask him those questions about the release form?"

"I'd be happy to, *darling*," Noah retorted. Apparently he'd heard the sarcastic simpering in her voice. Turning his back to her, he placed the clipboard on the table and addressed Delaney directly. "First of all, let me ascertain—is this advertising program geared for television? I'm assuming it is, what with the videotaping of our first encounter with the beverage."

"TV, yes. Radio, too. We hope to use it as a two-pronged campaign."

"Okay. I was wondering how, exactly, our images would be used in the commercial. I'm assuming our part is going to be spliced in with other material. I'd like to know what that material is going to be. I want to know the context."

"Of course." Delaney nodded. His hair moved around his narrow face, limp strands of blond silk. Once again Maggie pictured an Afghan. "I'm sure one of the people down in marketing could have gone over this with you—"

"Well, Mr. Delaney, I prefer to deal with the person in charge," Noah said evenly. He wasn't smiling as broadly as Delaney, but he looked more confident, which Maggie found interesting. Delaney had stolen Noah's sweetheart away. He presided over an enormous, successful corporation, lived in an exclusive community and had probably been born with a silver spoon—or, more likely, a silver candy dish—in his mouth. In contrast, Noah had grown up in desperate poverty, and while he'd reached a level of success that was impressive, it was nowhere near as exalted as Delaney's. Yet Noah seemed completely undaunted by his rival for Sisela's heart.

And Delaney seemed to consider them equals—which was particularly interesting because he had no idea who Noah and Maggie were, other than two people who'd tasted his company's new product. "I don't blame you, Mr. Davis," he said. "I like to deal with the people in charge, too. Are you folks from the city?" he asked.

"San Francisco," Noah told him.

"Great town," Delaney remarked, his smile widening. "Wonderful town. I love San Francisco!" Maggie sent him a mental message: *Go ahead, say your wife is from San Francisco.* But he didn't pick up on her brain waves. "'I left my heart in San Fran-cisco,'" he crooned off-key. "And what brings you to New York?"

"Business," Noah replied.

"What's your field?"

"I'm the marketing director of a solar technology company," Noah informed him. Maggie had to admit it sounded impressive.

"Hey! Good for the environment. I'm a big fan of the environment," Delaney boasted. "I love the en-vironment. I don't know if you realize this, but my first name—Cosmo—means orderly universe. When I think of the environment, I think of an orderly uni-verse."

"That's nice," Noah said, sending Maggie an edgy look. She smiled serenely. If Delaney was getting too weird for Noah, he could shut up and let her take over. But she wasn't going to bail him out. Not yet.

The two men hunched over the release form, pars-ing it clause by clause. They weren't discussing the environment or San Francisco anymore, which was probably just as well. Maggie had handled people much more eccentric than Delaney in her life, but Noah probably hadn't—although, given her behavior, Sisela couldn't have been the most normal woman in the great and wonderful town of San Francisco, and Noah had dealt with her.

Less than successfully, Maggie reminded herself as she furtively scanned the room. Bland drapes framed the walls of windows. Three-ring binders labeled with the names of Cosmic Candy's various products lined the built-in shelves on one wall. Delaney's desktop was neat in the extreme; his leather blotter, onyx pen-

holder and crystal paperweight looked lost and lonely
on the broad wood surface. The only item on the desk
that didn't seem to have come from the pages of a
high-end office-supply catalog was a pedestal candy
dish filled with Cosmic Mints.

She glanced back at the men. She couldn't believe
they'd found so much to discuss on the simple release
form. When she tuned in on their conversation, she
realized they had gone beyond the specifics of the
form and were analyzing the nature of civil litigation
in America. "Everything not nailed down becomes
an issue," Delaney was saying. "You must find this
in your line of work, Noah. Architecture is fraught
with actionable areas."

"Noah?" How had Sisela's two lovers wound up
on a first-name basis?

"Well, my part of the design work is usually in-
demnified," Noah told him. "It's the architects who
carry the high malpractice premiums. My company
has never been sued. If there's a problem with the
technology, we get it fixed. But there's no real lia-
bility if a solar panel doesn't work, right? The worst
consequence is that you might not have adequate hot
water in the building. There are backup systems in all
our designs, and if the panels aren't functioning prop-
erly, we take care of it. No one's ever had to threaten
a suit."

"We've never been sued, either," said Delaney.
"But I've got a legal staff looming over every decision we make. Health inspectors out the wazoo. Pack-
aging consultants, shipping consultants... It's hard to
believe I started this company as a college kid dealing
in chocolates on campus."

"Really? Is that how you got started?"

Delaney grinned. "Sweetheart deals. Guys would hire me to deliver chocolates to the girls they'd cheated on. Or they'd pay me to ship chocolates home to Mom on Mother's Day. The trouble was, most of the chocolate manufacturers took chocolate too seriously. I thought it needed some whimsy. My favorite book when I was growing up was *Charlie and the Chocolate Factory.* When I graduated from college, I bought a tottering candy company and rebuilt it with my own ideas."

"Wow," Noah said, his eyes glinting a sharp blue as he studied Delaney. "How did you manage to get the financing fresh out of college?"

"Oh, my father gave me a few million to play with. In that sense I wasn't like the hero of *Charlie and the Chocolate Factory* at all. I was rich. But I've gotten richer, thanks to Cosmic Candy. My father was wise to invest in me."

"I'd say so."

Maggie observed the men from her position several feet away. Noah looked fascinated by Delaney's story, but she sensed something else going on inside him. He was measuring Delaney, judging him. His expression was enigmatic, though—she couldn't guess whether he was giving Delaney a thumbs-up or thumbs-down.

She herself couldn't care less about Delaney's pampered youth, his father's wise investments or his favorite children's story. All she cared about was whether he was still romantically involved with Sisela Hansen.

"You know," he was saying, "I'm hosting a little

shindig tonight. Perhaps you and your wife would like to join us.''

''A 'shindig'?'' Noah shot a frantic look at Maggie.

She thought about Sisela—and then thought about other things: the ornate gates in the wall surrounding Delaney's mansion, the elitism of the residents of Bellewood, the hoity-toity atmosphere; and the fact that she was a working woman with an office smaller than a coffin and a set of scrapping brothers, one of whom's marriage was on the rocks. She was thinking of that obscenely overpriced grocery store with its gourmet salad greens and overweening attitude. That Delaney could live in a town where the supermarket had an attitude was reason enough for her to want to go to his ''shindig.''

''We'd love to come,'' she said, smiling warmly and returning to the table.

Noah gave her a long, quizzical look, then turned back to Delaney. ''Yes, we'd love to.''

''Great. I'm just having a few friends over—but I love to toss a surprise into the mix. It makes for the liveliest parties. Noah, I like the way you think, and...Ms. Davis?'' He angled his head toward her.

''Maggie,'' she said.

''Maggie, I'm sure I'd like the way you think if I had a chance to—well—to see you think.''

She bit her lip to keep from retorting that if he'd looked at her at all since she'd made his acquaintance, he would have seen her thinking plenty. She hadn't stopped thinking since she'd entered the lobby. For that matter, she'd been thinking since she'd arrived in New York yesterday. In fact, she'd been thinking pretty much all her life without a letup.

"Good. I'll count on you being there," Delaney said. "Black-tie optional. Seven o'clock. I live in Bellewood, just north of the city, in Westchester County. I don't know how familiar you are with the area—"

"We've been to the city before," Noah said smoothly. "I think I know where Bellewood is."

"I could have a driver sent for you. Where are you staying?"

"No, that's okay," Maggie assured him, concerned that Noah might let slip that they were currently ensconced at the cheapest motel in the Bellewood vicinity. "We've rented a car for our week in New York. If you could just give us the directions, I'm sure we'll find it."

"Certainly." He crossed to his desk, lifted the phone and pressed a button. "Sylvia, could you write out directions to my house for Noah and Maggie Davis? Thanks." He lowered the receiver and grinned. "So, we'll see you at seven tonight?"

"Sure," Noah replied, sending Maggie one more questioning look.

She nodded and gave Delaney her sunniest farewell smile. "I can hardly wait," she said.

"BLACK-TIE OPTIONAL?" she groaned once they'd emerged from the building into the balmy June morning. "*Black-tie optional?* What am I going to do? I've never been to a black-tie-optional party in my life. Silly me, forgetting to toss a cocktail dress into my suitcase."

"You were the one who said we'd love to go," Noah reminded her.

"That was when he said it was a shindig. I didn't know it was going to be some formal gala!"

Noah sighed. He'd thought the invitation had delighted her. But with women, you never knew. Ten seconds ago she could have been delighted, but now she was standing on a sidewalk in midtown Manhattan bemoaning the fact that she had nothing to wear. "Well, you said we'd go," he reminded.

"How can we not go?" She shoved a loose strand of hair back from her cheek. "If things had proceeded the way I'd planned this morning, Delaney and I would have had a little chat about Sisela and that would have been that. But instead, you had to sidetrack him with that ridiculous release form—"

"I didn't sidetrack him," Noah protested. "He and I had our own little chat. I've got to admit, I like the guy."

"The guy stole your fiancée!"

Noah took a deep breath. The air smelled of hot tar and auto exhausts. It burned his lungs, but he exhaled slowly, waiting to speak until he had the correct words in the correct order. "Cosmo didn't steal my fiancée," he said quietly. "A woman can't be stolen from a man. I didn't own Sisela. She was free to follow her heart."

"Even though she broke *your* heart in the process?"

"She didn't—" He caught himself before declaring that Sisela's disappearance hadn't broken his heart at all. If Maggie knew how unperturbed he was about Sisela's departure, she would question the entire purpose of this trip. And she'd be right. Noah wasn't really in New York to find Sisela anymore. He was looking for the route his own heart had taken so he could follow it as Sisela had followed hers.

A cab careered past them, blasting its horn at no one in particular. The noise startled Maggie, who flinched and clapped her hands over her ears. After a minute she lowered them. Her frown remained in place, scrunching her mouth into a pout that he would have liked to kiss if she'd been in a better mood.

She was most definitely *not* in a better mood. She was fed up with him and Delaney—and probably Sisela, too. And she had nothing to wear to the party.

"Why don't we go buy you something?" he suggested.

Her scowl grew dubious. "What do you mean?"

"Something to wear tonight."

She considered. Still looking doubtful, she shook her head. "Maybe we should just skip the party. There are other ways to find out if he's married to Sisela."

"But we want to go," Noah reminded her. In Delaney's office, she'd seemed downright enthusiastic about the prospect.

"Did you notice how he said '*I'm* having some friends over'? Not *we. I.* I wonder if Sisela's dumped him and moved on."

"We could find out tonight," Noah said.

That errant strand of hair licked her cheek again. She twirled it around her finger as she meditated. "There are more stores in Manhattan than in Bellewood—and I can't imagine a dress would cost more down here than up there." She eyed the revolving door into the building. "Do you suppose Laura would tell me where the good discount places are?"

"Forget about a discount place. You're going to your first black-tie-optional party. You need to look classy."

"Even if you put me in the most expensive designer couture, I'm not going to look classy," she warned. "And frankly, I don't feel like bankrupting myself just for this stupid party."

"I'll pay for the dress," he said.

She narrowed her gaze on him. "No."

"Two hundred a day plus expenses. Isn't that what we agreed on?" When she pursed her lips, he added, "A dress for Cosmo's party counts as an expense."

"Yes, but—"

"So, where should we go? What's a good store in New York? Bloomingdale's or something?"

She stared at him as if she didn't quite believe what he was offering. "You're not going to buy me a dress," she said uncertainly.

"Then you'll go to the party dressed like that," he said, gesturing toward her drab skirt and blazer.

"Noah—"

"Given what I'm spending on this whole scheme, the cost of a dress isn't going to make much of a difference."

She looked torn. Finally she let out a sigh and turned away. "I guess even Bloomingdale's has a clearance rack," she muttered. "Any idea where the store is?"

The first passerby they asked pointed them uptown. "Maybe fifteen short blocks. You can walk it from here," the woman assured them.

As they set off uptown, Maggie didn't try to lose Noah in the crowds. They walked side by side, Mag-

gie curling one hand around the strap of her purse
and letting the other swing at her side. It wouldn't
take much for Noah to slip his hand around hers, to
pretend they were still Mr. and Mrs.—*Ms.*—Davis. It
wouldn't take much at all, other than a death wish.
Even wrapped around her purse strap, Maggie's fist
looked lethal.

All right. She was steaming with anger, and he was
its cause and its object. He tried to list everything he'd
done that might have offended her: accompanying her
to New York City. Hitting it off with Cosmo Delaney.
Perhaps foiling her own strategy for finding out
whether Delaney was involved with Sisela. Offering
to pay for suitable attire for the party tonight.

Kissing her.

The last offense set off bells inside his head. That
was really what had her so surly: he'd kissed her. Not
only that, but last night he'd kissed her with heat and
passion and raw desire, and she'd kissed him back.
And to add insult to injury, he wanted to kiss her
again—and she knew it.

She had undoubtedly figured out why he'd presented them to the Cosmic Candy people as husband
and wife, why he'd maneuvered her into a role that
forced her to accept his attentions. Maybe his offering
to pay for her dress made her uncomfortable because
he'd kissed her. Maybe she saw it as personal, somehow; the sort of gift a man gave a woman he wanted
to take to bed.

Which, he supposed, he did. For the life of him, he
couldn't figure out why she turned him on so much.
He had to admit that, even simmering with anger, she
was something to behold. It took his full supply of

willpower to keep from brushing that untamed lock of hair away, from trailing his fingertips over her cheek and turning her face until his mouth could take hers.

Bloomingdale's loomed up ahead, a behemoth of a building occupying most of a city block. He nudged her through the door ahead of him and then they squared off. "Do you want to give me a maximum price?" she asked.

He smiled. Never having had the occasion to purchase a woman's dress, he had no idea what they cost. "Use your judgment," he suggested.

They wandered through the store, passing alcoves where gourmet foods, perfumes and accessories were displayed. Then up an escalator, into the women's fashions, where Maggie set to work, swooping down on one rack and then another with the efficiency of an assembly-line laborer. She lifted garments, studied them, put them back. She skimmed her hand across fabrics, shook her head at hemlines, plucked an occasional ensemble out to study in the light. She diligently checked price tags. A few outfits made the first cut, but most she tucked back onto the rack.

He loitered far enough away not to inhibit her but close enough to watch. The overhead lights made her hair shimmer. Her face was a study of concentration, her annoyance fading into brisk resolution. Without notifying him, she hoisted her armful of prospects and set off in search of a fitting room. Noah trailed her from a respectful distance.

What would Maggie look like all dolled up? he wondered. Not sleek and suave—but not pinchably soft, either. He imagined she would look…womanly, self-assured. Sexy in a way no slim, fleshless woman could ever match.

He noticed a couple of chairs near the fitting-room entrance. An older man was seated in one, reading the *New York Times.* He had the look of a *real* husband, waiting for his wife; the gold band on his left hand confirmed Noah's guess. Noah wondered whether Cosmo had noticed his and Maggie's lack of wedding rings. He wondered whether Maggie had noticed whether Cosmo was wearing one. Noah should have been more observant—but she was the professional. He was paying her to keep an eye out for such things.

The older man peered up from his paper as Noah took the unoccupied chair. Folding his paper, he nodded conspiratorially. "They take forever," he murmured, gesturing toward the fitting room.

"I'm in no rush," said Noah.

"Mine is trying on blouses. She'll be in there until sometime in the next century."

Noah grinned. "I guess it's important to make sure she's choosing the right one."

The man turned his gaze to the fitting room. So did Noah, expecting to see the older man's wife emerge. But Maggie did instead, dressed in a long-sleeved tunic of black silk, with elegantly blousy black silk trousers beneath it. The top was textured, with faintly shining threads weaving in and out of sight. The neckline was a semicircle, with a deep notch down the center front.

Noah's gaze slid to that notch and lingered for a long moment. Then he shifted his attention to Maggie's face. She stood in front of a three-way mirror near the fitting-room entry, her head twisted so she could peer over her shoulder to see how she looked from the rear.

He lowered his gaze to her bare feet. Her toes were round like the rest of her, her insteps arched. Then he traveled back up, imagining the feel of silk on her legs, the feel of her silky skin. Up higher, to the mid-thigh edge of the top, to the loose, bell-shaped sleeves that made her wrists look delicate, and to that daring notch between her breasts. In the mirror he saw her three times, from three different angles.

All of them were spectacular.

She examined her reflection for a minute, then turned to him. Her eyes were wide and she nibbled her lower lip. "What do you think?" she asked.

Noah didn't dare tell her what he thought: that she looked like a cross between an angel and pure sin. That the black silk was caressing her the way he wanted to caress her, that it was molded to her the way he wanted to mold his hands and mouth and body to her. That merely glimpsing her made him feel like a fifteen-year-old boy—all raging hormones and uncontrollable impulses.

He wasn't fifteen, though. He was an adult, but if the old gent sitting next to him didn't put his eyes back into his head real soon, Noah was going to punch his lights out.

He sent Maggie as calm a smile as he could manage. "Buy it," he said.

CHAPTER NINE

IT WAS A LUCKY THING Cosmo Delaney had such a long driveway, Maggie thought as Noah steered past the cortege of luxury cars and limousines lining the road. It led through the gate, bisected a meticulously landscaped front lawn and ended in a large oval in front of a mansion. If an auto thief stumbled upon this driveway, he would think he'd died and gone to heaven. The only ordinary vehicle on the property was Noah's modest rental car.

She wanted to be contemptuous of Delaney's swanky party with his swanky guests who had arrived in their swanky cars. She wanted to sneer at the palace looming at the end of the magisterial driveway. The house's three-story beige stucco facade was interrupted by six-foot-tall windows, its roof eaves were trimmed with ornate doodads, its broad marble front steps led through a forest of pillars to an elaborate portico. The building struck Maggie as a cross between the Parthenon and Buckingham Palace, neither of which she'd ever seen except in photographs but neither of which she could imagine being more impressive than this place was.

It was all so opulent, so ostentatious. So unlike anything Maggie was used to. The silk pantsuit she was wearing was out of character for her, too, as was the fact that, thanks to liberal applications of gel, her hair was actually holding its shape, scooped back from her face and held with gold-toned barrettes. The black leather sandals she'd found—marked down from eighty dollars to fifty—were almost Maggie's style. If they'd been fifty dollars marked down to thirty, she would have liked them better. But it had been Noah's fifty dollars, not her own.

That he'd spent so much money on her evening attire unnerved her. It was true, as he'd noted, that compared to what he was paying Finders, Keepers, the cost of her ensemble was a drop in the proverbial bucket. But it still made her uneasy to think he'd paid for the articles of clothing that draped her body, caressed her skin, whispered over her breasts—and pinched her outer toes the slightest bit. To have him buy clothing for her made her feel like his woman.

Which she wasn't.

Except for tonight, when she had to pretend she was.

She didn't want to think about the implications of their husband-and-wife pretense. She wanted to think only about her mission: to find Sisela, deliver the cheating blond singer into Noah's arms and then fly home to San Francisco, where her brothers were whining and fretting that the Tyrell universe was going to implode.

When she and Noah had returned to Bellewood after their shopping expedition, she'd telephoned her brothers from her motel room to see how Sandy was faring. For the next half hour, she'd had to listen to them explain to her, in varying shades of desperation, that Sandy was not faring well at all.

First, Jack had gotten on the phone and pleaded with Maggie to come home so she could talk some sense into Sandy and Karen. Then Neil had snatched the phone from Jack and moaned about how he honestly didn't want Sandy moving in with him. Then Jack had retaken the phone and reminded Maggie that, alone among the Tyrells, she knew how to get people to communicate and empathize and fall in love, or stay in love, or whatever the hell she was trying to do with her upstart detective agency. Then Sandy had gotten on the phone and told Maggie he was really fine. He'd sounded about as fine as a convict just sentenced to death.

Neil had grabbed the phone away and begged Maggie to call Karen. "You're the only one she talks to," Neil had told her. "I guess it's because you're both women or something."

"Or something," Maggie had muttered under her breath. Karen talked to her because she was the only Tyrell who had a functioning brain.

She'd told her brothers no. She was not going to drop everything, fly home and talk to Karen. She'd told them she loved them and she loved Karen, and she wanted to see Karen and Sandy work things out as much as everyone else did, but *no*. She wasn't going to skip out on her very first case just so she could fix her brothers' problems for them. If they had wanted her to work with them, they could have taken her into the agency as a full and equal partner, handling her own investigations, doing her bit for love and romance as a member of Tyrell Investigative Services. But they'd refused to make a place for her in their business, and now they were going to have to

fend for themselves. Much as she wanted to see
Sandy and Karen reconciled, she couldn't just walk
away from her client.

She especially couldn't walk away from him tonight, when she was supposedly married to him.

Unlike her, Noah looked as if he was used to at-
tending fancy parties at palatial estates. Dressed in a
sleek suit of midnight blue, a white shirt and a necktie
splashed with vivid colors in an abstract pattern, he
looked polished and suave and very much at ease.

"Are you okay?" he asked as he braked to a stop
in front of the pillared steps.

"Of course I'm okay."

A young man bounded down the stairs to the car
and opened Maggie's door for her. She smiled up at
the valet and he gave her a toothy grin. He looked
barely old enough to drive.

Before she could escape the car, Noah covered her
hand with his, holding her in her seat. He waited until
she glanced his way, then said, "You look terrific,
Maggie."

He sounded awfully eager to reassure her—which
meant she must look like hell. The smile she gave
him felt much more wooden than the smile she'd
given the valet. Sucking in a deep breath, she let the
kid help her out of her seat and waited while Noah
handed over his key. As he joined her at the foot of
the steps, the valet cruised around the circular driveway. Maggie wondered whether he resented having
to park a boring Ford sedan after all the Jaguars, Mer-
cedes-Benzes and luxury four-by-fours he'd jockeyed
around the driveway.

"What's our plan?" Noah asked as he gazed up at the massive oak double doors at the top of the stairs.

"We're going to go in," she said. "You're going to charm Delaney the way you charmed him this morning, and I'm going to prowl and snoop and see if I can find out anything about Sisela."

"We're a married couple from San Francisco," he recited. "What's your profession again?"

"I'm an office manager for a detective agency," she told him. She wanted to avoid talking about Finders, Keepers, but she also wanted to keep their fabrications to a minimum. The less she and Noah lied, the less likely they'd be to mess up their story. "We live in your apartment," she added. "We haven't been married long."

"But we're madly in love," he said, taking her hand and starting up the stairs.

Madly in love? Emphasis on *madly,* she thought as they nodded their thanks to the man who held open the front door for them. Voices enmeshed in conversation and laughter wafted down the entry hall from a room at the far end.

She strolled down the hall with Noah, taking a quick inventory of the doorways they passed, the paintings on the walls—more tasteful than the framed depictions of candy bars that decorated Delaney's offices—and the plush runner rug beneath their feet. "Pretty fancy, huh?" Noah whispered, giving her hand a squeeze.

For all his poise, she realized, he might be as awed as she was by the splendor of Delaney's house. Just because he looked like a million bucks didn't mean he felt comfortable visiting a millionaire's residence.

"It looks more like a museum than a home," she whispered back.

"It sure doesn't seem like the kind of house Willy Wonka would live in," Noah murmured.

"Maybe he inherited this place," she suggested, recalling that Delaney's father had bankrolled the fledgling Cosmic Candy Company. Delaney, Sr. must have had more than his fair share of hard cash. "Does it look like the sort of place Sisela would want to call home?"

Noah paused and frowned. "I don't know."

"What do you mean, you don't know?"

His frown deepened. He stared at the exquisite Chinese urn displayed on a table to his left, the gilt-framed still life on the wall to his right, the brightly lit room beyond the open doors at the far end of the hall. "I don't know."

Maggie shook her head. "You were going to marry her, Noah. How could you not know what kind of home she'd want to live in?"

"I..." He sighed, as if embarrassed to have to admit it. "Maybe it's just as well we didn't get married if this is the kind of home she'd want. She never struck me as pretentious, and her own apartment was pretty understated, but when we talked about the future, we never really discussed what kind of house we'd want to live in." He mulled over his thoughts, then resumed the long march to the room at the end of the hall. "She liked to live well—but so do I. But if I had enough money to live in a place like this, I sure as hell would be living somewhere else."

They'd reached their destination. The room resembled a ballroom—or perhaps an extremely posh gymnasium. It was certainly big enough to hold a Golden State Warriors game with the full complement of season-ticket holders. The ceilings were high, the far wall lined with more six-foot-tall windows interspersed with French doors opening onto a back patio. Brass chandeliers hung from the ceiling, and matching brass wall sconces illuminated the room from the sides. Stiff-looking chairs and sofas stood in conversation groupings throughout the room. Maggie could definitely picture Queen Elizabeth and her family sitting in those chairs, munching on cucumber sandwiches while the queen's dogs yapped and scampered, gnawing on table legs and peeing on the rugs.

If this was Delaney's notion of having "a few friends" over, someone ought to give him an accurate definition of the word *few*. Easily a hundred people swarmed throughout the room, sucking on cocktails and munching on canapés.

Maggie took a quick survey of the women standing nearest the doorway through which she and Noah had entered. They were tall, they were thin, they were leggy—and they all could have purchased their outfits at the size-eight-or-smaller boutique in Bellewood. Ignoring the envy that reflexively rose up inside her size-twelve body, Maggie shifted her attention from their lissome physiques to their faces. None of them looked like Sisela.

"I don't see Cosmo anywhere," Noah muttered.

She considered splitting up with him so they could work the room separately, then decided not to. She and Noah ought at least to stick together long enough to locate their host and say hello. Besides, she wasn't sure she trusted Noah to go off on his own.

She tried to convince herself the reason she didn't trust him was that he'd come close to making a hash of things that morning at Cosmic Candy headquarters. He wasn't a professional; he didn't know what he was doing when it came to investigative work. If she didn't keep him close beside her, he might say something wrong—although, in all honesty, she couldn't imagine anything he could say or do that would cause a major problem.

The only major problem, she acknowledged with a sharp pang of disgust, would be if Noah were to find Sisela when Maggie wasn't around to dowse any fires that might spontaneously erupt. If, all of a sudden, he found himself face-to-face with his host's wife—or plaything, or whatever she was to Delaney—and if Noah gathered her into his arms and yelled, "Darling, at last I've found you!" it would cause quite a stir. The situation had to be handled delicately.

Yeah, right. So what if Noah caused a stir? Delaney had spirited Noah's fiancée away while Noah had been performing good deeds in a flood-ravaged village in India. Why shouldn't Noah spirit his fiancée right back?

Maggie would be heartbroken—that was why not.

Ridiculous! Of course she wouldn't be heartbroken! The only reason that silly idea had even occurred to her was that she was so deeply immersed in her role as Noah's devoted wife.

But he wasn't her husband or her lover. That kiss had been a mistake. And tonight Maggie was going to find his *real* lover, the woman destined to be his wife.

A waiter swooped down on them, carrying a tray

filled with what appeared to be stuffed mushrooms. As he drew near, Maggie realized that the mushrooms were actually chocolate pieces. The waiter displayed the tray with a flourish, but Maggie shook her head. Ordinarily she would love chocolate, but not as an hors d'oeuvre.

Noah plucked a chocolate mushroom from the tray, bit into it and smiled. "Not bad. Try one, Maggie."

She shook her head again, then paused until the waiter had descended upon the next cluster of guests. "Delaney must have scrambled my brain. I can't remember ever saying no to chocolate before."

"You liked the mocha drink this morning."

"That was before I saw his corporate offices with all those paintings and candy dishes everywhere." She shied away from another waiter who swept past them carrying a tray of pink candies molded into the shape of cocktail shrimp, with a bowl of chocolate syrup instead of cocktail sauce. "This is weird. Do you really think Sisela would have hooked up with a crackpot like Delaney?"

"I don't think he's a crackpot," Noah defended him. "I think he's whimsical. And he's got vision." He circled the room with his gaze. "Other than that... Yes, for this much obvious wealth, I think Sisela might hook up with him."

"Let's circulate," Maggie said, tucking her hand around the bend in Noah's elbow and moving farther into the room. "Who do you suppose all these people are? They can't all be folks who wandered into that lobby this morning and sampled the mocha drink."

"They're his friends," Noah guessed, eyeing a tall, thin man with a shaved head wearing a powder-blue

raw-silk suit. Beside him was a woman clad in a dress
so ugly it had to have cost a fortune. She had glitter-
ing gold-enameled nails, gold stiletto-heeled mules,
and adorning her earlobes, boulder-size chunks of diamond. "This is his social set. Locals from Bellewood. People he plays with. Can't you smell the
wealth in here?"

"All I smell is chocolate," Maggie muttered, eyeing another woman dressed in a bizarre outfit resem-
bling Wilma Flintstone's cavewoman getup—only
this dress was silver satin, and the fur trim around the
halter neckline was undoubtedly real. Maggie almost
felt underdressed, despite the fact that she was wearing the most expensive outfit she'd ever owned.

Over the din she heard the soft tinkling sound of a
piano, and through the crowd she glimpsed what appeared to be a concert grand, angled against the far
wall. Apparently the music was being performed live.

When Maggie threw a party, she played CDs on
her stereo. Everyone came in jeans or khakis, and the
food consisted of cheese and crackers, carrot and cel-
ery sticks with dill dip, and her famous, artery-
clogging guacamole and taco chips—or if it was a
formal sit-down dinner, lasagna and garlic bread. But
Maggie wasn't wearing khaki or denim tonight. And
unlike at any of her parties back in San Francisco,
she was holding the arm of the best-looking man in
the room.

All in a day's work, she reminded herself.

Suddenly a boisterous guffaw cut through the bab-
ble of voices to her left. The sound was familiar, despite the camouflage of other voices churning the air.
"Delaney's over there," she whispered, motioning

with her head in the direction from which the laughter had come.

Noah nodded and ushered her through the crowd, around a pair of uncomfortable-looking chairs to a group holding forth near the piano. Maggie spotted the floppy blond hair of their host, then his long, pointy nose and his canine-damp eyes. He wore a white linen suit that could have costumed the Great Gatsby himself, and he held a martini in one hand and what appeared to be a chocolate-covered pretzel in the other.

Maggie would never eat chocolate when she was wearing white. The odds were too great that she'd get some on the fabric. Of course, Delaney was probably used to confronting chocolate as a regular laundry-day challenge—as if the kind of man who'd live in a joint like this would do his own laundry.

He spotted Maggie and Noah through the crowd. His smile grew warm and he gestured for them to join him. "You came! How splendid!" He beckoned them to his side. "Did you have any trouble finding the place?"

"No." Noah shook Delaney's hand and smiled. "No trouble at all."

"These lovely folks are visiting New York," Delaney informed the attractive brunette standing next to him. "Noah and Maggie Davis. Strangers in town, far from home—I thought they could use some fun. Noah, Maggie, this is the Countess Josefina Boursini."

"So pleased," Josefina Boursini said, her sultry voice flavored with a charming Italian accent.

Maggie shook hands with her, then studied her

while Noah greeted the countess. Was she Delaney's date for the evening? If so, where was Sisela? Had they gotten a divorce even more hush-hush than their marriage? Had they ever been married?

"Cosmo's parties are always so crazy," the countess was telling Noah, who seemed transfixed by her. "This time, with the chocolates. I tell you, I have never eaten a chocolate mushroom before. I think it is wonderful. I should have my cook use Cosmo's chocolate mushrooms in the marsala sauce. Dinner and dessert all in one!" She laughed uproariously at her own joke.

Maggie forced a smile. Her gaze wandered toward the piano and then to the French doors and the escape they offered. If Delaney was consorting with the countess tonight, Maggie didn't need to be here searching for Sisela. At best, she might hope to corner a member of the household staff and ask whether a gorgeous blond woman had been Delaney's companion before the countess had arrived on the scene.

Before Maggie could excuse herself and set off to find a servant to interrogate, Delaney spoke up. "I'd like you to meet my wife. She was here a minute ago and then I lost her. Josefina, did you see where she went?"

"To get some chocolate," Josefina said, peering over Maggie's head. "But look—she's coming over here."

Maggie turned around. So did Noah, his hand alighting gently on her shoulder. And then his fingers squeezed, hard.

She saw the statuesque blond woman weaving a path through the crowd. She saw the woman's elegant cheekbones, her delicate nose, her eyes as blue as Noah's but infinitely colder. The woman had on a white satin dress that scarcely existed. She was all arms and legs and fragile-looking collarbones. And silvery blond hair. And thin rosy lips. And those hollow icy eyes.

If Noah's hand tightened any more on Maggie's shoulder, he was going to leave a bruise.

He must really love her, Maggie acknowledged, fighting off a wave of dismay. Talk about heartbreak: The sight of Sisela Hansen sauntering to her husband's side had to be shattering Noah's heart. If it wasn't, he wouldn't be shattering her shoulder with his clenched fingers.

Sisela's gaze drifted to Noah and she nearly stumbled. She recovered smoothly, moving toward Delaney in silky strides. Her smile seemed frozen on her face, her eyes chilling to absolute zero. "Darling," she said quietly, drawing to a halt next to Delaney. "Who is this?"

"Surprise! These folks are visiting town. They're from San Francisco and I thought you'd like to meet them. My wife used to live in San Francisco," he told Maggie and Noah. Sisela's smile remained arctic and remote. "Sisela, this is Noah Davis and his wife, Maggie."

"Noah Davis," Sisela murmured. "What a pleasure."

"And my wife Maggie," Noah said, nudging Maggie forward.

"Your wife," Sisela echoed. "How lovely. I'm Sisela," she said, gathering Maggie's hand in hers. Sisela's slender, manicured fingers felt like leftover spaghetti, limp and cold from the refrigerator. "Cosmo loves giving me surprises."

"That must make life interesting," Maggie said lamely. She could do detective work, she could run an office, she could mend rifts among her relatives, but making scintillating small talk at unbearably awkward moments was not one of her talents.

Noah's hand relaxed against her shoulder, his fingers rubbing gentle circles into her skin. Was this his nonverbal way of apologizing for having pinched her? Or was he trying to soothe her? Or maybe just pretending, for Sisela's sake, that he adored his "wife" so much he couldn't stop touching her?

"So," Sisela said, apparently deciding that her obligations as a hostess entailed not allowing uncomfortable silences to last more than thirty seconds. "You're visiting New York?"

"Yes," Noah replied. Maggie was glad he'd answered. Her voice seemed to have evaporated.

"Are you tourists? Exploring the world?" One of Sisela's pale eyebrows arched ironically. Maggie assumed she was alluding to Noah's yearning to explore the world a year ago.

"No," Noah told her, his tone cool and even. "We're here on business. Isn't that right, Maggie?"

"Yes," Maggie managed in a rusty voice. She eyed Cosmo's drink covetously. She didn't like martinis, but at the moment anything wet and alcoholic would suit her fine.

"What kind of business?" Sisela asked. Her eyes were as hard as drills, boring into Noah.

Delaney seemed unaware of the tension between his wife and his guests. "Noah designs solar technology for architects," he explained. "Fascinating stuff."

"Really." Sisela tore her gaze from Noah and peered up at her husband. "Fascinating, I'm sure," she murmured enigmatically.

Another pause stretched between them, and Sisela seemed in no hurry to keep the conversation alive. Noah's fingers continued to trace tiny circles on Maggie's shoulder. The pianist embarked on a treacly rendition of "Breaking Up Is Hard to Do." Maggie felt a scream coming on.

She suppressed the urge with a smile. "Well," she said with artificial cheer, "I think I'll go get myself a drink."

"I'll join you," Noah said, nodding a farewell to the Delaneys and following her through the crowd. He caught her elbow when she was still several yards from the bartender and turned her to face him. She was startled to see him grinning—all dimples and mirth. "We found her," he said.

"Yes, we did. And she's married," Maggie reminded, irked by his smile.

He shrugged. "All that matters is that we found her. We set out on a mission, and we accomplished it. I'm feeling pretty damned good."

"All right," she said carefully. Would he still be feeling "pretty damned good" once the reality of his ex-fiancée's marital status sank in?

"In fact, I think we should drink a toast." He ushered her to the bartender's table, eyed the bottles arrayed across the linen and lifted a bottle of Bordeaux. He handed it to the bartender and said, "Two glasses, please."

The bartender filled two goblets with the red wine and presented them to Noah and Maggie. Dubious, she lifted her glass when he lifted his. "Here's to adventure," he murmured.

Before she could ask him exactly what he meant, he clinked his glass lightly against hers and raised it to his lips. His gaze never moved from her as he sipped.

THE DOUBT SEEMED TO FADE from her eyes as she swallowed a bit of wine. Her hair shimmered with tawny highlights; her mouth curved in a smile that was half-mystified and half-knowing. It occurred to Noah that Maggie was the most interesting-looking woman at the party.

Granted, some of the women were more classically pretty. Some were more strikingly beautiful. But none—including Sisela—conveyed such an aura of intelligence. None—including Sisela—made Noah want to kiss the taste of wine from her lips the way Maggie did.

"I'm going to find the ladies' room," she said.

Noah smiled. Obviously Maggie's thoughts hadn't been as sensual as his own.

He watched her disappear into the crowd, her glass held steady in her hand, her round hips shimmying as she walked. He took another sip of his wine and felt his spine go slack. His nerves had been twitching, he realized, but they were slowly calming down.

It was just as well that Maggie had given him a little space. He had to sort out his thoughts—and before he could do that, he had to get his adrenaline back to a normal level. Seeing Sisela had been so...odd.

Not shocking, really; he'd more or less expected to find her here. Not painful, either. He'd realized he wasn't going to be tormented by a reunion with the woman who'd jilted him as soon as he'd admitted that he hadn't been tormented by her jilting him in the first place. Part of his motivation to search for Sisela had been his fear that something terrible might have happened to her. Certainly he was relieved that she was safe and sound and obviously well cared for.

The other motivator had been his desire to remain with Maggie, to continue the adventure, to see it through. To try new things, to take chances, to say yes when a mildly lunatic millionaire extended a spur-of-the-moment invitation to a party. To spend as long as he could admiring Maggie's swaying hips, her lucid eyes, her skeptical smile.

He wondered how far she would have to hike to locate the facilities. In a house this big, she might take one wrong turn and be lost for hours. Then again, with all the waiters and butlers swarming around, surely she could find someone to tell her where the toilet was. She wasn't a man; she was allowed to ask for directions.

The voices around him blurred into a fog of chatter. He asked the bartender to top off his glass and then wandered away from the bar, wishing he could find a quieter place where he could sit and assess what he was feeling.

Sisela had looked not just well, but *good*. She was still a dazzling beauty, the kind of woman who caused people to stop and gape. Noah himself had gaped, almost astonished by the realization that she was truly breathtaking. He'd admired her the way an art aficionado might admire a painting in a museum, a masterpiece he'd admired during a previous visit. He would see it again and gasp at its brilliance—and then move on.

Had Noah actually intended to marry Sisela? He was confounded by his ignorance about her. They'd dated for more than a year, yet she was a complete mystery to him. They'd eaten together, gone to movies together, read the Sunday newspaper together, had sex together, talked about their dreams and then put togetherness on hold, going off on separate paths. He never would have guessed her path would end in a place like this. That was how little he'd known her.

After all of one week, he knew Maggie better.

He'd never gone to a movie with Maggie, or shared a newspaper with her, or had sex with her. Yet he felt he understood her. There was no pretense about her. No bull. She didn't hide behind her looks, didn't act deferentially, didn't opt for discretion when bluntness would serve her better. She didn't flirt, didn't play coy. And she didn't cut herself off from her family. In the past twenty-four hours, Noah had gotten to know more about Maggie's brothers than he'd ever known about Sisela's mother and father.

He rolled a mouthful of wine on his tongue and then let it slide down his throat. He was glad he'd come to Bellewood, glad he and Maggie had found Sisela—if only because in finding her, he'd found out a lot about himself.

Fresh air, fragrant with the evening scent of lilacs and newly mown grass, filtered in through an open

French door. Noah started toward the door, then paused when he spotted Maggie at the center of a cluster of people. He fell back a step so he could watch her without being noticed.

"Most detective work isn't glamorous at all," she was saying. "People think it's all like in the movies, but it isn't. Nobody would ever want to make a movie about ninety percent of the stuff we do. Computer checks, Internet searches... Not the least bit exciting."

Noah wondered whether she would categorize his case as exciting or glamorous. She looked glamorous enough tonight, with the shadowy black fabric of her outfit emphasizing her curves, that keyhole slit dipping down from the neckline in the most subtly erotic way. With her hair pulled back, he could see the sweeping line of her jaw, the feminine arch of her neck, the shell of her ear. When she talked, her eyes were luminous, brighter than the electric chandeliers overhead. Her cheeks glowed pink.

She sipped her wine, and he positioned himself behind a silver-haired gentleman in a tux so she wouldn't catch sight of him over the rim of her glass. Someone was asking her about the difference between police detectives and private detectives. "Police detectives are enforcing the law," she said. "They're solving crimes. Private investigators generally work in the civil area...." He heard her despite the low-level cacophony. Her voice was like a thread of optic fiber, winding through the noise, its tip gleaming with transmitted power.

When they'd first entered the party, she had seemed overwhelmed by the luxury of Cosmo Delaney's estate. Not anymore. She seemed calm and composed. The people surrounding her were clearly captivated.

He felt a tap on his shoulder. Spinning around, he found himself face-to-face with Sisela. "Can we talk?" she asked.

Maggie's animated features and glistening voice were still fresh in his mind as he gazed at the tall, elegant woman with whom he'd once believed he wanted to spend the rest of his life. Her face was remarkably impassive, he thought. Gorgeous and cool, giving nothing away.

"All right," he said.

Sisela worked her way over to the open French door, Noah trailing her. Her hips didn't sway the way Maggie's did—but then, Sisela had hardly any hips at all. He tried to recall the way she'd looked naked; given the skimpy dimensions of her dress, she was practically naked now. Had he worshiped her body? Had they been fabulous in bed?

He honestly couldn't remember.

Guests milled around the brick patio surrounding an illuminated swimming pool. With a small wave and a nod, Sisela acknowledged someone who called a greeting to her, but she continued to the edge of the patio, where she found an empty bench. Carved out of marble, it looked uncomfortable.

She sat on it, and Noah sat next to her. The bench was even more uncomfortable than it looked.

He decided to let her open the discussion. He had nothing much to say, other than that he hoped she was happy. But she'd sought him out, so she must have wanted to talk to him.

"Your *wife?*" she asked.

Noah could come clean with her. He had no reason to lie to her about Maggie. Nor did he feel any urge to make Sisela jealous. *He* felt no jealousy over the fact that she'd found true love with Cosmo Delaney. Mostly he felt settled, his past tied up in a neat parcel for storage, his future wide open before him.

Yet he didn't want to deny that Maggie was his wife. Lying wasn't his style, but...damn it, he liked thinking she belonged to him, if only for one day, one night.

He angled his head toward the house. "Your husband?" he said with a smile.

Her fingers twisted in her lap. He'd never seen Sisela fidget before, and the sight embarrassed him. He drank some wine, giving her a chance to collect herself.

"It was a crazy thing," she said. "Reckless. Just a wild impulse. I'm still not sure why—"

"He's a great guy," Noah said, bailing her out. He figured she was disowning her responsibility for the marriage to protect his feelings, but they didn't need protecting. "I like him, Sisela. And he certainly has a lot to offer." He surveyed the acres of lawn extending out from the patio and grinned.

"We were working together on a commercial," she said, fidgeting again. "It was my first job, a radio ad for Cosmic Star Crunch. I was down to my last dollar, and I thought you were never coming back—"

"What made you think that? I said I'd come back. I don't break my promises."

"Well, you went away, didn't you? You were gone, and I was lonely and out of money, and sud-

denly there was Cosmo. He was so kind and generous, and he just— I don't know—we just—"

"It's okay," Noah insisted. "I'm okay about it."

"Obviously," she said, her voice frosty. "You
have a wife."

Only for as long as I'm with you and your husband,
Noah thought ruefully. "I think we both made good
use of our year apart," he remarked, keeping his tone
soft to counteract the hardness in hers. "If our relationship couldn't withstand a year's separation, it's
just as well we both walked away from it."

"I walked away," Sisela argued. "You came after
me. I can't believe it's just a coincidence that you
crossed paths with Cosmo. You chased me down,
didn't you? You came after me."

"I— Yes," he admitted, unwilling to lie about that.
"I wanted to find you."

"Why? You were already married. Why did you
have to find me?"

He opened his mouth and then shut it. If he were
really married to Maggie, he wouldn't have bothered
to search for Sisela, would he? He would have been
too busy enjoying newly wedded bliss with his bride.

"I wanted to make sure you were safe," he replied,
glad that that, at least, was the truth. "When you
didn't show up at Romeo's when we'd promised to
meet, I was afraid something might have happened to
you."

"You obviously weren't afraid of something happening to me during the year you were away," she
said bitterly. "You got married."

"So did you, Sisela," he said mildly, although her
hypocrisy irked him. "I don't understand why you

sound so resentful. It seems to me we both landed on our feet.''

"I'm not resentful. I just..." She twisted in her seat. "I just wish you hadn't found me, that's all.''

"Why? Are you running away from something? Trying to hide something?''

"No. I just..." More fidgeting. Her fingernails were polished a pearly white; her hands looked as smooth as porcelain. He wondered if she was still playing the piano, still singing for her own enjoyment. "Everything is fine. It's done. I'm happy, and I want to put yesterday behind me.''

"Good," he said, unable to keep his irritation out of his voice. "That's great. I want to put yesterday behind me, too.''

"Then perhaps you and your wife ought to leave,'' she said. "You've done what you set out to do—track me down, corner me in my own house, at my own party, and make me feel wretched. So why don't you go?''

Noah sighed. He didn't mean to make her feel wretched. He covered her restless hands with his until they fell still. "We'll leave soon," he assured her. "As soon as I can tear my wife away from her audience.''

"Your wife is on her way over right now," Sisela said, pointing with her chin. Maggie was strolling along the edge of the pool toward them.

Noah released Sisela's hands and stood, his mouth curving naturally into a smile. How delightfully human Maggie looked, compared to Sisela's ice-goddess perfection. Maggie held her head high, her shoulders back, her body moving sensuously in the black silk. Her steps were slow, her smile spellbinding.

"Hello, Maggie," Noah said, extending his hand to her.

"My feet are killing me," she muttered through gritted teeth. "How are you?"

When she didn't take his hand, he slid his arm around her shoulders. She felt so warm. Sisela would probably give him frostbite if he touched her. "Actually—" he directed his gaze toward Sisela "—I'm a little tired. Would you mind if we left?"

Maggie eyed Sisela, then Noah. "Oh, and I was just beginning to enjoy myself."

She must have surmised that his desire to leave had something to do with Sisela. He could tell by the glint in her eye, the teasing edge of her smile. "Your feet hurt," he reminded her. "I'm sure you want to take your sandals off."

"I'm sure I do," she said, bending over and sliding the straps over her heels. The tunic's neckline drooped, affording him a glimpse of the creamy flesh of her breasts. The muscles in his groin pulled tight.

He wanted to leave, all right. Not because of Sisela, but because of Maggie. Because he wanted to make love to her, and he shouldn't want that, he couldn't want it—and maybe if they left, he would be able to stop thinking of her as his wife.

"Ah." She sighed. He made the mistake of glancing down, and saw her wiggling her liberated toes. He'd never cared one way or another about women's feet before. But he'd never seen feet as sweetly plump as Maggie's. "I feel much better. I think the pianist is going to play some dance music. We could stay and dance." She smiled at Sisela. "Do you like to dance?"

Sisela looked acutely peeved. She shot Noah an eloquent frown. "I think we really do have to leave," he said, tightening his hold on Maggie and guiding her away before she could say anything more.

After a few steps she balked and dragged him over to the grass. "My feet are really sore," she complained. "Those bricks were hurting."

"I'm sorry." The grass was as smooth as green velvet. He looked down and saw her toes curling into the soft, fragrant stalks. He felt her sigh in the curve of his arm.

"It didn't go well, did it?" she guessed.

"What didn't go well?"

"Your reunion with Sisela. She looked upset."

"No. She's fine. She's very happy with Cosmo," he said swiftly, hoping to reassure Maggie.

She peered up at him again, no hint of teasing in her expression. "She isn't happy, Noah. The woman was radiating waves of misery."

"No." He didn't want to think about Sisela's self-inflicted misery. He wanted to think only of Maggie, with her bare feet and her round eyes and her wine-darkened lips. He wanted to think of her lush body and the way she filled his arms as he turned her to face him.

He wanted to think, for just this one night, that she was his woman and he was her man, that he could kiss her until they both wanted to die from the pleasure of it.

CHAPTER TEN

HE WAS KISSING HER to score points with Sisela.

He was kissing her because the wine had muddled both their minds.

He was kissing her because they were posing as husband and wife.

By the end of the first kiss, Maggie no longer cared why Noah was kissing her. She forgot to care. She forgot the pain where her sandals had pinched her toes and the fact that she was standing on some gazillionaire's lawn in the midst of a hotsy-totsy party, kissing a man with the bluest eyes and the most seductive mouth she'd ever known.

Oh, God, could Noah kiss! With one nip of his teeth he could make her stomach flutter; with one sweep of his tongue he could make her sink against him and moan. With the movement of his hand along her back he could make her long to tear her clothes off; with the movement of his knee between her thighs he could make her think that after tearing her clothes off she ought to throw herself into the pool to keep from burning up.

But she wanted to burn, if only for a minute or two. Even though she realized Noah was kissing her for all the wrong reasons, she wanted his mouth on hers, drawing her out, drawing her in. She wanted this. She wanted him.

He kept one hand at the small of her back, refusing to let her put even an inch of space between their bodies, and slid his other hand up into her hair. It was all going to tumble down, she knew. Her precariously pinned and lacquered locks were going to collapse around her face. She didn't care about that, either. For the chance to kiss a man like Noah, she would gladly endure a lifetime of bad-hair days.

His chest exuded heat, as if he were burning, too. Maybe they should both jump into the pool and extinguish the fire.

Better yet, maybe they should just keep kissing like this for all eternity—or at least for the rest of the night. They should just keep stoking this passion, fueling it, feeling the flames lick higher and higher until the conflagration devoured them. Tomorrow morning, Cosmo Delaney's gardener would find a little mound of ashes on the lawn where they'd been standing. Beside the ashes, he'd see a pair of black dress sandals.

Her breasts were as hot as Noah's chest. Her nipples tingled from the heat. Her mind melted from it. Her lips molded to his, fused to his, taking his tongue and then offering her own. In the distance, someone must have opened one of the doors, because Maggie heard the sound of the piano through a burst of voices and laughter. The tune was a schmaltzy version of "Love Has No Pride."

The music wrapped around her, imbued her with its haunting sorrow. But it also reminded her that she *did* have pride.

She eased back from Noah and hid her face in his

shoulder as she struggled to catch her breath. It had
been intensely, sublimely wonderful kissing him, but
it wasn't real. She wasn't his wife; she was his em-
ployee. And she'd done what he'd paid her to do:
She'd found his true love—who just happened to be
married to someone else, but that wasn't Maggie's
fault.

She had pride, and her pride told her that Noah was
kissing her for show.

He twined his fingers gently through her hair. She
heard the rasp of his breath, felt the insistent swell of
his arousal against her. That was biology, not love,
she reminded herself. That was Noah responding to a
kiss and thinking about the woman he'd once loved
enough to propose marriage to: Sisela Hansen.

"I think we should go," Maggie whispered into
his neck.

"Yeah."

She pulled away. A shiver gripped her shoulders as
she eased out of his arms. His eyes slowly came into
focus on her. He looked stunned—as if maybe he'd
expected to see someone other than her. Someone tall
and blond and beautiful.

She wasn't sure he understood that when she'd said
they should go, she hadn't meant they should go back
to the motel and pick up where they'd left off. But to
spell that out for him while standing barefoot in the
middle of the vast lawn of Delaney's estate would be
tactless—especially since, now that he realized exactly whom he'd been kissing, such a lecture probably
wasn't necessary. He was coming back to his senses,
just like her.

Her fingers curling tightly around the straps of her

sandals, she padded across the lawn, appreciating its cool, springy texture against the soles of her feet. She assumed Noah was following her, but she didn't glance over her shoulder to check. She didn't want to see his befuddled expression, or—worse—his disappointment that Maggie wasn't the woman he'd actually wanted, the woman he'd been dreaming of for the past year.

She entered the house, sauntered through the crowd while conscientiously avoiding eye contact with any of the guests, and darted down the hall to the front door. On the portico, she asked the valet to fetch Noah's car. "The cheap, rented Ford," she told him.

"Your Rolls is in the shop?" he asked with a wink.

"No. I lent the Rolls to the Queen Mum for the summer," Maggie retorted, leaning against one of the pillars and letting the mild night air wash over her. She ought to have been famished—all she'd eaten that evening had been something that looked like a baby carrot but tasted like orange-flavored marzipan. What she wanted right now was a *real* carrot, or maybe some Brussels sprouts, along with a glass of plain skim milk.

The valet bounded down the steps to the driveway and set off on a long hike to wherever it was he'd parked Noah's car. Maggie watched him until he'd vanished into the shadows, then gazed up at the stars dotting the night sky before scanning the manicured front yard. She wondered whether Noah was going to join her. He should have come through the oak double doors by now. Perhaps he'd thought long and hard about the woman he'd kissed and the woman he'd *wanted* to kiss and had detoured back to the poolside patio to plead his case to Sisela.

And why shouldn't he? True love and destiny were powerful forces—even when an impetuous, wrong-headed marriage stood in the way.

She didn't mind if Noah went back to Sisela. She'd had no right to desire him, and she'd been a fool to let him kiss her, both yesterday and today. If word ever got out that she'd locked lips with a client during her search for that client's misplaced lover, her business would be destroyed before she'd even finished settling into her office.

For the sake of Finders, Keepers, she had to be glad Noah had decided to try to make things right with Sisela. She felt kind of sorry for Delaney. And she felt seriously resentful of Sisela—not because Noah had gone back to her, but because the woman had selfishly abandoned one man for another, and at least one of those two men was going to wind up hurt.

Of course, Delaney had plenty of money to cushion his crash. And Noah had so much charisma Maggie was sure he would find some other woman to salve his wounds if Sisela ultimately chose Delaney.

And that woman wouldn't be herself, she vowed.

She saw headlights circling the driveway and nearing the front steps. If she wanted, she could drive back to the motel herself, instead of loitering on the porch while Noah remained in the house taking his psychic temperature. But just as the valet stepped out of the car, Noah materialized behind her.

"I was thanking Cosmo for inviting us," he informed her.

How courteous, she thought wryly. "What excuse did you give him for our departure?"

"I said you were tired."

Her feet were tired, she admitted silently. Her brain was tired. Her toes stung, and so did her heart, no matter how many times she tried to persuade herself it didn't.

Noah touched her elbow as they descended the steps together. She steeled herself against her body's instinctive response to him and shut her mind against the memories of how wonderful it had felt to kiss him. He helped her into the passenger seat, then climbed in behind the wheel and steered away from the mansion. As they coasted down the long driveway, the lights of the party receded behind them and the interior of the car grew darker and moodier.

"Something's wrong," Noah murmured.

Instinctively Maggie peered at the dashboard, searching for a red warning light. "Are we out of gas?"

He chuckled, although he seemed pensive. "I'm talking about you and me, Maggie. I thought we had enough fuel between us to run the Indy 500 without a pit stop, but now I don't know. Are we out of gas?"

"There is no 'you and me,'" Maggie argued.

"What was going on by the pool, then?"

"You were..." She scrambled for a tactful way to put it. "You were overcome with emotion after seeing Sisela."

"Oh. I was 'overcome.'" He ruminated on that idea for a while, then shrugged. "And you? What was going on with you?"

"I was flying high from having solved my first case."

"I see." He steered through the towering gates and turned onto the road. "And so...what? I was overcome, you were high, and we just lost control of ourselves?"

"Exactly."

"I've been wanting to take you to bed all evening," he said so bluntly, Maggie flinched.

"No," Maggie argued, because it was too preposterous to be true. "You've been through a lot, Noah. You got jilted by your fiancée. You were so devastated by her betrayal, you hired me to find her. You chased me across the country. And when we finally found her, it turned out she was already married to a megamillionaire twit."

"He's not a twit. He's a terrific guy."

"He needs a haircut." Maggie scowled. "You've been on an emotional roller coaster, Noah. Admit it."

"I'm perfectly calm." He flicked the directional signal and gave the wheel a smooth, flawless turn, as if to prove how calm he was.

"You're in shock." She couldn't accept any other explanation for his recent behavior. Until he'd followed her east, he had never revealed even a glimmer of personal interest in her.

From the moment he'd entered her office, Maggie had understood that he was completely and unshakably committed to Sisela. Sisela had made a major mistake by marrying someone else in his absence, and he was going to have to plumb the depths of his soul to forgive her, but that nonsense with Maggie by the pool? Just as he'd held her while she'd cried a few

days ago, tonight she'd been the one providing a ref-
uge for his overflowing emotions.

"Do you mean to tell me," he said, sounding almost unnaturally calm now, "that you don't think
something phenomenal happened when you and I
kissed?"

"It was very nice," she conceded.

"Very nice?"

"Very, very nice."

"Two verys?"

Exasperation overtook her. "Noah, what is your
point? Do you want me to say I was turned on? I'm
human—of course I was. So were you. But that's not
what we're dealing with, here."

"What are we dealing with?"

She knew he wasn't stupid. He was being deliberately dense, forcing her to spell everything out. All
right, then, she'd put it together for him, letter by
letter. "First of all, I'm working for you. Second—
and more important—you're in love with Sisela."

"No, I'm not."

"Okay—you're in flux at the moment," she elab-
orated. "But it was hardly a year ago when you asked
her to marry you, and it was just a week ago when
you came back to America to plan your wedding.
She's bruised your feelings, but that doesn't mean
you don't love her."

"My feelings are fine, and I don't love her." His
equanimity slipped a little; she could hear the edge in
his voice.

"Well, then, I've got to ask what kind of person
you are if you could fall in and out of love with a
woman so easily."

"Trust me," he said tightly. "It's pretty easy to fall out of love with someone who breaks her promises. Especially when she marries someone else behind your back."

"All right," Maggie allowed, growing progressively calmer as Noah's composure eroded. "Maybe you're wounded enough to believe you don't love her anymore. What does that make me, besides being the detective you hired? I'm supposed to be the woman you take to bed to make you forget about how Sisela hurt you? I'm the one you have sex with to erase all memories of her?"

Noah took the turn too fast; the tires squealed before he slowed down and straightened the wheel. No more flawless driving, Maggie thought grimly. "I was hoping you'd be the woman I took to bed because we wanted each other," he retorted.

"I'm a little more complex than that, I'm afraid," she said. "I don't just sleep with guys because it's something I feel like doing at a particular moment."

"Fine," he said through clenched teeth. "Forget the whole thing, okay? It was great kissing you. Thanks for finding Sisela. We'll settle accounts back in San Francisco."

"Fine," she agreed. Her attempt at remaining poised wasn't going to succeed. Anger crackled in the car like electricity; she could practically see the sparks. Noah's outrage seemed to have resulted from her refusal to sleep with him—which proved all over again how right she was to refuse. And her anger arose from the understanding that he was using her. She hadn't minded his using her when he was paying her two hundred dollars a day plus expenses. But using her for a romp between the sheets?

He and Sisela deserved each other. Two self-centered jerks.

Her toes started stinging again, tender from the chafing of the sandal straps. Her eyes started stinging, too. She realized with a wretched sigh that her heart had gone well beyond stinging to the most harrowing anguish, raw and tender from having rubbed the wrong way against Noah Davis.

NOAH SPRAWLED OUT ON his sofa, clad in a pair of cutoffs and his favorite faded Stanford University T-shirt, nursing a beer and wondering why, after staring at his television screen for three prime-time hours, he couldn't remember a single image, a single character, a line of dialogue. If he were given to overindulgence, he would be drinking his twelfth beer instead of his second. As it was, his hair was a mess, his jaw hadn't been touched by a razor in two days and his floor was blanketed with scattered sections of the Sunday newspaper, all of them leafed through, none of them read.

The only thing he'd read—several times—was the final, itemized bill he'd received from Finders, Keepers in yesterday's mail.

Damn it to hell.

He understood that when a person took risks, the biggest risk was of failure. He'd acknowledged going in that there were many possibilities for failure: that Maggie wouldn't find Sisela, that Sisela would *wish* Maggie hadn't found her, that *he'd* wish he hadn't found her. And that he would spend a lot of money and come up empty.

Empty. That was how he felt. His adventure was over, he was home, he had an invoice from Finders, Keepers; he couldn't bear the thought that tomorrow morning at eight, he would have to scrape off his weekend growth of beard, don a suit and tie and go back to Solar Systems. He was going to have to return to the life he'd had a year ago; the safe, sane, tidy life of going to work, arranging big-money deals that preserved the ozone layer, and stopping at Romeo's after work for an espresso—only this time, with no one sitting across the table from him.

Certainly Maggie wouldn't. She'd made her position quite clear the morning after the party, when they'd driven to La Guardia Airport, returned the rental car and boarded a plane to San Francisco. She hadn't said much during the drive, but after he'd rearranged their seat assignments during check-in, she'd been stuck beside him for the five-and-a-half-hour flight home. She'd been able to fake a nap only so long before the uncomfortable seat had gotten the better of her and she'd had to stretch.

He'd launched into a conversation. "What happens now?" he'd asked.

"When we get back to San Francisco?" She'd stretched and faked a yawn. "I add up my expenses, print out a bill and mail it to you."

The small, hard, airplane pillow had mussed her hair. He'd wanted to comb his fingers through it, to feel the rippling curls against his palms.

"I wasn't asking about Finders, Keepers, Maggie," he'd said. "I was asking about us."

"'Us'?" She'd let out a caustic laugh. "There's no such thing as us."

"Last night there could have been."

"Last night you were showing off in front of the woman who walked out on you," Maggie had reminded him, her voice losing its angry undertone. She'd sounded thoughtful, wistful and unexpectedly forgiving. "Here's the deal. You hired me to do a job, I did it. Maybe it didn't come out the way you wanted. I know I was really hoping it would have come out differently. My very first case—and I couldn't... Well, I'm sorry about that."

"Forget about it," he'd told her. "I'm not discussing Sisela. I'm discussing you and me."

She'd shaken her head. "The reality of you and me is, you were using me. That was our arrangement. It accomplished your goal, and I got paid for my time, and that's the black-and-white of it."

"When I kissed you..." He'd felt a hum in his body just remembering their kisses—a hot, heady current. "I sure as hell wasn't using you, Maggie."

"Last night you wanted sex. I guess maybe I did, too. But I don't make a habit of having sex without love. I'm sure sex with you would be wonderful...." A delicate flush had darkened her cheeks. "But we aren't in love, Noah. We have no relationship."

She'd been speaking the truth. They had no relationship. He'd never even thought of her in the context of love. And given that he'd been paying her and she'd accomplished what he'd hired her to do... Damn. Maybe he *had* been using her.

The local eleven-o'clock news broadcast began. Tipping his bottle back against his lips, Noah swallowed some beer. He wondered if he'd ever been in love. If he could bear Sisela's defection with so little disappointment, surely he couldn't have loved her. And before her? There had been girlfriends, but no one he'd ever want to wake up next to for the rest of his life.

"And in a lighter vein," the perky blond anchor-woman said, making Noah wonder what dark news had been reported while he'd been daydreaming, "do you ever find yourself thinking about the one who got away? That long-lost love, that first big crush? Well, there's a detective agency in town devoted to finding the sweetheart you let slip through your fingers. Here to tell you all about it is our Consumer Beat reporter, Sarah Cummings. Sarah?"

The camera switched to another perky blonde, indistinguishable from the first, but this one was standing in the doorway of Maggie's minuscule office. "Hi," the new perky blonde said into the microphone she held below her chin. "I'm at the local detective agency Finders, Keepers, where the sleuth in charge, Maggie Tyrell, is making a career of bringing separated lovers back together again." The camera cut to a shot of the exterior of the building. "Maggie is the daughter of John Tyrell, founder of Tyrell Investigative Services, one of San Francisco's largest detective agencies. But, unlike her brothers, who still run the family firm, Maggie isn't interested in tracking down troublemakers. She wants to bring about happy endings for her clients."

Noah sat upright and balanced his beer bottle on the floor between his feet. He stared as the camera cut once again to Maggie's office—this time with Maggie in it. She was smiling sassily, her hair tumbling down around her shoulders, her eyes bright and her lush body concealed under a plain knit top, linen slacks and a blazer.

He had always heard that people looked heavier on TV. But Maggie didn't look heavy at all. She looked strong and healthy and substantial. No gust of wind could knock her over. No "troublemaker" could put one over on her. She was Maggie Tyrell, and she could do anything.

She was talking, and he sat forward to listen. "You know John Greenleaf Whittier's poem about how the saddest words are, 'It might have been'? So many people wind up thinking about what might have been if only they hadn't lost someone they loved. But they move on, they lose touch and then they live their lives with a degree of regret. I started Finders, Keepers so people can find out what might have been—and they can still make it happen. I find the lost lovers and they take it from there."

"What made you decide to pursue this area of detective work?" the reporter asked.

Maggie gazed directly into the camera—directly into Noah's eyes. "I'm an optimist," she said. "And I believe in true love and destiny."

His heart twisted in his chest. When he'd been engaged to Sisela, he'd never thought much about love—because, he supposed, he didn't really believe in it. Surely the example of his parents hadn't proved that true love was worth betting on. But when Maggie talked about it with such conviction, he wanted to believe. When he watched her and thought of her opinionated attitude, her high-wattage personality, her concern about her brothers, her determination to do her job and to stay away from uncommitted sex...

He could almost believe. Almost.

He didn't know how she'd managed to get the publicity of a puff piece on the local TV news show, but the story was a well-presented promotion. Maggie looked great, she sounded even better, and the cameraman had shot her office at such an angle that it actually appeared larger than a gym locker. Noah felt happy for her.

But more than that, he felt sorry for himself. Sorry that she was there, in the little box across the living room from him, and he was on the couch, all alone. Sorry that he hadn't told her how much he admired her when they'd been together; how much she amused him, how much she challenged him. How much she turned him on—and not just with her kisses. Everything about her—her personality, her bullheadedness, her intelligence and her compassion—aroused him.

He'd lost someone. Not Sisela, but someone who could make his life different, better, full of adventure. When he'd had her, he hadn't realized how much she could mean to him, how much delight he could take simply from being with her.

So he'd lost her.

But he could find her. He didn't have to hire a detective agency. He knew where she was, how to reach her, how to work his way back into her life.

CHAPTER ELEVEN

IF YOU HAD TO BE STUCK with a brother whose marriage needed resurrecting—and you were the only person in the universe who could help—you might as well have a sister-in-law who worked for one of the city's local TV news shows.

Maggie hadn't expected any huge gestures of gratitude from Karen and Sandy after the long evening she'd spent negotiating a reconciliation between them. All she'd done was invite them both to her apartment and then refuse to let them leave until they were communicating again. She'd acted as an interpreter, and occasionally as an editor, improving on their words. She'd poured tea, she'd poured bourbon, and she'd threatened to pour a pitcher of ice water onto Sandy's crotch after the third time he pointed out that since he and Karen were exceptionally compatible in the sack, he really didn't see why they couldn't just overlook the trivial stuff like his habit of forgetting anniversaries and dinner dates.

After about four hours and a gallon or so of tea and bourbon, Maggie had gotten Karen to admit that she'd married Sandy knowing that he was absent-minded, that, in fact, she'd thought his chronic befuddlement when it came to certain matters was adorable and dear. Maggie had also gotten Sandy to admit that when a man loved a woman, he had to exert himself to do the things that made his woman happy, even if those things were as challenging as remembering their wedding anniversary.

Karen and Sandy hadn't exactly kissed and made up, but they'd left Maggie's apartment together, which was something. A simple thank-you for her diplomatic intervention would have sufficed. But the next morning, Karen had phoned Maggie and asked if she would like the station to do a human-interest story on Finders, Keepers.

"Are you kidding? I'd love it!" Maggie had shrieked. For better or worse, she'd tied up her one and only case, and no new customers were pounding on her door, begging her to accept large wads of legal tender to find their misplaced paramours. If a snappy little story on the eleven-o'clock news could generate some interest in her firm, she might be able to stay in business for another month.

The Monday morning after the story was broadcast, customers started pounding on her door.

Two people were actually waiting for her when she arrived at her office at nine-thirty. By the time she'd gotten one a cup of coffee and shoehorned the other into her office, two more had arrived. By noon she'd talked to a dozen potential clients. Four cases she chose to start on immediately. The rest she sorted in order of difficulty, filling her calendar with work for the next several months. Paying work. Full-price five-hundred-dollars-a-day work.

She'd barely had a chance to consume half the sandwich Neil had brought her from the deli on the corner when the line began to form outside her door again. Eight more prospective clients stood patiently in the hall connecting her office to the rest of Tyrell Investigative Services. Jack was reduced to offering them coffee while they waited, just as Maggie used to bring cups of coffee to clients waiting to see Jack.

The irony amused her. The demand for her services invigorated her. In fact, she'd have been unequivocally elated—if she weren't so damned depressed.

She was enraged that Noah Davis could have the power to depress her. Who was he, after all? Just a client like all the other hopeful men and women queued up in the hallway. Noah Davis had helped her launch her business, but she'd found his lady and sent him a bill, and she really had no reason to be thinking about him anymore.

Still, she couldn't stop herself. While she'd been overseeing the Karen-Sandy negotiations, she'd wanted to shake them by their shoulders and scream, "What's wrong with you two? You love each other, you have each other, and when you kiss it means something. Be grateful for what you've got. It's a hell of a lot more than I have!" When she'd unpacked from her trip to New York and hung the silk pants outfit in her closet, when she'd reviewed her charges and printed out Noah's bill, when she'd sat at her desk and stared at the poster of Nureyev and Fonteyn and recalled the first time Noah had marched into her sight, cramming himself into the folding metal chair and blocking her view of the dancers...

He was a client—emphasis on *was*. And he obviously had some growing up to do about love....

He was nothing to Maggie. Nothing at all.

The person currently in her sight was a dumpling-

faced grandmother wearing a chunky-beaded neck-
lace and feather earrings. "Herman taught me how to
drive," she was saying. "I thought if our relationship
could survive driving lessons, it could survive anything. It had to be true love. But then he took the
train to Chicago for his uncle's funeral, and I never
saw him again. I suppose he must have fallen in love
with someone in Chicago...."

Maggie nodded sympathetically as she typed Mabel
Montgomery's meandering tale into her computer. So
many other people had sad stories—how could she
possibly feel sorry for herself? Unlike Mabel, Maggie
had never suffered any delusions about Noah's feelings for her. Their relationship—if *relationship*
wasn't too strong a word—hadn't survived three days
of sleuthing on the East Coast; driving lessons would
have pushed them over the edge. It wasn't as if Maggie had loved and lost Noah.

"I'll see what I can do," she assured Mabel. "I've
got other cases ahead of yours, so it may be a couple
of months before I can start searching for—" she
skimmed the print on her monitor for his name
"—Herman Hubbard. I won't start billing you until
I'm working on your case, of course, and I'll send
you a breakdown of my hours."

"No problem," Mabel said, her feathers quivering
whenever she moved her head. "I've waited forty-
five years. Lord knows, if I hadn't seen that news
report on Finders, Keepers on TV last night, I might
have spent the rest of my life waiting. A couple more
months isn't a big thing."

Maggie smiled and rose to escort Mabel to the
door—an extraneous gesture, since one step would

carry Mabel out of the office. But besides being courteous, Maggie wanted to check the hallway to see
how many more people were still waiting for a few
minutes of her time. It was nearly four o'clock, and
she was ready to collapse from the exhaustion of listening to so many people tell her about their romantic
debacles and missed opportunities.

Three people now stood in the corridor: her brother
Jack, holding a stack of empty coffee cups, an elderly
gentleman decked out in the sort of summery pastels
and plaids that led her to believe he'd come to her
office straight from the golf course, and a third man,
young, dressed in a suit that marked him as upper-
level management. He had black hair and blue eyes
and a slightly crooked, gloriously dimpled smile.
When he saw her, his eyes glittered like stars on a
clear night.

Maggie scowled. What was Noah doing here? If
he'd come to argue over the bill, he shouldn't have
bothered. They could have dealt with any discrepan-
cies over the phone.

She couldn't even bear to look at him. Just one
glimpse of his dimples sent her spinning back in time
to a night beside a swimming pool, with his arms
around her, his mouth covering hers. One glimpse of
his eyes, and her head echoed with his rough-edged
plea: *"I've been wanting to take you to bed all evening."*

The nerve of him, showing up at her office! How
dared he reenter her life when she was so busy de-
spising him?

She smiled and nodded at the elderly gentleman.

"Hi. I'm Maggie Tyrell. Would you like to step inside?"

"Thanks," he said, moving toward her.

She led him into the office and slammed her door with telling force. Sending her client another quick smile so he'd know her anger wasn't directed at him, she pointed toward the chair Noah had once fatefully occupied, and then sidled around the desk to her own chair.

The fellow, Walter Notera, related his story. It was unique to him, but similar in certain ways to every other story Maggie had heard that day. He'd loved Hilda Gertner, but they'd been of different faiths and her family had refused to let him court her. The Korean War had put him in uniform, and when he'd returned home she'd been married and gone. He'd wed a fine woman, they'd had a nice life together, but his wife had passed away two years ago and he'd been thinking a lot about Hilda, wondering what ever had happened to her; was she happy, had she lived a nice life, too?

Maggie drew up a contract and promised Mr. Notera that she would do her best to find the answers to his questions about Hilda.

She dawdled through her session with Mr. Notera, hoping that if she took long enough, Noah Davis wouldn't still be waiting outside her office when she finished. She asked Mr. Notera dozens of questions about Hilda—what she'd looked like, what her address had been when he'd left town, what her parents' names had been. Had Hilda gone to college? Did she have any siblings? Had she been interested in pursuing a career?

She'd wanted to teach school, he'd told her.

Maggie stalled for a few more minutes, slowing her typing as she entered the information into a computer file. "I can't start the search right away," she told him. "I've got several clients ahead of you. But I'll call you as soon as I'm ready to open your case."

"I appreciate it," Walter said. "If Hilda's happy, I don't want to bother her. But I keep thinking, what if she's alone? What if she's been thinking about me?"

"I'll do my best to find out," Maggie assured him. Despite the fact that she'd listened to so many poignant stories that day, Walter Notera's account made her eyes moist. She was a softie when it came to thwarted love, to painful loss. She knew people could recover from heartbreak—Mr. Notera had enjoyed his "nice" marriage to his "fine" wife, after all—but if there was any way to undo a mistake from one's past, to go back and make it all come out right...

Kissing Noah Davis had been a mistake. Desiring him had been a mistake. Letting him hold her the evening she'd gone to his apartment, gazing into his blue, blue eyes and wondering what her life might have been like if a man like him had ever loved her— Oh, yes, she'd made mistakes.

She couldn't go back to fix the past, but she could ensure that she didn't make any more mistakes in the future. Which would be a whole lot easier if Noah had given up and left the hallway. But when she opened her door and bade Mr. Notera goodbye, she saw that Noah was still there, alone this time, slouching against the wall with his hands in his trouser pockets. His tie was loosened, his collar button undone and his hair mussed, as if his lengthy wait had tuckered him out. But his eyes were uncannily alert, focused on the door as she opened it, and then focused on her.

"Can I help you?" she asked, sounding as impersonal as a telephone operator.

"Yes." He pushed away from the wall, shrugged his jacket higher on his shoulders and stalked down the hall toward her office.

She didn't want him there. Once he was inside that tiny room she would have no way to escape him. But she couldn't allow him to discuss his business in the corridor, within earshot of her brothers.

Gritting her teeth, she followed Noah into her office and moved directly to her chair so the desk would serve as a barrier between them. He closed the door behind her, then twisted the bolt, locking them inside.

She swallowed hard. Why had he locked the door? Why did the metallic click of the bolt sliding into place seem to draw the walls inward, forcing her and Noah even closer together?

She remained standing, flattening her hands against the surface of her desk so she wouldn't clench them into fists. Ordering herself to stay poised and professional, she asked, "What can I do for you?"

He remained standing, too. He reached into an inner pocket of his jacket, pulled out the invoice she'd mailed him and tossed it onto the table. *Good,* she thought. *He's come to argue about the bill.* She could handle that much more easily than any personal issue he might want to raise. Money was simple.

"A couple of weeks ago," he said, his voice so

familiar it pained her to listen to him, "I came here looking for a woman."

"I remember," she said curtly.

Unfazed, he continued. "I still don't have her."

"That's not my problem, Noah. You hired me to find her and I found her. It's not my fault that things didn't work out." *You bastard,* she added silently. *Coming here and complaining about Sisela after you failed to get me into bed!*

"No," he said evenly, his eyes on her face, his mouth shaped into that half smile that exasperated her because it was so damned sexy. "As it turned out, Maggie, *I* found her."

"What's your point? Do you want *me* to pay *you* for dogging me all the way to Bellewood?"

He shook his head. His smile didn't seem to change, but another dimple sprouted in one corner of his mouth. "It's you, Maggie. You're the woman I was looking for."

"What?" Her voice rose an octave and faded into an undignified squeak.

"I found you. And then I lost you. I'm willing to pay this bill—" he jabbed his finger at the invoice on her desk "—but I need to know how to get back the woman I lost."

"You never..." This time her voice was an octave too low. She cleared her throat and clung to the edge of the desk to keep from collapsing into her chair. "You were looking for Sisela. You weren't looking for me."

"I was looking for the woman I needed in my life. I might have been a little bit confused regarding the details, but I was looking for the right woman."

"Noah." Her voice was neither too high nor too low this time; it was too weak. It couldn't sustain his brief name, let alone a complete sentence.

"So maybe I was confused. But I'm not confused anymore. I saw you on TV last night and it all came clear to me. *You're* the one I needed to find. And then I lost you, Maggie."

"You never had me to lose."

"I'd like to correct that," Noah said. "The first part."

"You want to...to have me?" Well, she knew he did. He'd been pretty straightforward about that.

"You were supposed to help me find my woman. And that's exactly what you did." He inched around the desk toward her, leaving her no opportunity to elude him—as if she would want to. On the whisper-thin chance that he could be speaking the truth, she was willing to stand exactly where she was, to let him come close.

But not too close. Not close enough to hurt her. "This makes no sense, Noah. I know we— Well, we—"

"Kissed," he murmured. His voice was so low, so intimate, the mere word struck her like a match against flint, igniting a tiny flame inside her.

"Well, yes, we kissed. But—" she inhaled deeply "—we were pretending to be married. You were in love with Sisela. You wanted her back so badly, you paid for an extra ticket and flew across the country just so you could be there when I found her."

"I didn't pay," he reminded Maggie with a self-deprecating grin. "I used my frequent-flyer miles."

"Whatever." He really wasn't that close to her, yet

he felt close. Closer than two people should be when they were standing several feet apart. "I'm sure you don't—well, love me." She faltered slightly over the word *love*. "Two weeks ago you were engaged to marry Sisela."

"Two weeks ago I hadn't seen Sisela in more than a year. And she was married to someone else." He did move closer then, leaned toward her, extended his hand to her cheek and traced down to her chin with his index finger. "Two weeks ago I met you. A lot can happen in two weeks." His finger continued downward to the curve of her throat, sending shivers of heat along her nerve endings. "Don't you realize why I traveled to Bellewood? Not to be with Sisela. To be with *you*."

"No." She couldn't risk believing him. It would hurt too much if she trusted him and he betrayed her.

"I didn't realize it myself, not at first. But I understand now. It was *you*. I wanted to be with *you*."

"But I'm not—I'm nothing like Sisela," she said.

"Thank God." He reached out with his other hand and caressed the other side of her face.

"I mean, I'm— Look at me, Noah. I'm no fashion plate."

He shook his head, molded his hands over her shoulders and pulled her toward him. "You're beautiful," he murmured, then covered her lips with his.

This was insane. He couldn't really mean what he was saying. Not that she was hung up about her weight or fixated on her appearance, but she was aware of herself, her strengths and limitations, and she knew damned well that men like Noah didn't think women like her were beautiful.

Except that his words seemed torn from his heart, and his kiss was honest. It felt so good, so right. Feeling his arms close around her and his mouth open over hers, feeling his tongue claim her just felt...*true*. She sensed conviction in Noah's kiss, along with passion and hunger, and maybe even love.

Two weeks ago he'd come to her looking for the woman he needed. How could either of them have known it would lead to this? Surely he'd been no less surprised by this truth than she was.

Yes, she acknowledged. It was the truth. This kiss—this deep, dazzling, devastating kiss—contained the truth.

He relented, leaning back only far enough to peer into her eyes. He must have seen trust in them, and acceptance, because his smile returned, reassuring and dangerous at the same time. He touched his lips to her forehead, to the bridge of her nose, to one cheek and then the other and then her mouth again, filling her with long, greedy strokes of his tongue.

Her legs gave way and she sank against her desk. He slid his hands down her arms to her waist, lifting her to sit on the desk and pressing against her knees. He shoved her skirt's hem up until it was bunched around her hips, then eased her legs apart and stepped between them.

He was hard. She felt the bulge of his arousal through his trousers, through her panty hose. It made her aware of her own arousal, the ache low in her belly, the tension in her thighs as he leaned into her. He glided his hands as far down as her knees and then up again, up over the rumpled fabric of her skirt, over her waist to her blouse, to her breasts.

She gasped as he massaged them with his hands, and gasped again as he finessed the buttons of her blouse. He was still kissing her as he pulled her blouse free of her skirt and reached behind her to unclasp her bra. His fingers grazed her skin and she sighed. Her breasts fell free and she trembled, swaying toward him. He cupped his hands beneath the full, round flesh, kneading it, making her moan.

He bowed, pushing bits of clothing out of his way so he could kiss a path down to her breasts. His mouth was hot, his tongue wicked as he teased and tantalized, skimmed and sucked. "Noah," she breathed, raking her fingers through his hair, then shoving his jacket off his shoulders. She needed to touch him the way he was touching her. She needed to kiss his chest, to make his nipples hard and tight. She needed to know he needed her as much as she needed him right now. Her entire body shimmered with love and longing, and she needed him to be where she was, feeling what she was feeling.

"Hey, Maggie?" A voice penetrated the door.

She let out a ragged breath, her fingers clenched around Noah's collar. He buried his lips in the hollow between her breasts.

"Maggie, you still in there?" Jack.

"Yes," she mumbled.

The doorknob rattled. "Can I come in?"

"No. I'm busy," she said. Noah laughed soundlessly, nuzzling her breasts with his lips.

"I guess you must be. You had quite a spectacular day, huh?"

"Spectacular," she agreed, then bit her lip as Noah ran one hand down to her leg.

"Well, we're ready to shut down for the day, okay? Make sure you lock up when you leave."

"Uh-huh."

Trying unsuccessfully to ignore the imprint of Noah's palm on her thigh, she listened to Jack's receding footsteps and attempted to clear her mind, to come up with a sensible suggestion. They should go get some dinner, she thought vaguely. They should talk a bit more about Noah's unexpected new sentiments, and their implications, about what he and Maggie might each be looking for in a relationship... Then his hand came to life on her leg, rising higher, pulling her panty hose away so he could reach between her legs, and she decided that the only thing they should be doing was this.

He rubbed her. She shuddered. Her fingers shook so much, she nearly tore a button off his shirt. He straightened, taking her mouth with his once more and giving her more room to open his shirt.

His thumb moved against her and she moaned. "Noah," she whispered. "Noah, I—"

"Wait," he whispered back. Even if her brothers were no longer in the vicinity, even if she and Noah were all alone except for Nureyev and Fonteyn and the fish swimming across Maggie's screen saver, the moment was too intimate for anything but whispers. Whispers and touches and kisses and more touches.

Both his hands were on her now, sliding under her hips and tugging down her underwear. Both her hands were on him, struggling mightily with his belt buckle. "Wait," he pleaded, letting go of her to reach into his pocket and pull out a condom.

"You came here for this," she accused quietly, not

sure whether to be angry or relieved that he'd brought protection.

"I came here for you." He dropped the foil packet on her desk, then helped her with his fly.

She kicked off her panty hose. He shoved down his slacks. She slid her hands under his shirt and felt his skin, satin-smooth and hot. Lean muscles flexed and shifted beneath her fingers. His nipples tightened just as she'd wanted them to; his shoulders knotted beneath her fingers. Through his skin she felt the vibration of a quiet groan.

He brought his hand to her again, and this time there was no lingerie in his way. This time his fingers could explore her, brush against her, slide into her until she was writhing, groping for him, closing her hands snugly around him and drawing him toward her. "Now," she breathed, or maybe it was his name she was saying. She didn't know. She couldn't think. She could only arch on the desk, her body reaching for his, dying for him to fill her.

And then he did, slow and hard and possessive. He caught his breath as her body absorbed him. Closing his eyes, he rested deep inside her for an endless moment. Then he inhaled again, and she realized she'd have to breathe, too, if she didn't want to faint.

He lifted her arms around his shoulders, then planted his hands on the desk on either side of her and began to move. She clung to him, circled his hips with her legs and welcomed him again and again, each thrust bringing them closer, bringing her higher. She forgot that they were both still half dressed, that they were in her stuffy, ugly office, that Noah was standing and she was quite possibly wrinkling his invoice, to say nothing of her skirt. It didn't matter. All that mattered was Noah, his body, his powerful love-making.

She closed her eyes and held him tighter. He surged deeper, faster, and she stayed with him, her need growing fiercer, more desperate, her blood searing her veins. Her body tensed, then soared, throbbing in a release so glorious she moaned into his shoulder. Above her, Noah stiffened and then let go, pulsing into her as she pulsed around him.

Another endless minute passed before he moved. She carefully relaxed her embrace. His skin was damp with sweat, his eyes still shut as he labored to breathe. A long time passed before he opened his eyes, gazed at Maggie and grinned.

"I've never done this on a desk before," he confessed.

"You weren't on the desk," she reminded. "I was."

"All right, then. I've never done it with a lady on a desk."

She laughed. Making love with Noah this way had been absurd—but then, the notion that Noah could love her was equally absurd. If one absurdity was possible, why not the other?

He remained inside her as he righted himself. She kept her legs wrapped around his waist, denying him the chance to withdraw. Circling his arms around her, he dropped a kiss onto her forehead. "What happens now?" she asked, almost afraid of his answer. Even after what had just occurred, she couldn't believe he actually loved her.

"We go to my apartment and try doing it on a bed."

She laughed again. "How ordinary."

"No." He softened and slid from her, then brushed her brow with another light kiss. "It won't be ordinary. Nothing about any of this is ordinary." He scooped her underwear from the floor and handed it to her.

She didn't realize how uncomfortable the desk was until she climbed down from it. Her back was sore; her rear end, numb. She'd never felt so wonderful.

But still...now that Noah wasn't distracting her with his physical prowess, she found herself entertaining doubts. How long had Noah dated Sisela? And been engaged to her? And even after all that time, it had turned out not to be true love.

"Why me, Noah?" she asked, bracing herself for whatever he would say.

He paused, his shirt buttoned halfway and his tie dangling around his collar, and scrutinized her in the glaring office light. "Why you?" he asked, then frowned. For an instant she feared that he didn't understand what she was asking and she was going to have to elaborate. But he spared her that ordeal. "You excite me," he said simply. "Every minute I spend with you is an adventure."

His reply wasn't the flattery she'd expected. It wasn't the declaration of passion she might have hoped for. But once again, Noah won her over with his stark honesty.

She had never before thought of herself as exciting—but she liked the idea. And she had to admit that falling in love with Noah might just turn out to be the biggest adventure of her life.

CHAPTER TWELVE

BEDS WERE DEFINITELY better than desks.

Noah lay sprawled across his wide bed, appreciating the firm mattress, the crisp sheets, and most of all, the woman curled up next to him, cozy and pliant and magnificently naked, breathing in the deep, steady rhythm of sleep. The glowing red digits on the clock radio beside him told him it was a little past midnight. He'd dozed for a while, but he hadn't shared a bed with a woman in a long time, and Maggie's presence had awakened him.

Not that he was complaining.

Her hair frothed around her shoulders and his—ripples of gilded brown. Her eyelashes were ridiculously long, delicate dark fringes against her cheeks. Her lips were plump and slightly puckered, as if she were dreaming about a kiss.

There was more of Maggie than he was used to in a woman. More hair, more bosom, more bottom. More words, more spunk, more energy. Making love with her was like diving into a tropical sea—she was warm and wet, full of life and mysterious currents that carried him helplessly, willingly along.

When they'd arrived at his apartment, he'd been determined to slow down, to make love to her comfortably, thoroughly, at a leisurely pace. But once she'd removed the last of her clothing and he'd seen her full, firm breasts, the soft curve of her belly, her strong, solid thighs and that dark tangle of hair between them, he'd practically lost his mind. They'd tumbled onto the bed, and she'd run her hands over his skin, scraping her fingernails lightly down his back, skimming her palms over his legs, gliding her lips over his chest.... Well, how was he supposed to go slow when Maggie was doing such amazing things to him?

It hadn't been comfortable. Sex with her was too intense an experience, too ferociously pleasurable to be comfortable, even if they were doing the deed on appropriate furniture. Maybe sex wasn't supposed to be "comfortable"—although he wasn't sure he'd want to attempt it with her on a desk again.

Her hand stirred against him, tracing the ridge of his lowest rib. She blinked her eyes open and smiled at him—an enigmatic, sublimely feminine smile.

"Did I wake you?" he asked.

She shook her head and her hair swept over his shoulder, turning him on as much as her roving fingers did. "I was dreaming that we were making love," she murmured. "It was such a wonderful dream, I started wishing it would come true."

Oh, God. Another unseen Maggie riptide was threatening to sweep him out to sea. "You're insatiable," he teased, although the accusation applied as much to him as to her. Just the silky coils of her hair and the meandering path of her index finger on his chest were enough to arouse him fully.

"No," she argued, still smiling, still sketching sinuous lines across his skin. "I'm really not."

"Then let's go back to sleep," he said, testing her.

"Let's talk," she countered, directing her hand lower, under the sheet he'd drawn over their bodies. His muscles clenched as her hand skimmed across his abdomen.

"Okay," he said tensely, forcing himself to breathe. "Talk."

"About what?"

"Tell me about—" he scrambled for a subject "—your brothers."

"My brothers?" With her fingers she skirted the edge of his groin, then roamed back up toward his chest. "What about them?"

"How's the one with the marital problems doing?"

"He and his wife are back together. They say they're working things out. Their condition has been upgraded from critical to stable."

"They're not out of the woods yet?"

She shook her head, then touched her lips to his cheek. "It's sweet of you to ask." Her hand paused near his heart, and he covered it with his own so she wouldn't go exploring down below again—at least not until they were ready to shift from talk to action. "If my brothers knew what we were doing in my office this afternoon, they'd kill me."

"I think they'd be more likely to kill me," he countered. He'd chatted for a few minutes with her brother Jack while he'd been waiting for Maggie to finish with the lovelorn fellow who'd been ahead of him in line. Jack had seemed like a nice guy—quite possibly the kind of guy who'd kill anyone who fooled around with his baby sister. Noah considered overprotectiveness an asset in a brother.

"No," she said, pressing another kiss to his chest and causing the muscles below his waist to tighten again. "They'd kill me, because I'm family. You, they'd only castrate."

"What a relief," he joked, his voice fading to a silent groan as Maggie slid her toes over his instep and up his shin.

"Tell me about your family," she urged him. "Does your mother still live in—where was it? Butte City?"

"She's in a condominium in Sacramento," he said. "I bought it for her a few years ago. She went back to school and got certified as a home-health aide."

"Good for her."

"It's better than counting on getting any money from my father."

"Where is he?"

Noah sighed in disgust. "Who the hell knows?" He heard the bitterness edging his voice. It was an emotion he would have preferred to keep as far as possible from this night and this woman. But she'd asked, and he couldn't help himself.

She propped herself up on one arm and peered down at him. His body felt chilled without her cuddling against him, and his soul felt chilled when he saw the concern in her face. His eyes were accustomed to the dark; he could see her expression plainly enough to know it was filled with pity.

"When was the last time you saw your father?" she asked quietly.

"Does it matter?"

"Yes."

"When I was fifteen," he told her. "Half a lifetime

ago." He let out a long, steadying breath, as if he could exhale his anger. "When I bought the condo for my mother, she finally gave up and stopped waiting for him. She left no forwarding address." He took another long, cleansing breath. "I suppose if he really wanted to find her, he could."

"If he wanted to," Maggie agreed. She settled into his arms again, using his shoulder to cushion her head. "I can't begin to guess how you turned out so well. With a father like that, who taught you how to be a man?"

He laughed, but his laughter held an incredulous undertone. He wasn't sure he'd turned out well at all. "When I was ten, my mother signed me up in the Big Brothers program," he told her.

"That was smart of her."

"I was furious. I didn't want a Big Brother." What he'd wanted was his father, and if he couldn't have that, he hadn't wanted anybody else. He'd thought the children who participated in the Big Brothers/Big Sisters program were losers, poor kids from broken homes. Being part of it had seemed to Noah like a badge of dishonor.

But his mother hadn't given him a choice, and he'd been determined not to make her life harder than it already was by kicking up a fuss. "My Big Brother was a professor at the state university in Chico. He was a divorced guy with a lot of time on his hands."

"Did you like him?"

Noah twined his fingers through her hair. It occurred to him that he and Sisela had never had a discussion like this. She'd never questioned him about

his past. No one ever did, so he never talked about
it.

But Maggie was an investigator, probing, prying,
trying to uncover the truth. And although he didn't
exactly want to talk about it, he was touched that she
cared enough to ask.

"He was an okay guy. All I wanted to do was
sports, but he wasn't interested in sports." Her hair
twined around his fingers, cool and soothing. "I
mean, he took me to a few baseball games, but he
wasn't much of a jock. He taught environmental sci-
ence at the college."

"Solar power," Maggie guessed.

Noah nodded. His thumb glided into the crease behind her ear and she snuggled closer to him. "He got
me interested in the subject. He told me my mission
was to save the world." He grinned, remembering.

"Well, you're certainly doing him proud."

He snorted. "I wanted to save the world, but even
more than that, I wanted to earn a good living. I was
poor and I hated it. I always thought my mission in
life was not to be poor anymore." He ran his thumb
behind her ear again just because he liked the way it
made her soften against him. "I forgot about saving
the world for a long time. If there hadn't been a flood
in a village in India, I might never have gotten around
to saving anything."

"Sooner or later, you would have found something
to save," Maggie told him. "Once that urge is in you,
it doesn't just disappear."

"It can atrophy," he argued. "Mine was pretty far
gone. I'd gotten my education, landed a high-powered
job, found a woman to marry. I wanted the safety of

all that. I wanted to know what I would be doing every day for the rest of my life. And I wanted to get paid a lot of money.''

"But then you left."

"One final fling before settling down for good."

"Is that what you thought marriage to Sisela would be? 'Settling down'?"

He twisted his head to look at her. "Why shouldn't it be that?"

"I don't know." She shrugged, her entire body shifting against him. "'Settling down' sounds so dreary. I want to get married someday and have children. But I'd hate to think I had to 'settle down.'"

He considered the woman in his arms and smiled. He couldn't imagine Maggie settling down, either. She was too dynamic. She had too many ideas, too many plans. Detectives weren't designed for settling down, he supposed—even if they specialized in helping separated lovers reunite and "settle down."

"If marriage isn't settling down, what do you think it is?" he asked, wondering why, considering his experience with the subject, the very mention of marriage didn't make him want to run screaming into the night. Even the most dangerous subjects were fascinating when Maggie was talking about them.

"Marriage," she answered, "is happily ever after."

"Oh." Now there was an odd concept.

She said nothing for a minute. Her hand started to move on him again, less erotic than consoling. Measuring each word, she said, "You probably don't believe in 'happily ever after.'"

This time he was the one to rise off the bed. She

sank onto her back beside him and he gazed down at her. Her eyes were wide, mesmerizing in their intensity. Her knowing smile was gone.

She was right. He didn't believe in "happily ever after." He had no idea what true love was, let alone whether it existed in the real world. He used to think stability and contentment would be enough to satisfy him. But then he'd wanted one last adventure. And that adventure had made him want more.

Adventure didn't seem like a happily-ever-after pursuit. If his mother's marriage had been something of an adventure—full of risk and doubt—it had also been the very antithesis of "happily ever after."

He was convinced that security was more attainable than happiness. That was why he'd set his sights on security. Noah had always been practical—until the adventure bug bit him. "No," he belatedly answered her. "I don't think I believe in 'happily ever after.'"

She reached up, bringing her hand around to the nape of his neck and drawing him down to her. He kissed her and realized that one thing he did believe in was kissing Maggie Tyrell. He believed that she was a good woman and that making love with her was a good thing; that when he lost himself in her, he wasn't really lost.

He kissed her again. He could make a religion of this, he thought—the Maggie religion. He could believe in her strength and her intelligence, in her matter-of-fact confidence. He could believe that when she held him, when her arms closed tight around him and her body moved beneath his, there was no truth left but to sink himself into her—so deep, so completely that he had only one faith and that was her....

He wouldn't dare believe in everlasting happiness, but he could believe in happiness today, maybe even happiness tomorrow. He could believe that happiness was possible with Maggie Tyrell, a woman brave enough to ask him anything.

She shuddered, her fingertips biting into his shoulders, her body convulsing around him as a dark cry tore from her, and he gave himself over, let go; let himself believe in this, in her.

"HEY, MAGGIE, YOU GOT a minute?"

Maggie glanced up from her monitor, where she'd been running an Internet search on behalf of Stuart Roth, a bond trader who had broken up with his high-school sweetheart twenty years ago and, ten years later, had realized what a bonehead move that had been. It had taken another ten years for Maggie's face to appear on his TV screen, and now Stuart was gladly shelling out five hundred dollars a day for her to locate Candace Reinback, who two decades ago had been the prettiest girl in Mill Valley.

But Maggie hadn't found Candace's name in any of her data searches so far. Her gaze blurry from staring at her monitor, she raised her eyes to find her brother Sandy looming in her doorway, tall and handsome in his gangly way, his shirt rumpled and the lace of one of his canvas high-tops untied.

"Sure, I have a minute." Actually, she didn't, but she was overflowing with benevolence. Spending a night in the arms of a man like Noah Davis could do that to a woman.

Sandy shambled into the office, stubbed his toe on

her desk, cursed and sank into the visitor's chair. "This room is too small," he announced.

"Tell me something I don't know. You guys want to give me a bigger room? I could take that room next to Neil's office where we keep all the stationery supplies and the coffeemaker. Better yet, I could take Neil's office and *he* could move into the coffee room. Of course Jack would probably charge me an arm and a leg in rent. He's a lousy landlord, isn't he?"

Sandy sent her a quick smile, then shrugged. "You could talk to him about it," he said, which made Maggie suspect that he hadn't really heard much of what she'd said.

"What's up?" she asked solicitously.

"Well, it's just that..." He shifted in the chair, noticed his shoelace was undone and banged his elbow against the desk when he bent over to tie it. Straightening, he said, "I'm blowing it with Karen."

Maggie hid her dismay. "What makes you say that?"

"Remember last Sunday, when you said you were going to dump ice water in my lap?" He squirmed some more in the chair, causing the hinges to squeak. "Well...it's just that... Well, last night Karen said she had a headache."

Maggie struggled to translate his statement into plain English. Karen was refusing her husband sex? "Maybe she really did have a headache," Maggie suggested.

"She's never had a headache before," he complained.

"Come on, Sandy! *Everybody* gets headaches

sometimes. She's in a high-stress job. Maybe she was tired, and—''

"Maggie, if we don't have sex, our marriage might not survive. I'm not what she wants. She wants some guy with enough gigabytes of memory to bring her flowers on her birthday and diamonds on her anniversary. I'm not that guy. But I thought, well, we had the other thing going for us. But after last night... And besides, remember what she said on Sunday? You said it, too. 'You can't build a relationship on just sex.'"

Maggie sighed in sympathy, then realized she was sighing as much for herself as for Sandy. Last night with Noah had been heavenly, but was it enough to build a relationship on? Noah didn't believe in happy endings. He had no experience with true love. He'd never had the opportunity to witness a strong, solid marriage—as if marriage to Maggie was something he would even consider.

"So what are you saying, Sandy? You think Karen faked a headache as an opening salvo in divorce proceedings?"

Sandy flinched, then crumpled. "I love her so much, Maggie! But I can't help thinking that if she doesn't love me, the kindest thing I could do would be to let her go."

"Sandy." Maggie resisted the urge to leap over her desk and throttle her brother. "If you love her, fight for her. Give the fight everything you've got—including the flowers and the diamonds, damn it! If you give up, you lose her. If you don't give up, maybe you don't lose her." She waved toward her computer. "Do you know what I've got here? I've got the files of a dozen clients who let someone go and are now regretting it with all their hearts. Ask me if they're happy they gave up. Ask me if they wish they'd stuck around and fought for their loved ones, instead. For God's sake, Sandy, I don't want you coming in here a year from now and offering me five hundred dollars a day to track Karen down so you can try to win her back.''

Sandy blinked. Maybe she wouldn't have to throttle him. ''You'd really charge me five hundred a day? No favors for brothers?''

''I've done you more favors than you deserve,'' she reminded him. ''And if you don't think Karen would be worth five hundred a day, then maybe you're right. Maybe this marriage isn't worth saving.''

''She's worth the sun, the moon and the stars,'' Sandy said passionately.

''Flowers and diamonds might do the trick. Actually, I don't even think she wants diamonds. What she wants is for you to remember what matters to her.''

''Sex used to matter to her.''

''Then woo her. Seduce her. Make her know how much you love her.'' Maggie's phone rang. ''If that doesn't work,'' she added, reaching for the phone, ''give her two aspirin and a back rub.'' She lifted the receiver to her ear and looked at the door, signaling Sandy that she wanted him to leave. ''Finders, Keepers, can I help you?'' she recited into the phone.

''Hi, Maggie.''

Hearing Noah's voice made her grin. She was glad she didn't have a mirror in front of her, because she had no doubt it was a soppy, sappy grin. Even Sandy, oblivious and dense, gave her a funny look before he trudged out of her office. "Hi, Noah," she murmured, staring at Nureyev and Fonteyn on the opposite wall. Maybe Maggie and Noah weren't ballet stars, but her memory, far more efficient than her brother Sandy's, vividly remembered every embrace from last night— the exquisite ones, the graceful ones, the pawing, panting, greedy, sweaty ones. Her cheeks grew hot as she relived each embrace in her mind.

"Are you free tonight?" Noah asked, forcing her attention back to the present.

"Tonight?" Squaring her shoulders, she retorted, "What kind of woman do you think I am? You think you can call me at the last minute and I'll drop everything and come running? Actually, I was planning to wash my hair tonight."

He laughed. She did, too. "It's not the last minute," he protested. "It's at least four hours before the last minute."

"Well, then, I might just be free. Assuming what you've got in mind is more interesting than a shampoo."

"I just got a call from Cosmo Delaney," Noah said.

Maggie fell silent. Her goofy, infatuated smile faded, and her cheeks cooled. When she thought of possible reasons why Delaney would have contacted Noah, none of them pleased her.

Delaney could be upset about Noah's having misrepresented his reason for being in Bellewood, insinuating his way into Delaney's party under false pretenses. Or he could be contemplating a lawsuit claiming that Noah had been stalking Sisela, or that Noah had tried to break up the Delaney marriage.

As Noah's paid henchwoman, Maggie could be facing a lawsuit, too.

But maybe the possibility of legal troubles weren't what alarmed her most. Maybe it was something as stupid as insecurity. If Delaney had called Noah, it could have been to say, "She was yours before she was mine, and you're welcome to her."

If Noah had to choose between Maggie and Sisela, surely he'd choose Sisela.

Maggie's thoughts were racing far ahead of her. "What did Delaney want?" she asked cautiously, swallowing the catch in her voice.

"He and Sisela are in San Francisco. He wanted to get together for dinner. I'd like to bring you with me."

"Why?"

"Why?" He sounded bemused. "If he's bringing Sisela, I want to bring you."

"A double date?" Maggie rolled her eyes. "You know, you don't have to pretend we're married anymore. That ruse served its purpose, but there's no reason to keep up the act."

"I wasn't thinking of that," he explained. "I was thinking that I'd like to have you with me."

"Pretending to be your wife?"

"Not pretending anything. Just being the woman I want sitting next to me at dinner." He hesitated. "Is there a problem, Maggie? Would you really rather wash your hair?"

Lord, no. She'd rather be sitting next to Noah at dinner—or anywhere else. "Okay," she said. She could stand playing Noah's wife for another evening. She only had to make sure she didn't become too immersed in the role.

"They're staying at the St. Francis. Cosmo suggested that we meet for dinner there, around seven. Would that be all right?"

"Sure."

"I'll pick you up at six forty-five."

"Okay." She sighed and wiped a stray tear from her cheek. "I guess I'll have to get all dolled up again, huh?"

"I've seen you all dolled up," Noah said in a husky tone, "and it's a magnificent sight."

Now that he was flattering her, she didn't have to take him too seriously. Her mind clarified itself and she considered the entire situation. "Did Delaney tell you what he was doing in town?"

"As a matter of fact, no. He said he wanted to discuss it over dinner."

She relapsed into panic. What if Delaney planned a violent confrontation over dinner? What if, in the middle of one of the hotel's luxurious dining rooms, Delaney suddenly hurled himself at Noah, grabbing him by his collar and screaming, "You tried to break up my marriage! Prepare to die!"

"Did you mention to him that you were going to bring me?" she asked anxiously.

"He said Sisela would be there. I assume that means you'd be welcome, too. Back in New York, Cosmo seemed to like you."

"That was when he thought I was someone else."

Noah chuckled. "Who cares what he thinks, any-

way? I want you there because *I* want you there. Isn't
that a good enough reason?''

Though it didn't allay her fears about Delaney's
purpose in coming to San Francisco, it was a good
enough reason to spend the evening with Noah.

"Six forty-five," she said. "I'll be ready, all dolled
up."

"I'll see you then," he promised. "And after dinner, if you'd like, I'll take you back to my place and
wash your hair for you."

Closing her eyes, Maggie pictured him and her in
his shower, naked, with hot water streaming down
over their bodies and his fingers twining through her
hair.... She decided she could survive even an intimate dinner party with Cosmo and Sisela Delaney if
her reward was a personal shampoo from Noah.

CHAPTER THIRTEEN

GOD, BUT SHE WAS BEAUTIFUL.

Noah tried not to stare, but her beauty stunned him. It wasn't as if he'd never seen her before, yet tonight, wearing a simple dress of forest green that altered the color of her eyes somehow, and with her hair swept back and a thin gold chain around her throat...

Next to her, Sisela looked wan and drawn, her fashionably fat-free body looking as if it had been constructed out of Tinkertoys. Sisela's cheeks were pink, but the pink had been applied with precision—two perfectly matched cosmetic ovals that emphasized her chiseled cheekbones. Maggie's cheeks were naturally rosy, as if she'd been strolling through an orchard on a brisk autumn day.

Seated on Noah's left at the spacious circular table, Cosmo Delaney peered up from his menu and smiled impishly. "They've got a dessert here called Too Much Chocolate," he announced. "Everybody save room. We've got to try that."

Sisela smiled delicately. Maggie eyed Noah; her smile was far more eloquent than Sisela's, and it was meant for only him. It said she thought Cosmo was odd but harmless and even charming in his own way. It said she would rather be dragged down the zigzags of Lombard Street by her heels than forced to order a dessert called Too Much Chocolate. It said there was someplace she'd rather be than in this opulent hotel restaurant, and she'd want Noah with her in that place, and she'd want them both to be wearing a whole lot less than they were wearing right now.

Or maybe he was just imposing his own fantasies on her.

"This is great," Cosmo murmured enthusiastically. "I love San Francisco. I don't know why Sisela agreed to leave this city, just for me. I guess you must love me, hmm?" he asked his wife.

"I guess," she replied, her smile thinning.

"If I could move my entire business to the Left Coast, I'd consider it, just for the chance to live in San Francisco. Sometimes I think it's not such a crazy idea. Cosmic Candy has got a lot going on in California, a huge, powerful market we're building. The mere definition of the word 'cosmic' is terribly Californian."

"Yes, we're all very cosmic out here," Maggie joked. Noah wondered if Cosmo and Sisela could hear her wry undertone. She turned to Sisela. "Do you miss San Francisco?"

"There are some things I miss about it," she said, gazing at Noah.

He held his face impassive and gave Maggie's knee a squeeze under the table. If Sisela was going to give him looks like that while her husband sat next to her, this was going to turn into a very unpleasant dinner.

Even if his ex-fiancée didn't keep sending him vaguely imploring looks, Noah wasn't sure what kind of dinner it was going to be. He was curious to know why Cosmo had wanted to hook up with them.

Cosmo had said he'd explain over dinner, which implied that he was here on an actual mission, but Noah couldn't begin to guess what it might be. And the longer he sat next to Maggie, aware of the way her hair coiled over her shoulders, the fullness of her lower lip and the tantalizing swells of her breasts inside the slim-fitting bodice of her dress, the less he found himself caring what Cosmo might want with him.

A waiter appeared at their table, noiseless and obsequious. Cosmo selected a bottle of wine from the list, and they ordered their food. The waiter scurried away, leaving the four of them to regard each other over the linen-draped table.

Evidently determined to be a good host, Cosmo broke the brief silence. "We've accumulated a few more usable man-in-the-street interviews for our Cosmic Mocha Drink promotion," he said. "I think it's going to be a strong product. What do you think, Noah?"

Surely Cosmo hadn't invited him to dinner to discuss gourmet cocoa. "Maggie and I sure liked the stuff, didn't we?" He glanced at her.

The smile she gave him this time was unreadable—the sort of smile that implied that her thoughts were miles away from the subject of cocoa. "It was delicious," she agreed.

"And with all the upscale coffee bars sprouting up everywhere," Cosmo continued, "and the flavored brews selling so strongly, I think coffee is the gourmet beverage of the future. What do you think, Noah?"

Noah pretended to consider his answer, although

he was actually using the time to consider his host. Why was Cosmo asking him his opinion? Why did he think Noah could possibly have anything useful to say on the subject, other than what he and Maggie had said on video a week ago?

"I'm no expert," he conceded, choosing his words carefully, "but it seems to me you've got an advantage in that your product is something consumers could enjoy in the comfort of their own homes. They can pick it up at the supermarket, bring it home and drink it in their favorite easy chair. With a box of Cosmic chocolates within reach."

"Absolutely!" Cosmo pounded the table with his fist for emphasis. Fortunately, the tablecloth muffled the sound and cushioned the heavy silverware.

The waiter approached with their wine, and Cosmo subsided in his seat. He sampled the wine, nodded his approval and sat with bristling impatience while the waiter filled the other goblets. As soon as the waiter had departed, Cosmo leaned forward, all revved up, his wispy blond hair glinting beneath the overhead lamp. "A gourmet indulgence savored in the comfort of one's own home. What do you think, Sisela? Doesn't that sound right to you?"

"Absolutely," she echoed him, although with less exuberance.

"The entire concept has to be that you don't have to get dressed, get into your car and drive someplace to drink your Cosmic Mocha. You don't have to shave, you don't have to put on lipstick and make yourself presentable. It's right there in your own kitchen, and you can drink it in your pajamas—or in your birthday suit if you like. You can drink it in the tub, or in bed, or in your recliner. That's it!''

That's what? Noah wondered, shooting a perplexed glance at Maggie. She appeared equally mystified, her smile quizzical.

The waiter returned to their table with salads—flat crystal plates heaped high with what looked like weeds to Noah. He gamely stabbed a spiky specimen with his fork.

Cosmo grazed contentedly on his salad for a while, reminding Noah of a steer. Sisela used the edge of her fork to scrape the dressing off a clover-like plant before nibbling it daintily. Maggie ate her salad without a peep.

Was she enjoying this dinner? Was *he?* Noah's mind wandered, as he'd imagined hers wandering, to other places he'd rather be—for instance, his bed, with her next to him. Or better yet, underneath him or on top of him. Cosmo Delaney wasn't bad company, but he was a bit peculiar. And Sisela... Sisela sat across from Noah, pale and waiflike, an anemic reminder of his formerly anemic dreams and goals. He could hardly believe that at one time he'd wanted nothing more than the safety of marriage with her. He'd actually thought he could make a life with a woman who scraped vinaigrette off her salad greens!

''Well, all right, then,'' Cosmo said, vigorous enough for both Delaneys. He nudged away his empty salad plate, patted his mouth with his napkin and beamed a megawatt grin at Noah. ''Here's the deal. I didn't just happen to be in San Francisco, Noah. I came here specifically to see you.''

Noah returned his smile, but anxiety nipped at him.

Here was the deal, all right: Cosmo was going to call him to account for having tracked down Sisela, for having misrepresented himself in order to discover the whereabouts of his former lover, now Cosmo's wife.

For once Noah didn't dare glance at Maggie. He kept his attention riveted on Cosmo. If bullets were going to fly, Noah didn't want any of them hitting Maggie. He had to keep her out of this, even if it meant lying to Cosmo about her involvement. Noah had deceived the guy once; he'd have no qualms about deceiving him again, especially if his reason was to protect Maggie.

"I know more about you than you realize," Cosmo said, lifting his wineglass and cradling the bowl with his long, slender fingers. "I've been investigating you."

Noah swallowed a curse. He supposed there was some ironic justice in it, a perversion of the Golden Rule. Cosmo was doing to Noah what Noah had done to him.

If Cosmo had investigated Noah, he must know that Noah had once been engaged to marry Sisela. So why was she present? How could she sit placidly at this dinner table in these posh surroundings, observing her husband as he skewered the man Sisela herself had betrayed? She wasn't exactly an innocent bystander in the sorry scenario. She was the chief instigator. Where was her shame?

"Scholarship student, UC Berkeley followed by an MBA at Stanford. You grew up dirt-poor, but you've hauled yourself up into the stratosphere."

Swell. Before Cosmo accused Noah of being a home-wrecker and a con artist, he was going to recite

Noah's life history. "I didn't haul myself up," Noah argued, trying not to sound too defensive. "I worked hard and got some lucky breaks."

"You were brilliant and talented. You've gone far."

Now, if he got one more lucky break, he might only be arrested and sent to jail on a stalking charge. If his luck had run out, Cosmo was probably going to grab the sterling-silver knife from his place setting and plunge it between Noah's ribs. Noah was going to bleed to death in a dining room at the St. Francis Hotel.

"I think you could be a genuine asset to the Cosmic Candy Company."

"Look, I'm sorry that I— *What?*"

"I've come to San Francisco to make you a job offer," Cosmo announced, shooting a cocky smile at Sisela as if to say, *Didn't I tell you this was a terrific idea?*

If Sisela thought it was a terrific idea, she didn't verbalize her opinion. She flickered a faint smile at her husband, then directed her gaze to Noah. Her smile vanished, to be replaced by an expression of beseechment.

What was she asking of him? What was she trying to say?

He didn't care. He was too intrigued by Cosmo's unexpected offer. "What kind of job?"

"Marketing."

"Marketing what?"

"Director? Vice president? Would that work for you? We can work out the title later."

"Noah," Maggie murmured.

He grinned and patted her hand to silence her. If she had misgivings, he'd give her a fair hearing—later. Right now he just wanted to enjoy the completely absurd notion that he could manage Cosmic Candy's marketing program. "You're thinking about a regional director or something?"

"I'm thinking about a national 'director or something.' I don't see why not. But given your knowledge of California, we could certainly focus on the West Coast and expand the market here. We need a bigger plan nationally, though. I think you're the fellow who could come up with one."

"Uh—Mr. Delaney." Maggie tugged her hand out from under Noah's. He could tell from one glimpse of her face that she was annoyed by his attempt to stifle her. "Cosmo," she corrected herself as the rangy blond executive turned to her. "If you've done research on Noah, you would know that he specializes in solar-power projects."

Cosmo nodded his reassurance. "Yes, I do. It seems fateful to me that he should move from a company called Solar Systems to one called Cosmic. I mean, there's karma at work, here."

"You're going to give him a job because of karma?" Maggie scowled.

Noah tried to hush her with a nudge under the table. She didn't have to be so skeptical, at least not right away. But she must have sensed his foot's approach, because she shifted her legs in her chair so he couldn't reach her.

Cosmo smiled deferentially. "I trust my instincts, Maggie. I always have, and they've served me well. I don't necessarily choose my staff based on the usual

criteria. I go by instinct. I get an intuition that someone has energy and ideas, someone can shed light on
a situation, someone can bring a new perspective to
the table. I make a lot of my decisions that way. It's
how I wound up marrying Sisela. We didn't need a
long courtship. I saw her, I knew she was the one and
only woman for me and we got married. It's the way
I do things.''

Noah practically heard the metallic crunch of Maggie's thoughts colliding inside her skull. He could
guess what she was thinking, because he was thinking
the same thing: that if Cosmo had married a devious,
two-timing lady like Sisela based on his instincts, his
instincts weren't worth trusting. If he could be so
wrong about Sisela, he could be wrong about Noah.

Except that Noah actually wanted to give serious
thought to Cosmo's job offer. Not because he had any
experience in the chocolate business—Maggie was
right about that—but because the job would open him
to a new adventure.

His course would be safer if he remained at his
current job. He was successful at Solar Systems, earning good money, admired and respected in the firm.
Why rock the boat?

But then, why *not* rock it? He didn't have to worry
about making his mother's life more difficult—not
anymore. He didn't have to bet his future on one rigid
plan and stick with the hand he'd drawn until the deal
was done. Surely he could spread his bets, take his
chances and not worry if one of his wagers went
south. When you counted too much on only one out-
come, you didn't necessarily wind up any safer. His
mother was proof of that.

Cosmo's voice dragged him from his ruminations. "The truth is, Sisela thinks it's a marvelous idea, too. I don't always bounce all my intuitions off her, but since she'd met you at the party—and this was really an off-the-wall idea—she and I discussed it at length. She's with me a hundred percent on this. Aren't you, sweetheart?"

Sisela gave Noah a smile. He recognized that smile. It was her one-corner-higher-than-the-other smile, a smile that meant, *You know what's going on here, Noah. You know what I'm thinking.*

Noah didn't know what she was thinking, but he felt a chill run down his back when she said, "One hundred percent."

"You'd love having Noah working for us, too," Cosmo told Maggie, exerting himself to sell her on the idea. "For example, you'd get all the chocolate you could ever want. Employees get a free supply. It's one of the benefits, along with health insurance and an excellent pension plan. Some of my people think the free chocolate is the *best* benefit. Isn't that true, Sisela? Half of them work for me for the chocolate. You married me for my chocolate, didn't you?" He winked at his wife.

Noah knew why Sisela had married Cosmo, and it wasn't for his chocolate. Noah suspected that Cosmo was smart enough to know why Sisela had married him, too. However strange Cosmo seemed, he wasn't an idiot. He and Noah had talked at length that morning in New York. Cosmo had told him about how he'd parlayed his love of chocolate and flair for business into a hugely successful company—a privately held one of which he was the sole proprietor.

"I don't come cheap," Noah warned him.

Cosmo laughed. "I know. I had you investigated, remember? Look, I don't think this lovely dinner is the appropriate place for us to start negotiating terms. I've planted a seed, and I want you to water it and see if it takes root. Now, I've promised Sisela that the rest of this trip belongs to her. We're going to do the tourist routine—Golden Gate Bridge, the Alcatraz tour, Coit Tower and Fisherman's Wharf. She wants to visit her old haunts—the school where she used to teach, Seal Rock and some romantic little coffee house that used to be one of her favorite places when she lived here. What was it called, dear? Hamlet's? Othello's?"

"Romeo's." Sisela locked gazes with Noah for a fraction of a second and then averted her eyes.

Noah stared at her, willing her to lift her eyes to him again. She became absorbed in an intense study of the tablecloth.

He was stung. He shouldn't have been; he and Sisela were over, done, kaput. She had chosen a life of wedded bliss with Cosmo, abandoning Noah to something much better—not just a chance to meet Maggie, but an entirely different direction for his own future. If he felt anything for Sisela, it should be gratitude for setting him loose when he himself might not have realized the need to break free.

But still, it bothered him that she was going to share Romeo's with Cosmo. Noah himself had shared Romeo's with Maggie—but that had been different. She'd been his private investigator then, not his friend, and certainly not his lover. She'd met him there only to discuss business. If he'd found himself fascinated by her then, it had been an intellectual fascination. He'd been captured by her transformation from a frazzled woman in overalls using a stapler as a hammer, to a well-groomed professional who really seemed to know what she was doing.

Having an espresso with her at Romeo's hadn't meant anything. He was sure it hadn't.

"Romeo's. That's it," Cosmo said. "I knew it was some Shakespearean hero. Sisela says the cappuccino is outstanding there."

"The espresso's better," Noah said tightly.

"Is it? You know the place, then. Perhaps I should try the espresso. What do you think, Maggie? Which is better, the espresso or the cappuccino?"

Maggie's gaze journeyed from Noah to Sisela and back again. She arched her eyebrows in wry contemplation, then said, "Actually, I don't think either of those drinks is as good as Cosmic's Mocha Drink."

"Ah! Brava!" Cosmo clapped his hands together in delight. "Maybe I ought to offer *you* the marketing position, Maggie."

"No, thanks. I'm happy where I am," she said, then leaned back so the waiter could place her entrée in front of her.

"Of course, as Noah's wife, you're entitled to some input as to whether or not he accepts a job with me."

She watched the waiter delivering the other entrées, then smiled coolly at Cosmo. "I think this should be Noah's decision," she said. She shot a brief glimmer of a smile at Noah, then addressed Cosmo. "Noah has to decide what he wants. It's completely up to him."

Yes, it was completely up to him, Noah thought uneasily. Maggie didn't want to be a part of his decision—because she wasn't exactly a part of his life. Not quite. Not yet. That was another decision he had to make.

Last night that decision had seemed perfectly clear. Last night, with her in his arms, he'd wanted nothing more than her. He'd wanted to find peace with her, security, passion, risk, excitement, serenity. He'd wanted more than he'd ever had, more than he'd ever believed possible. With Maggie, he'd believed it was all attainable.

But now...now he wanted to learn more about this strange new career opportunity Cosmo had extended. He wanted to lash out at Sisela for refusing to meet his gaze. He wanted to know that, whichever way he turned, Maggie would be at his side. He wanted to give her something beyond his ability to give: the promise that he could live happily ever after with her.

At the very least he wanted her to say, "Yes, Noah, I think you should accept Cosmo's offer," or, "No, Noah, I think you should stay at Solar Systems." He wanted her to be that much a part of his life.

He hadn't asked her to be, though. She wasn't his wife. Whatever he ultimately chose to do, he was going to have to do it on his own.

"YOU THINK IT'S CRAZY," Noah said, escorting Maggie up the front walk to her apartment building, a cozy five-story unit in the Sunset neighborhood. "You think I should turn Cosmo down, don't you?"

The night was warm, but Maggie felt cold. She wanted to hug herself—or maybe Noah—for warmth.

But she couldn't. Even if she wrapped herself in him, she wouldn't feel warm. The iciness was inside her.

She'd been fine until Cosmo had mentioned Romeo's, and Noah and Sisela had shared a look across the table. It was at that moment that Maggie had realized how much unresolved history still existed between the two of them. The spark was still there. Maybe it was a spark of anger, maybe a spark of blind rage. But it hadn't yet burned itself out.

She supposed she shouldn't have been surprised. No matter what had happened between her and Noah last night, no matter how glorious the lovemaking had been, how intimate the conversation, how natural it had felt to sleep all night long in his arms, he wasn't over Sisela yet. No matter how loudly he'd insisted that he was, he wasn't.

People didn't hire Finders, Keepers to find their ex-lovers unless they still cared about those ex-lovers. Now that Maggie had active cases filling her days and more cases crowding her calendar, she could draw certain generalizations about the sort of client who signed a contract with her agency. That client was someone for whom the spark still glowed—someone eager to fan that spark back into a flame.

Intellectually, she could accept that. She could acknowledge the memories that linked Sisela and Noah. One mention of Romeo's, one hint of their romantic past, and it was only natural that all the old feelings stirred to life. It was only logical, and Maggie prided herself on her logic.

But emotionally... Emotionally, she was shriveling up inside.

"I'll admit, Cosmo really took me by surprise,"

Noah continued, oblivious to her mood. "But it seems to be the way he operates. Totally by instinct."

"A pretty stupid way to run a major business if you ask me," she muttered.

"But it works for him. Look what he's done with Cosmic Candy in all of, what? Ten years?"

"Ten years plus a little infusion of cash from Daddy."

"All right, so maybe he didn't do it single-handedly. But his instincts are good. I'd like to hear his entire offer, just out of curiosity." Noah arched an arm around Maggie's shoulders. "I thought it was nice that he wanted to include you in the decision."

"He thinks I'm your wife," Maggie retorted. "He had to include me." He'd included his wife, too. And she was one-hundred-percent behind the idea. Maggie's shoulders stiffened at her memory of Sisela's major contribution to the discussion. She dug in her purse for her key and turned to face Noah beneath the overhang above her front door. "If Delaney really wanted my input, I would have told him I thought it was the most harebrained idea I'd ever heard. It makes no sense at all. It's stupid."

"Why is it stupid?" Noah peered down at her as if he truly cared about her opinion.

"Besides the fact that you know nothing about the candy business?"

"I know marketing. I know how to promote a product."

"Architectural solar panels are a little different from Cosmic Star Crunch."

"The principles are the same," he insisted. He cupped his hand to her cheek, brushing back a curly lock of hair. His palm was so warm, it threatened to thaw the ice inside her. One touch from him could do that to her.

"You're well situated at Solar Systems. They love you there, don't they?"

"That gives me a strong starting point for negotiations with Cosmo."

"Plus..." She swallowed, then forced out the words. "There's a bit of personal history lurking in all this."

"What?" He brushed his fingertips into her hair. "You mean Sisela?"

"Yes. I mean Sisela."

"That's history," he declared. "Your word, Maggie. 'History.'"

"Oh, really? Do you think she really thinks it's terrific that you might work for her husband? Do you think she really gives a damn who works for him? If it was anyone other than you, do you think she'd give a rat's ass who he hired?"

Noah didn't automatically reject her assertion, which meant he recognized a glimmer of truth in it. His eyes looked shadowed in the evening light, dark with thought. "Whether or not she gives a rat's ass about me is irrelevant," he finally said. "I'd be working with her husband. She'd have nothing to do with me."

"Don't be naive, Noah. She's got her own reasons for wanting you to work for Cosmic Candy."

"Maybe her reason is that she knows I'm a damned good person to have in a company. Maybe she knows I'm smart and capable." But he didn't sound entirely convinced, himself.

It wasn't Maggie's job to convince him. Her job, as far as he was concerned, had been to bring him and Sisela back together—and she'd done a superlative job of it.

Her job as far as *she* was concerned was to protect herself. She wasn't Noah's wife. She wasn't the love of his life.

He was going to do whatever he was going to do. And she was going to avoid getting hurt—if it wasn't already too late.

CHAPTER FOURTEEN

NOAH UNDERSTOOD THAT he'd lost Maggie again somewhere along the way. He just wasn't sure how, or why, or whether he was going to have to hire an outfit like Finders, Keepers to get her back.

He lay awake late into the night wondering how he'd gotten from those golden opening minutes of the dinner party, when he'd looked at her and felt his blood heat with lust and pride and an array of other, unfamiliar emotions, to this postmidnight moment alone in his bed, separated from her by several city miles and a ton of bewilderment. Was she staring at the ceiling above her bed the way he was staring at the ceiling above his? Was she as lonely as he was? Was she wishing she'd said yes when he'd asked if he could accompany her upstairs to her apartment?

The problem was, he didn't exactly blame her for saying no. The last time she'd said no to him, she'd stated her views about sex quite clearly. It wasn't an act she engaged in casually.

Well, he didn't engage in sex casually, either. He thought it was one of the most magnificent experiences life had to offer, and he shared it only with women who mattered to him.

For Maggie, though, mattering to him wasn't enough. Noah knew it. He'd known it last night when she'd asked so many questions and forgiven him his answers. He'd known it days ago, on the plane home from New York. He'd known it the first time she kissed him. He'd probably known it the first time he'd seen her.

Maggie wouldn't have sex with a man she didn't love.

Which meant she loved Noah.

He wasn't sure what he felt for her, though. He wasn't sure he was able to love anyone. All he'd seen of love as a child was that it had tethered his mother to his careless, irresponsible father and brought her misery.

Noah hadn't loved Sisela—but he hadn't had to love her to believe he could make a successful marriage with her. If he hadn't loved Sisela, whom he'd asked to be his wife, he couldn't imagine how he could love Maggie, whom he'd only just met.

So he didn't blame her for saying no to him tonight, for backing off and putting some distance between them. She didn't trust their relationship. She didn't have faith that he could love her the way she needed and deserved to be loved.

If only he didn't want her so much. If only thinking about her going about her life without him didn't upset him. If only he could detach himself from her without suffering from a sharp, soul-deep ache and a mind-paralyzing panic.

It was like trying to breathe in a vacuum. He was all alone; there wasn't another molecule in his tight, dark universe. Without Maggie in it, he would suffocate.

The hell with it. He couldn't have Maggie, because

to have her on her terms was impossible for him, and to have her on his would be unfair to her. So he was just going to have to find another source of oxygen.

A new job might make breathing easier. Unlike love, job opportunities were something he could comprehend, something into which he could enthusiastically throw himself.

He was bemused by Cosmo Delaney's offer of employment—but then, Cosmo obviously had his own weird way of running his business. Intuitions, hunches, first impressions: whatever basis he used to make his decisions, they had led him to Noah. And Noah, although more pragmatic and logical than Cosmo, knew without a doubt that he could handle any marketing position Cosmo offered him. He could make money as easily for Cosmic Candy as he could for Solar Systems.

He had no idea whether he'd like working for Cosmo Delaney, let alone whether he'd have to move out of San Francisco, adopt a different corporate identity and tolerate Cosmo's apparent eccentricities with a smile. Still, why not hear the man out? Why not at least explore the idea?

Of course, it would be much better if he could share it with Maggie.

He glanced at his alarm clock. All of three minutes had passed since he'd decided he was going to stop thinking about her, and there she was again. Maggie. With her intelligence, her daring, she had the ability to make any experience more exciting.

Locating Sisela wouldn't have been fun if Maggie hadn't been a part of it. The adventure hadn't been flying to New York, tracking down Cosmo and crashing his party. The adventure had been doing it all with Maggie.

Damn. Maggie was all he wanted to think about. Maggie—her sweet, firm body, her infectious smile, her earnest commitment to the people she cared about, the heat of her taking him in, surrounding him, cresting with him. He wanted Maggie in his bed right now. He wanted to hear her gasp with pleasure, wanted to feel her fingers pinch his shoulders as she clung to him. He wanted her mouth fused to his and her wild mane of hair spilling into his face.

He just didn't want to have to think about love. He didn't trust it. He didn't believe in it. Did that make him evil?

Sisela had never demanded that he love her. Sisela had probably never expected love; she'd probably never needed it. She'd been like him in that way. Too bad she'd skipped town behind his back, though.

Too bad? What was he thinking? He didn't want to go back to the way he used to be before Maggie, before Finders, Keepers, before he'd spent a year rebuilding a flooded village. He didn't want to go back to having an espresso every evening at Romeo's with the same courteous waiter hovering discreetly over his table and the same blond woman seated across from him. He didn't want his life to be easier or simpler or predictable the way it used to be. He wanted to take chances.

Following up on Cosmo Delaney's job offer would be taking a chance. Even if chocolate couldn't save the world, Noah had to take the chance that Cosmic Candy Company might open new doors into a new future. He could experiment. He could expand his horizons. He could eat chocolate and call it a professional obligation.

And if Maggie wasn't going to be part of his life, he sure as hell was going to have to find new ways to make his life exciting.

Considering a new job with Cosmo Delaney might be a way.

MAGGIE DIDN'T WANT TO answer her phone. She had enough clients to keep her busy for months. If she took this phone call, all she'd get for the effort was a new client to occupy the next empty square on her calendar.

No way could the caller be Noah. Not after she'd sent him away last night. And he was the only person she'd want to hear from now, the only caller who could cheer her up. So really, what was the point in answering?

The phone rang a second time, reminding her of the point: She was a professional running a business, and since she didn't yet have the cash flow—or the square footage—to accommodate a secretary, she was going to have to answer her own phone.

Reluctantly, she lifted the receiver and mumbled, "Finders, Keepers, can I help you?"

"Maggie, it's Karen. I'm pregnant."

Maggie nearly dropped the phone. She gulped in a deep breath and focused on Rudolf Nureyev. *Karen? Karen and Sandy? Pregnant?*

She took another deep breath to steady her voice and asked, "Are you sure?"

"The thingie turned blue and I'm nauseous."

Under other circumstances, Maggie would have

been ecstatic. But Sandy and Karen hadn't yet patched up all their differences—and besides, nothing short of Noah's stampeding her office, flinging himself at her and roaring, "I love you, damn it!" would make her ecstatic. "Does Sandy know?" she asked her sister-in-law.

"Not yet. I just turned the thingie blue this morning. I must have gotten pregnant before he forgot our anniversary."

"Well, now that you and he are back together again..." Maggie recalled Sandy's complaint yesterday about how he and Karen were not nearly as back together again as he would have liked.

"I don't know what to do," Karen moaned. "We still have a lot of problems. I don't know what to do about this, Maggie."

"What do you mean, you don't know what to do about this? How many options are there?" Maggie believed all women had the right to make their own choices in such situations—but this was her brother's wife. This would be her first niece or nephew. As far as Maggie was concerned, there were only two options: to have the baby as a happy couple or to have the baby as a not-so-happy couple.

"I was sort of hoping maybe you could talk to Sandy."

"Talk to him?" What little joy Maggie took in Karen's news was dimmed by a looming shadow. Why did this blessed event not feel like a blessing? "You want *me* to talk to Sandy? About what?"

"You could..." Karen sighed. "You could tell him I'm pregnant."

"I think you're supposed to be the one to tell him that."

"But he listens to you."

"Do you think that if you told him this he *wouldn't* listen?"

"Maggie, please," Karen wheedled.

Maggie suppressed a groan. If she didn't help Karen, something awful might happen. Karen might make a disastrous choice. And after all, wasn't it Maggie's job to bring lovers together? If ever her expertise was required, it was now, with these two mule-headed people who had so much at stake.

"Sandy and I will probably botch everything without your help," Karen added, as if she could sense that Maggie needed just one more nudge.

"You and Sandy have to learn how to make your marriage work on your own. I can't keep running interference for you," Maggie lectured her halfheartedly. If Karen and Sandy couldn't make it work, Maggie couldn't *stop* running interference for them— not with a baby on the way.

"I know, I know." Karen sounded contrite. "It's a mess, for sure. But until we get it all straightened out, couldn't you help me out just this once?"

Just this once? Maggie swore softly at how many times she'd helped Karen and Sandy out. "All right," she agreed, feeling a bit nauseous herself. "I'll tell him. But you and he are going to have to take it from there."

"Thanks, Maggie."

"And I'm telling him only because it's my job to keep lovers from screwing up their lives."

"You do that job so well," Karen assured her. "I

appreciate this, Maggie. If you can break the ice with him, I'll be able to take it from there. I hope," she added pensively.

Maggie lowered the phone into its cradle, then lowered her chin into the cradle of her hands and stared at her favorite poster. Nureyev and Fonteyn made passion look so elegant, she thought dismally. They made it look pretty and graceful and easy. But nothing was easy. Nothing about her brother's marriage. Nothing about keeping lovers from screwing up their lives. Nothing about love itself was easy.

She might not be able to salvage her brother's marriage, but she was certainly willing to give it her best shot. So why couldn't she salvage her own relationship with Noah? Why couldn't she keep him and herself from screwing up?

A broken sigh escaped her. She recalled, once again, the looks Noah and Sisela had exchanged over dinner last night. She recalled his determination to find Sisela in the first place. She recalled his tender lovemaking—and his inability to utter the words he knew she needed to hear.

What was left to salvage?

"I'm in love with him," she whispered to the dancers.

They didn't respond, but her heart did. Her heart told her that by waiting for Noah to admit he loved her, she was being as stubborn as Karen, who thought receiving flowers on her anniversary was the only acceptable proof of Sandy's love for her. Maybe Sandy forgot calendar dates; maybe he wasn't sentimental. But he loved Karen, and he expressed that love in his own unique way.

Noah couldn't say he loved Maggie. He couldn't admit he was even capable of love. He was confused, he was distracted by Sisela—but surely it was possible that what he felt for Maggie was the real thing.

Shoving away from her desk, she stood. She would deal with the father-to-be first. If he acted like a jerk, she'd just whip him into shape.

Down the hall, she saw Neil ushering a client into his office. She recognized the gentleman, a lawyer who used the firm on a frequent basis. She didn't like this guy's attitude. He always called her ''honey'' and asked her to bring him coffee.

Now, of course, she didn't have to run and fetch for him. She was her own boss, the savior of lovelorn fools. She strode past him to Sandy's office, feeling powerful.

As usual, her brother was hunched over his computer, squinting at the spreadsheet that filled his monitor. ''Sandy, I've got to talk to you.''

He nodded without turning.

''You're pregnant,'' she said.

He flinched, snapped his head up and gaped at her. ''What?''

''You're pregnant. Well, Karen is. But she's giving you half the credit.''

''She's pregnant?'' He leaped out of his chair so abruptly it skidded into the wall on its casters. He banged his hand on the computer keyboard, obliterating his spreadsheet. He stormed toward Maggie, eyes blazing. ''Are you sure?''

Maggie braced herself. Sandy had never indulged in lunatic behavior before, but he'd never been an expectant father before, either. For that matter, he'd never been in as much trouble with Karen as he was right now. The situation had disaster written all over it.

"Now, Sandy," Maggie said in her most ameliorating voice. She wanted to pet him, as if he were a wild dog she could tame with a few well-placed caresses. "Before you react, you ought to—"

"We're pregnant?" He swooped down, caught her in his arms and spun her around the room. "We're pregnant? I can't believe it! Ya-*hoo!* We're pregnant!"

"*I'm* not pregnant," Maggie protested, trying to wrestle out of his grip. Now that she knew he was happy, she could revert to crankiness. "Let go of me, Sandy! Put me down. I'm not part of this 'we.'"

"You're going to be an aunt." He released her, only to grab his chair and spin it around, instead.

"I might not," she said, capturing his attention.

He stilled the revolving chair and frowned. "What do you mean, you might not?"

"Karen thinks your marriage is still a mess. She was afraid to tell you about the baby herself, so she asked me to break the news. And she's not sure what she's going to do about it."

"Not sure—?" Sandy's face grew pale. "Oh, my God. I've got to go to her, Maggie." He groped in his trouser pocket for his keys. "Right now. I've got to convince her that I love her and this baby is the best thing that ever happened to us. What should I do, Maggie? How can I convince Karen I love her?"

Maggie checked herself before supplying him with what seemed like an obvious answer. "What do you think you should do?" she asked.

He ruminated for a minute. "I should bring her flowers, huh?"

She almost smiled. "That would be a good start."

"More than flowers?" He tried to read Maggie's face, but she refused to give him any hints. "A bottle of champagne?"

"She's pregnant, dummy. She can't drink champagne."

"Oh, yeah. Right. Uh…" He ruminated some more. "Earrings?"

"You don't have to spend a fortune on her, Sandy. All she wants is to feel appreciated."

"Flowers," he murmured, nodding and pushing past Maggie as he headed for the door. "Flowers and appreciation. Yeah, I can handle that. I can show her I appreciate her. Lots of flowers. Red roses…" And he was gone, leaving behind a welcome tranquillity.

Maggie sent up a silent prayer that Sandy and Karen could mend their marriage for their baby's sake, if not their own. Then she crossed to Sandy's computer, called up the spreadsheet he'd been working on and saved it to a file for him.

Saving his files, she could do. Saving his marriage? Maybe.

Now it was time to apply her lifesaving techniques to herself.

NOAH HAD BEEN THRILLED when she called. And then not so thrilled when she'd brusquely rejected his suggestion that they meet at Romeo's after work. "I don't want to meet there," she'd snapped. "I'll meet you anywhere but Romeo's."

Well, okay. At least she wanted to see him. After

she'd all but barred the door to him last night, he ought to be grateful that she was willing to meet with him at all.

He'd suggested a café at the Cannery on Fisherman's Wharf. She'd promised to be there at 6:00 p.m., and then she'd hung up before he could say anything more. He'd been vacillating between "thrilled" and "not so thrilled" ever since.

Maggie could drive him insane with all the emotion she churned up inside him. Why couldn't he have stuck with his pursuit of stability? Why couldn't he have opted for a small, placid pond instead of the Pacific at high tide?

Because he wanted the Pacific. He wanted excitement. He wanted Maggie.

He arrived at the café at six o'clock sharp. She wasn't there, and he suffered another twinge of unruly emotion as he paced in the entry. Then he saw her swing open the door and step inside.

She looked disheveled. Her hair appeared to have gone one-on-one with an egg beater and lost. Her blouse was wrinkled, her skirt slightly askew, and he suffered a sharp twinge of arousal as he recollected the last time he'd seen her in work apparel. He remembered wrinkling a different blouse of hers, skewing a different skirt.

Smiling, he strode toward her as she entered. He wanted to haul her into his arms and kiss her hard, but doubt gnawed at him. After last night, after she'd said no, he was hesitant. He would have to follow her lead.

The hostess ushered them to a small table near the window. Through the glass he could see one of the wharves extending into the turquoise water of the bay. A trawler was parked alongside the wharf, a sea-stained vessel rigged with ropes and spools of net.

Ordinarily Noah wouldn't even have noticed the boat. That evening, though, he felt like a tourist, a stranger in his own city. Maybe it was because he wasn't fluent in the language of the only person in his presence who mattered. Maybe it was because whenever he was with her, the world seemed altered somehow.

She took her seat and smiled at him. Her smile made his temperature rise.

"I'll have a glass of Chardonnay," she told the waiter who approached their table. Noah asked for a Scotch on ice. The waiter whisked away, leaving them to each other.

Maggie seemed edgy. She traced an invisible pattern in the tablecloth, then glanced out the window. If they were at Romeo's, perhaps they'd both feel more comfortable. But Maggie had insisted that they meet elsewhere.

"Why not Romeo's?" he asked after an endless length of silence.

An anxious smile crossed her lips. She was spared from answering by the appearance of the waiter with their drinks. As soon as he was gone, Noah leaned forward and gathered Maggie's hand in his. "Why not Romeo's?" he repeated.

She didn't pull her hand away. She didn't pull her gaze away. "Romeo's belongs to you and Sisela," she said.

Was that what this was about? Had Maggie shut him down last night because Sisela had been at dinner with them? "Sisela is history," he reminded her. "And she's married, remember?"

"If she weren't married—"

"She'd still be history." Saying it somehow convinced him that it was the truth.

"I want…" She sighed shakily, then steadied herself with a sip of wine. "I wanted to see you tonight as a professional," she murmured. "I mean, I called you because…" Her voice faded into the air. Her smile was so brave it nearly broke his heart.

"You called because?" he prompted.

"Because it's my job to bring people together."

This sounded promising.

"When it's meant to be," she continued. "When destiny demands it. When two people are fated to be together."

A little less promising, he amended. He wanted to be with Maggie—he wanted it in his brain and in his toes and in every cell and sinew in between. But *fate* and *destiny* were charged words—and he wasn't sure he believed in them any more than he believed in true love or "happily ever after."

"I've got this huge client list all of a sudden," she said. "Dozens of people want me to straighten out their love lives for them. Not that I'm complaining. I'm glad to do it, and—" she grinned slyly "—unlike some people, they're paying me the full rate." Her smile faded. "But even if they weren't, well, I love doing it. Straightening out people's love lives is something I do well."

Noah didn't want her straightening out his love life. All he wanted was *her,* having a drink with him, describing her day to him, returning to his apartment

with him and letting him make love to her. He wanted
her sleeping with him and waking up with him. He
wanted her naked in his arms all night and ready to
take on the world with him when they rose the next
morning.

He didn't want anything more than that.

And she did.

"Last night," she continued, then took another for-
tifying sip of wine. "Last night, I got the impression
that Sisela wasn't exactly history to you."

"I can't speak for Sisela," he conceded. "I can
only speak for myself, Maggie. And—" *I love you.*
That was what she wanted to hear. He wanted so
badly to give her what she wanted.

She gazed expectantly at him.

Why couldn't he lie? It would be only one small
fib, a gift to Maggie, something to make her feel wonderful. Something to make her toss aside her doubts.
Something to make her waltz out of this café and into
his bed.

If he were just a bit of a bastard, he'd say it without
a qualm.

"You're the only woman I want," he said instead.
Not quite what she longed for, but at least it was the
truth. Unlike his father, Noah wasn't going to lie to
a woman, no matter how much she wanted to hear
lies and believe them. Noah would give Maggie everything he could, even if everything he could give
her fell short.

She said nothing. She trailed her fingertip along the
rim of her wineglass. He imagined that fingertip trailing up his arm, down his chest, all over his body.

"Yesterday, you were the only woman I wanted.

Tomorrow you'll be the only woman I want." *Please, Maggie, let that be enough. I can't do any better than that.*

Her eyes glistening, she studied her wineglass, then lifted it to her lips. It wasn't enough. He was going to lose her—the most courageous woman he'd ever known, the most challenging woman, the gutsiest— simply because he couldn't utter a lie.

Standing, he clasped both her hands in his and lifted her to her feet. "This isn't about destiny and fate," he whispered. "It's about you and me."

She raised her eyes to him.

"You said your job was bringing people together. Bring us together, Maggie. You can do that, can't you?"

She already had done it, he realized. All that was left for her to do was the most difficult thing he'd ever asked of any woman: to accept him as he was.

"I can do that," she murmured.

CHAPTER FIFTEEN

"I'M GOING TO NEW YORK," he said.

Maggie eased out of his arms and sat up. He lay on his back, his hands folded beneath his head and his smile hopeful. In the two weeks since she'd decided to risk her heart and soul on Noah, she had only grown more convinced that he had the most beautiful smile in the world, the most beautiful eyes. Every morning when she woke up in his bed, she found herself astonished that she was with him—this stunning man who didn't even seem to care that she was chunky and frizzy-haired and about as glamorous as a fire hydrant.

He hadn't told her he loved her. He couldn't—she knew that. But just because he couldn't speak the words didn't mean he didn't feel them. People had different ways of expressing love. Her brother Sandy couldn't say it the way Karen wished he could, but he loved her just the same.

Admittedly, Sandy was trying harder. He was bringing Karen flowers every day now, and Maggie had recited the old line about being careful what you wished for. Karen had apologized. She wouldn't complain, she said, except that in her delicate condition she found the flowery perfume nauseating.

But they were making progress. And Maggie knew,

she just *knew,* that she and Noah were making progress, too.

Every time he kissed her he was telling her he loved her. Every time he touched her, every time he moved his hands over her body, every time he sank into her and groaned, every time he held himself back for her, denying himself his release until neither of them could bear it any longer, until she was burning up inside, until they were both on fire.

Well, he must feel *something* for her. When he was good and ready, she hoped he'd be willing to call it by its proper name.

The air in his bedroom was milky with the early-morning light that filtered in through the curtains. The alarm wouldn't go off for another hour.

He'd eased her out of sleep a few minutes ago. Drowsing next to him, her back against his chest, she'd felt him brush his lips over her bare shoulder and she'd decided that if he was going to be acting that way, it would be worth her while to wake up. Instinct had made her turn in his arms and give him more to kiss. He'd browsed along her collarbone to her throat and then down, covering her breasts with light kisses and then not-so-light kisses. She'd felt his teeth tugging at her nipples, the rough flick of his tongue on the inflamed tips. And then he'd journeyed lower, keeping his hands on her breasts as he caressed her belly with his mouth, as he stroked his tongue between her legs.

She'd arched and shuddered beneath him. She'd begged him to stop. She'd begged him never, ever to stop. Strange, incoherent pleas had tumbled from her lips as he deepened his kisses, kneaded her breasts, used his legs to pin her to the bed.

He'd made her feel things she'd never felt before. Deep, wrenching sensations. Shockingly lovely sensations. Powerful spasms that shook her from her scalp to her insteps, that stole her breath and made her pulse rocket.

When, after an endless moment, she'd decided that she wasn't going to die of bliss, she'd pulled him up onto her and opened to him, but he'd shaken his head, kissed her brow and rolled off her. "That was for you," he'd whispered. "Just for you."

He had to love her. A man didn't give such selfless pleasure to a woman he didn't love.

At least that was what she'd thought as they cuddled together and unwound in the silent predawn light. She'd closed her eyes, tucked her head into the crook of his neck and breathed in the scent of him—clean and male and minty. She loved his smell, his warmth, the firm contours of his chest, the strength of his arms around her. She loved him for what he'd just done to her.

Until he spoke.

Now she scrutinized him warily, wondering whether his lovemaking hadn't been just for her, after all. Maybe he'd done that because he wanted to soften her up, to prepare her for bad news.

"New York?"

"Cosmo Delaney and I have been talking," Noah told her. "He wants me to fly East so we can discuss this new job."

She exerted herself not to react negatively. Noah hadn't mentioned the Cosmic Candy job possibility since the night she'd decided to follow the "destiny" Noah swore he didn't believe in. Apparently he'd been in touch with Cosmo Delaney but had decided not to tell her.

"When—" Her voice cracked, and she swallowed. "When are you going?"

"Friday evening, on the red-eye. I can't take any more time off from Solar Systems, so I asked him if we could get together on the weekend."

"You've worked all this out with him." She prayed Noah didn't hear the hint of panic in her voice. To her ears, it was as sharp as the sound of shattering glass. She and Noah had been intimate for two weeks. They'd spent every night together, occasionally at her place but mostly at his. They'd slept together, had sex together, eaten breakfast and bickered over the newspaper together. They'd met for dinner every evening after work—not at Romeo's but at her office or his. Some nights they'd gone out, but more often they'd stopped at the grocery on the way home, picked up fresh shrimp or pasta or a chicken for roasting. They'd cooked together, eaten together, washed the dishes together—and tumbled into bed together.

She knew every square inch of his body. She knew the knotted muscles in his shoulders, the density of his hair, the heat and power of his arousal. She knew that all she had to do was start unbuttoning her blouse and he'd be hard—and all she had to do was think of him hard and she'd be even more aroused than he was.

But she hadn't known this: that he'd been in communication with Cosmo Delaney, discussing a job prospect three thousand miles away. Noah hadn't bothered to mention that.

It hadn't merely slipped his mind, either. He'd assumed she would be upset, so he'd fattened her for the kill by making love to her in a way that would reduce her to mush. *"Just for you,"* he'd said.

And the job at Cosmic Candy Company was just for *him*.

"So," she said, keeping her tone pleasantly bland, "you're going to New York. Is this a done deal, or are you still negotiating?"

He reached up and tucked a lock of hair behind her ear. She steeled herself against responding to his touch. She didn't want to sigh and melt into his arms, but she didn't want to recoil, either. "There's no deal," he told her. "I'm just flying to New York so we can talk."

"People can talk on the phone," she noted wryly. "You're going to do more than talk."

"He wants to talk in person," Noah explained. "He's booked a flight for me. I owe it to myself to hear him out, Maggie."

Yes, he owed it to himself. Much as she hated to admit it, working at Cosmic Candy could be the opportunity of a lifetime for Noah, even if the head honcho was a flake. Hadn't Cosmo batted around titles like "director" and "vice president" when he'd wined and dined Noah in San Francisco? For all Noah's success at Solar Systems, the solar-panel company was small stuff compared to a national chocolate company looking to expand its market share. Not only would Noah get a fancy title, but he'd get an entire continent to play with and a chance to design and implement his own marketing strategy. Maggie was no expert on big business, but if she were a marketing professional, she'd want a job like the one Delaney was dangling in front of Noah.

But he was going to New York.

He was leaving her.

If he loved her, he would have demanded her opinion about whether or not he should go, and he would have given it as much weight as he gave his own. Maybe he would have asked her to accompany him to New York. Delaney still thought she was his wife, after all, and Delaney apparently believed men should take their wives on business trips. He'd brought his wife with him to San Francisco two weeks ago.

His wife. Sisela.

The sound of shattering glass echoed in her head, and she saw the splinters forming, piece after piece, into a cracked, fragile but recognizable shape, to form the truth. Noah wasn't in love with her. He didn't believe in love. He'd started life as a desperately poor kid who had little faith in people or emotions but who placed his trust in financial security. He'd had a useless, irresponsible father and a mother who'd kept him fed but failed to instill in him any confidence that relationships could work. And he'd decided that he would never be poor again.

Cosmo Delaney was offering Noah something Maggie never could. He didn't want the love she could give. He wanted the safety of an influential, high-paying job.

"Okay, then," she said brightly.

He lifted both hands to her face, cupped her cheeks

and urged her down to him. "Okay, then *what?*" he asked.

"Okay, so you'll go to New York. Maybe it's your destiny." Her eyes burned with tears, and she hid her face against his chest so he wouldn't see them.

"I don't believe in destiny," he reminded her.

Perhaps he didn't, but she did. But destiny sometimes traveled a crooked path. Noah's true destiny might have been to run Cosmic Candy's national marketing program. Maggie's success in locating Sisela had led to his hooking up with Cosmo Delaney.

It was still destiny, and she'd still helped Noah to realize it. And for all she knew, Sisela was still a part of it.

He combed his fingers through her hair in a pattern that simultaneously soothed her and turned her on. "You don't want me to go," he guessed.

I want you to love me. I want you to say you'll stay in San Francisco and build a life with me. I want you to promise you'll come back. I want you to promise you'll meet me someplace at the appointed hour and make me your wife. "I want you to do what's right for you," she said.

He kissed the crown of her head. His fingers danced in her hair and he shifted under her, urging her legs apart with his knee. That was all it took to reignite her. Damn him for being able to reach her so easily, so quickly. Damn him for being able to move her against him until her heart was pounding and she was gasping, aching, wanting him.

Didn't he know this was love? Couldn't he get it through his thick skull? She didn't need flowers or anniversary presents or a pregnancy. All she needed was for him to recognize what they had together, to treasure it, to accept it.

All she needed was for him to whisper, "I love you, Maggie. I'll come back."

But he wouldn't say it. He couldn't.

COSMO HAD ARRANGED FOR a room for him in Bellewood—not at the cheap motel where Noah and Maggie had stayed when they'd been there before, but at a luxurious bed-and-breakfast called the Holliwell Inn, located in the heart of town. Actually, Cosmo had invited Noah to stay in his mansion for the weekend, but Noah had declined. This was a business trip—no matter that it was scheduled for a weekend, and no matter that Cosmo was unorthodox in his business dealings. For a job interview, Noah didn't want to be sleeping in the home of his prospective boss. It just didn't seem professional.

Besides, Delaney's house was a bit much. Noah would likely get lost trying to find his way to the bathroom. Or he'd fall into the pool. Or he'd get to thinking about the last time he'd stood next to that pool, kissing Maggie, and he would forget all about why he'd come to Bellewood.

He wished she'd been a little more enthusiastic about his trip here. As he unpacked his suitcase, hanging his suit in the antique armoire in one corner, tossing a spare T-shirt across the quilt on the four-poster bed, he contemplated the way Maggie's mood had changed the instant he'd told her he was going to meet with Cosmo. He wasn't sure why she'd become so distant. It wasn't as if she hadn't known about the job possibility. She'd been right beside him the evening Cosmo had first proposed the idea.

Surely she couldn't be angry just because Noah hadn't told her about Cosmo's subsequent telephone calls. Those were business discussions—nothing that would have interested Maggie.

Sisela had never asked him about his career plans, and it hadn't occurred to him that Maggie would want to know all the details of his and Cosmo's negotiations. It wasn't as if he'd deliberately hidden anything from her; he simply hadn't thought to mention it.

After perching his toiletries bag on the shelf above the ornate pedestal sink, he crossed the spacious room to the window, which overlooked the town green. The lawn was as lush as velvet, the trees dense with leaves. It was a much nicer view than the parking-lot vista his motel room had overlooked the last time he'd been in town.

Would Maggie have liked the view, or would she have thought it pretentious? She hadn't been terribly enamored of Bellewood, he recalled. But then, she'd spent her time there hiking for miles through the town, hobnobbing with Cosmo's party guests and fretting over her brother's marital problems.

And doing her job, Noah reminded himself. Finding Sisela. Earning her money.

He ought to be concentrating on his job, too. He'd managed to doze for a couple of hours during the flight—Cosmo had booked him a first-class ticket, so the seat hadn't been too uncomfortable. He could conduct a reasonable discussion with Cosmo in a couple of hours, jet lag notwithstanding. A few cups of coffee, a shave and shower and he could conquer the world.

Too bad Maggie wasn't here to conquer it with him. Of course, if Maggie had been here, conquering the world would be the last thing on his mind. He'd be more interested in conquering her erogenous zones.

He swore under his breath. Why did thoughts of Maggie keep popping into his head? He had to stay focused on the job.

Turning from the window, he gazed at the wide bed. He pictured Maggie sprawled out on the quilt, her hair splayed across the piles of pillows, her breasts spread round against her rib cage as she gazed up at him. Sex, he realized, was the only place she hadn't gone cold on him since he'd told her about his impending trip East. Her chatter had dwindled—her effusive descriptions of her clients and their long-lost loves, her analysis of her brother Sandy's newfound attentiveness to his wife, her jokes about her brothers Jack and Neil, her insinuations that if her business continued to grow she was going to have to hire one of them as an assistant....

But her laughter had dried up. Everything had, except for the sex. In that one area she was still his, still soft and warm and loving, still willing to let him make her happy.

What had he done wrong? Why was she disappearing on him?

Not now, he chided himself. Right now he had to concentrate on pumping some caffeine into his system and organizing his thoughts on how to strategize Cosmic Candy's marketing, how to expand the West

Coast markets, how to get Cosmic Star Crunches and Cosmic Mocha Drinks into every kitchen in every town in the country. He could worry about Maggie later. After he'd nailed things down with Cosmo.

Coffee, he resolved. Coffee and Cosmic Candy. Adventure awaited him. He'd figure out the rest later.

MAGGIE HADN'T SLEPT WELL last night. It had taken her no time to get used to sleeping in Noah's bed, in his arms. It had taken no time at all to realize that she could spend the rest of her life very happily sleeping with Noah—except that the bastard had left her.

He thought he'd only flown to New York to discuss a job with a crackpot mogul. But she knew the truth: he'd really, truly left her. He'd left a woman who could give him all the love in the world, because he didn't believe in love.

Well, good riddance to him, she thought miserably, staring at the mess she'd made of the Saturday newspaper. Sections lay strewn across her kitchen table, the pages wrinkled and creased, a photograph of the mayor framed in a brown ring left by her coffee cup. If Noah Davis wanted to thwart fate, if he wanted to contradict destiny, that was his choice. A stupid choice, for sure—but all his.

She heard the buzz of her doorbell and groaned. It was nine-thirty—not too early for visitors, but she was gloomy and her head was throbbing. Since she wasn't expecting company, she figured the caller would be one of her neighbors begging for an egg or a copy of last week's *People* magazine. For the sake of community peace, Maggie would have to act civilly.

Raking her hair back from her face with her hands, she shoved away from the table and stomped down the hall to the door. Peering through the peephole, she saw her brother Jack.

Great. Just who she wanted to see. Her smug older brother looking bright-eyed and bushy-tailed. He wouldn't have traveled all the way to her apartment this early on a Saturday morning for an egg or a magazine. He'd probably come to bug her about something.

Well, at least she didn't have to look presentable for him. Letting her hair tumble back into its matted tangle, she shrugged her oversize T-shirt higher on her shoulders and yanked open the door. "What do you want?"

Jack accepted her surly greeting with a smile. "Good morning, sweetheart. I smell coffee. Offer me a cup and I'll say yes."

"Go away," she said, not really meaning it.

His smile widened. "Why, thanks, I'd love some!" He swept past her and down the hall to her kitchen, swung open the cabinet where she stored a motley assortment of mugs and helped himself to a cup of coffee. "I come to you with love in my heart," he said, pivoting toward the refrigerator to get the cream. "So be nice."

"I don't want to be nice," she argued. No woman whose heart had just been broken was required to be nice to her brother.

Jack dug a teaspoon from the silverware drawer, then sat at the table and stirred his coffee. Maggie refilled her own cup, made a desultory attempt to straighten the newspaper, then gave up and shoved it onto the floor. She planted her mug on the table, slumped in her chair and glowered at Jack.

"Did he break up with you?" Jack asked.

Maggie pursed her lips. She had stopped discussing her love life with her brothers her final year of high school, when the three of them had greeted her date for the senior prom with baseball bats and told him they expected their sister to be treated like a lady, or else. Poor Steve Nyland had spent the entire night of the prom glancing nervously over her shoulder and asking if any of her brothers had ever been convicted of assault.

They meant well. They were just a little too protective. So she kept certain details of her life to herself.

Thus, Jack's question took her by surprise. "Did *who* break up with me?"

Jack tried hard to look innocent and unconcerned. "Whoever. Some guy." At Maggie's stony frown, he shrugged. "That client of yours. His name was Noah, wasn't it?"

She bought time by sipping her coffee. Black and strong, it scalded her tongue, but she didn't stop sipping until she'd marshaled her defenses. "Jack, what business is this of yours? Are you investigating me?"

"I met him outside your office that day when the hordes stampeded, remember? He told me he was a client of yours, but I haven't been a P.I. ten years for nada. I asked a few questions, he let a few things slip. The guy was hot for you."

She sighed. Of course Jack had figured it out. He'd learned the detective trade, just like Neil and Sandy and Maggie herself, at their father's knee. "He was hot for me," she confirmed. "Now he's cooled off. It's not a big thing."

"For the past two weeks you haven't been home at night," Jack asserted.

Anger flared inside her. He really had been snooping! "How do you know that?"

"I tried phoning you a few times."

"You never left a message."

"I didn't have a message to leave. I was only trying to find out if you were there. I did a few surveillance runs, too. You weren't home, Maggie. I knew it. And I know you're an adult and you're entitled to a sex life—"

"And some privacy," she snapped.

"Hey, I didn't ask any questions, did I? I didn't break in and check your phone book. I am exercising discretion, Maggie."

"Yeah, right."

"But the past couple of days you've looked a little down in the mouth. So I thought maybe the guy was treating you wrong, and I ought to look into it."

"He didn't treat me wrong." She sighed, watching her breath ruffle the surface of her coffee. "I knew going in it wasn't going to last." That was the truth. She'd foolishly taken her chances that something might change, that he might see the light—that the light he saw might be love.

"He broke your heart."

"He did not. He went to New York to pursue a job opportunity," she said.

"I could kill him for you," Jack offered.

She wanted to be angry. Her brother had no right poking his nose into her personal business, meddling in her social life, sitting in judgment on her choices of male companions. She really wanted to lash out at him.

But she was too touched. Her brother—all her brothers—might be royal pains in the butt, but they loved her. Jack loved her enough to volunteer to commit murder on her behalf.

"You don't have to kill him," she said, giving Jack a sad smile. "I'll recover."

"Well, then." He sat straighter, took a swig of coffee and grinned. "It's time to discuss what I really came here to talk about."

Her defenses rose again. "What?" she asked warily.

"Finders, Keepers."

She waited. Her heart had room for three things in it: her family, which was the main reason she hadn't shoved Jack out the door and thrown the dead bolt; Noah, who was on the other side of the country, chasing his own dreams without regard for her; and Finders, Keepers. Finders, Keepers was hers. She'd conceived it all by herself, she'd given birth to it and it was hers.

Jack could kill Noah if he had a mind to. But if he so much as threatened Finders, Keepers...

"I want in."

"What?"

"I want you to merge with Tyrell Investigative."

Her head jerked up. She gripped her mug and glared at him. "You want me to merge my company with yours?"

"We were wrong not to keep you in the family firm from the start, Maggie. I'm here admitting it. We were wrong. You were right. Your company is flying high. You've got more clients than you can deal with—"

"I'm dealing with them all!"

"One at a time. Maybe two at a time. You're in that crowded little closet—"

"Because that was all the space you'd give me!"

"Bring your outfit into Tyrell Investigative and I'll give you the conference room. We can convert that into your main office. It's a bigger room than my office, even."

"No."

"Don't be stubborn, Maggie. Think about it. We could take some of your cases when our loads are a little light. You could catch up. We subscribe to databases you can't afford right now, and we could contribute our expertise and all the stationery supplies—"

"Other than being able to filch your stationery, what would be the advantage to me?" she asked wryly.

Jack laughed and came up with one more. "You'd be back in the family firm."

That, she had to admit, was an advantage far more valuable than access to paper supplies and databases. Despite how much her brothers exasperated her, she loved them. She could always count on Jack, Sandy and Neil not only to drive her insane but to stand by her and fight for her and love her.

"I'd be an equal?"

"You'd be president of a subsidiary," Jack proposed. "That's a better title than Neil's."

"I'm better than Neil," she muttered, unable to hide her smile. "I deserve a better title."

"It's yours."

"He wouldn't mind?"

Jack laughed. "He's probably going to hire you to find him a wife."

Maggie rolled her eyes and snorted. "I wouldn't want to subject anyone in the sisterhood to him." Her smile fading, she drank some coffee and considered Jack's offer. She still felt a sharp, agonizing despair over Noah's defection, but this was like a shot of whiskey, dulling the edge of her pain. She might not be able to manage her own romances, but she was damned good at managing other people's. And if her brothers contributed their intelligence and technical support when the load got too heavy, she could be even better.

"So?" Jack asked. "Are you in? Or should I say, 'back in'?"

"I'm not going to make coffee for your clients."

"The president of Finders, Keepers? Of course not. You'll make coffee only for your own clients." He winked.

"Let me think about it." She stood, crossed to the counter and emptied the coffee decanter into her mug. She wanted to weep from all the emotions churning inside her. She was filled with so much love she was close to bursting from it—but not enough love to keep Noah by her side. Not enough to keep her eyes from filling with tears.

She barely heard the scrape of the chair as Jack pushed it back and stood. She barely heard his footsteps on the tile floor. Only when she felt his arms around her in a brotherly bear hug did she realize how close he was. "I'm still willing to kill him for you," he vowed. "Or maybe just castrate him. Which would you prefer?"

She recalled the first time she'd seen Noah, filling the doorway of her office. He'd arrived just minutes after Jack had spotted her teetering on her desk and told her he wanted to be close by in case she fell. She was falling now, and Jack was there to catch her.

She rotated in his arms, rested her head on his shoulder and let the tears come. "I'm so glad you're my brother," she whispered.

"I'm glad I'm your brother, too. Neil, Sandy and I don't like it when other guys give you a hard time. We claim exclusive rights in that area." He gave her a squeeze. "Yeah, I think I'll castrate him. Killing him would be too kind."

"Thanks," she murmured, knowing he would understand what her gratitude was for and how very deep it ran.

CHAPTER SIXTEEN

STRETCHED OUT ON THE BED, his head half buried in a multitude of flouncy pillows, Noah groaned. He'd had a long day after enduring a long overnight flight. He should be ready to plunge into sleep.

But he couldn't. His brain was working overtime and his nerves quivered with excess energy. His head hurt. His stomach hurt a little, too—probably from eating too much chocolate.

He had spent the day with Cosmo at his gaudy mansion, munching on candy as they'd reviewed Cosmic Candy's current marketing programs and discussed past campaigns that had succeeded and those that had failed. They'd talked about the company's projected earnings, its manufacturing facilities, its effort to establish a niche somewhere between the inexpensive candy sold in supermarkets and drugstores and the gourmet chocolates sold in specialty boutiques. In the middle of the afternoon, just as they'd finished analyzing the strength of imported European chocolates among the affluent, Cosmo had beckoned Noah outside, stripped off his shirt and dived into the pool. "Come on in!" he'd hollered to Noah. "There are swimsuits in the cabana if you want to change."

"No, thanks," Noah had said, settling himself onto

one of the lounge chairs that flanked the pool. "I don't want to change."

I don't want to change, he thought now, watching the light in the windows darken as dusk gave way to night. He'd undergone a huge change over the previous year and an even bigger change over the previous few weeks. He wasn't sure he wanted to go through any more changes right now.

Working for Cosmo Delaney would be an adventure. But as Noah considered the prospect, it just didn't strike him as the exciting ride he'd imagined it would be when the opportunity had first presented itself.

Why? Why didn't he want to change anymore?

The phone on his nightstand rang. It was an ersatz antique contraption of brass and wood with ivory trim, a modern Touch-Tone telephone disguised as a nineteenth-century model to fit in with the room's quaint decor. The shrill chirp of the bell was late-twentieth-century, though, and it made Noah's head hurt even more.

He lifted the receiver and tucked it against his ear. "Hello?"

"Noah?" A satiny voice glided through the wire. "Noah, it's Sisela."

Just what he needed, he thought churlishly. He was three thousand miles from home, trying to figure out what he was going to do with his life and how he was going to feel cheerful about it. He didn't need Sisela confusing matters.

"I'd like to talk to you," she said.

"Fine. Talk." Rude, but he wasn't in the mood to be charming.

"Can I come up?"

That jolted him. He'd assumed she was calling him from her home. Her statement implied that she was in fact calling from one of the genteel parlors on the first floor of the inn.

He sat up and regrouped. He was tired, unshaven, shoeless and fatigued. He didn't want to go downstairs. Having Sisela come up to his room didn't seem particularly discreet, though. "I don't think—"

"I'll be right up," she decided for him. Before he could argue, he heard the click of her hanging up.

He lowered the phone and shoved his hair back from his brow. What the hell did Sisela want with him? How had she and her loony husband managed to infiltrate his life so thoroughly?

He knew how. Maggie. He'd walked into that cluttered, windowless office of hers on Van Ness and seen her lively hazel eyes and her glorious hair, her defiantly full curves and her equally defiant smile, and he'd wanted to have an adventure with her.

He still thirsted for adventure. But the adventure he was experiencing now—this trip to Bellewood to ponder employment with Cosmo Delaney—didn't include Maggie. This adventure was a solo outing, and while he'd liked going it alone when he'd set out for the Far East and India, that was before he'd learned what an adventure could be like with Maggie.

A knock on the door dragged him from his thoughts. He padded barefoot across the braided rug that extended from the bed to the door, and opened it.

Sisela looked pretty. Her hair was silky and sleek, her tall figure draped in a gauzy dress that was diaphanous enough to reveal the slender silhouette of her body. Her eyes were artfully made up, her legs flawlessly smooth. He remembered that she used to have her legs waxed every few weeks back in San Francisco. He remembered that the feel of her skin used to excite him.

Not anymore. Nothing about her excited him now. He stared at her and felt no connection at all. She might as well have been a model in a magazine ad for overpriced perfume.

She entered the room, gazed around and moved to the washstand. She adjusted a crystal dish of potpourri, then checked her reflection in the mirror above the sink. Turning, she smiled at Noah. "How are you?"

"I'm tired," he said bluntly.

"You're angry with me."

"We don't need to have this conversation, Sisela." Once again he was being rude, but he was too weary to care.

Still smiling, she waltzed over to his bed and sat. He deliberately headed for the chair near the window. Unlike the phone, the chair was probably as antiquated as it looked. Straight-backed, its seat upholstered with a millimeter-thick pad covered by a musty tapestry, it was far too uncomfortable to have been bought for any reason other than that it was authentically old.

"I don't want you to be angry with me," she pressed on. "I don't want any bad feelings between us."

"Fine. No bad feelings." He yearned to rest his hands on the arms of the chair, but unfortunately the chair had no arms. He'd been more comfortable straddling the folding metal chair in Maggie's office.

He rested his hands on his knees instead. The position felt stiff and tense. He propped one leg across the other knee and planted his hands on his shin. Still stiff and tense.

"It would be a shame if we couldn't get along," she said.

He studied her in the light from the bedside lamp. Yes, she was pretty—in a strangely static way. He rummaged deep in his memory to recall why he'd fallen for her, why he'd asked her to become his wife. Stasis, perhaps. The assurance that she was what she was, that she would never make too many demands on him, that she would never expect more than he could give—that he wouldn't have to give too much.

He felt as if his heart were twisting inside his rib cage, wringing itself out, tying itself into a knot. A year ago, he hadn't known how much he was capable of giving. He'd given his mother support, both familial and monetary. But his soul had been vacant. There, he'd had nothing to give.

Until he'd stumbled upon a flooded village in the hills of eastern India.

"I told you why I did what I did," she continued, crossing her legs as if deliberately offering him a glimpse of her thighs.

"You told me," he agreed. "But I've got to say, after getting to know Cosmo, I think you made a wise choice. He's a great guy. Generous to a fault. And obviously smitten with you."

"He is a great guy," Sisela agreed, absently running her index finger from her knee up her thigh to her hem and back down again. "You'll enjoy working for him. With him," she amended. "You're both so smart, such creative thinkers. I tremble to think what the two of you can accomplish together."

"I'm not taking the job," Noah said. He hadn't consciously realized until that moment that he'd made up his mind. But as soon as the words were out he knew they were right.

Sisela's perfectly shaped eyebrows rose. "You're not? But you have to!"

Her reaction amused him. "Why do I have to?"

"You just do, Noah! It's such a perfect idea! The two of you working together, joining forces... It's so perfect."

He felt marginally less stiff, no thanks to the chair. Something about Sisela's ardent defense of her husband's job offer tickled him. "Oh, I don't know that it's so perfect. It has potential, but there would be drawbacks, too."

"What?" She leaned forward, her eyes as sharp and cold as chips of blue ice. "What drawbacks?"

"For one thing, I don't want to leave San Francisco." That was another truth he hadn't realized until he'd spoken the words. "I love San Francisco. I don't want to live in New York."

"Cosmo can work around that, I'm sure," she insisted. "You could maintain an apartment in New York and keep a home on the West Coast, too. Actually, that would work well. You could fly to New York when business demanded and have a pied-à-terre in the city. And then your wife wouldn't have to be uprooted."

His wife. He almost laughed out loud at the irony. He'd never really thought about how much he loved San Francisco until Maggie—his make-believe wife—had entered his world.

"So you could live out there with her, if that's what she wants, and just fly to New York when business required it. That would be fine. Maybe even better than relocating her here."

Something clicked inside his head. "What do you mean, 'maybe even better'?"

"She wouldn't be happy here," Sisela declared.

"Oh?" Noah suspected that Maggie would be happy anywhere. She was the sort of woman who made her own happiness. No doubt she'd prefer to remain close to her brothers, but if destiny compelled her to move to New York City—or to Bellewood, or to Halore, India, or to any other place in the universe—she would find a way to make herself happy.

Sisela leaned farther forward, her dress sliding down to cover her legs and simultaneously gapping on top to provide a glimpse of her breasts. "I've got a lot riding on your decision, Noah. I want you to take this job with Cosmo. It was my idea. I told him you'd be perfect for it, and eventually he came to agree with me. You've got to take it."

Another click in his skull. Sisela had persuaded Cosmo to offer Noah the job? Why?

The only answer he could think of was so distasteful, he clenched his teeth to keep from cursing. He gazed at the splendid-looking woman before him, the woman he'd once chosen to marry. The woman he'd chosen because he'd never believed in love.

The woman he'd chosen because *she* hadn't believed in love, either—or so he'd thought. "You didn't tell him to offer me the job because you love me, did you?" he asked.

She trilled a laugh. "Oh, Noah, you can't be serious. I thought having you work for Cosmic Candy would enable us to renew our friendship. But love? Surely we're beyond that."

"No. We're not. Do you love me?"

She regarded him curiously. "I used to think we'd get married. Isn't that enough?"

It had been enough when Noah hadn't realized there could be more. Suddenly he felt a heavy pang of sadness for Sisela at the understanding that it was still enough for her. She wasn't beyond love, but love seemed to be beyond her.

"No," he said quietly. "It's not enough."

"Then what do you want me to say?" If she leaned forward any farther, she was going to somersault off the bed. He sensed that she was trying to reach him without actually standing and hurling herself at him. "Do you want me to say I love you, Noah? Do you want me to say I love Cosmo? He's a good man. He's a wonderful husband. I'm lucky to have him. But I miss you. We had something good, too."

"Not good enough."

"Noah—"

"I'm married," he said. Like so much else he'd said tonight, the words felt true in his heart. "Maggie is my wife. And I love her."

Sisela stared at him, clearly baffled. The way she was gaping at him, he felt he must have transformed before her eyes.

He *had* transformed. No doubt about it. He'd discovered, to his great astonishment, that he believed in true love after all.

"I've got to go home," he said abruptly. His headache had vanished; his chocolate-glutted stomach had stopped rumbling. He was suddenly invigorated, exhilarated, so full of energy he felt powerful enough to fly back to California merely by flapping his arms. He leaped up from his chair and crossed to his suitcase, which sat on a luggage stand beside the armoire. "I've got to go," he repeated, nearly knocking Sisela off the bed with the suitcase as he flipped it open atop the quilt.

"You really love her?" Sisela asked, sounding more puzzled than disappointed.

"I really do." He loved Maggie's fire and her passion, her brains and her guts, her body and her soul. Her convictions and her commitment. He loved her for having more faith in him than he'd had in himself. He hadn't known he could love a woman this way. But she'd known all along.

She'd loved him so much, she'd let him leave her. She'd had so much faith in him, she must have trusted that he would figure out the truth on his own—and if he never figured out the truth, she would never manipulate him into pretending he had.

He didn't have to pretend. This was no game of make-believe. As he tossed items willy-nilly into his bag, his entire being pulsed with the reality of it. He loved Maggie. She had made him realize how much love he could give.

He all but forgot Sisela was in the room. As he snapped the bag shut and swung it off the bed, he was startled to find her standing near the door, still staring at him. "Tell Cosmo thanks for the offer," he said. "Tell him I'd be happy to do consulting work for him if he wants. Never mind—I'll tell him myself. I'll give him a call and we can work out an arrangement. Freelance, though. On my terms." A whole new adventure began to unfold before him: consulting work. He could be his own boss, just like Maggie. Maybe he could even do some work for Finders, Keepers. He was the best example of her skill at finding lost lovers, wasn't he? He'd been lost, but thanks to her, he wasn't lost anymore.

Two TRANSCONTINENTAL flights in two days would have been enough to stagger the toughest man in the world. But Noah was running on sheer adrenaline as, his jet lag doubling back on itself, he disembarked from the plane at San Francisco International Airport at 6:00 a.m.

At that hour on a Sunday morning the streets of the city were eerily empty. A few diligent joggers loped along the sidewalks, panting and sweating; a few derelicts stirred to life under their blankets of newspapers. But most of the city was still asleep.

Noah drove directly to Maggie's building, double-parked when he couldn't find a space on the street and entered the vestibule. He pressed the button beside her mailbox so long he was afraid he might awaken her neighbors, but she didn't answer.

If she wasn't home, where could she be?

With another man? No. He refused to even consider the possibility.

He hurried back to his car and got in. Even the most devoted entrepreneur wouldn't be at her desk at six o'clock on a Sunday morning, but since he lacked a better idea, he drove across town to the building on Van Ness where her office was located. The ground-floor lobby was open, but no one was in sight. His footsteps echoed as he crossed to the elevator and rode upstairs. The main entry to Tyrell Investigative Services was locked.

Riding back downstairs, Noah felt the first wave of exhaustion hit him. Love made a person behave irrationally, he acknowledged. Just as his mother had lived her life foolishly because she'd loved Noah's wastrel father, now Noah was acting like a fool, chasing around the city on no sleep, searching for the woman he loved.

And why not? Why not act like a fool for love? All his life he'd worried about his mother's insufficient grasp of reality when it came to his father—but maybe the love she'd harbored for Noah's father had been one of the few sources of joy in her life. Maybe what had kept her going from day to day hadn't been

Noah's caution and his eagerness not to trouble or disappoint her, but instead had been her love for his father.

Perhaps the reason Noah had resisted love was that he hadn't wanted to relinquish his sanity. But it was too late. He was in love and he was going to keep racing around the city like a lunatic until he found Maggie.

In the lobby of the building, he found a public phone with a directory. He leafed through the pages until he reached "Tyrell," and scanned the column of listings. Was her brother Jack really a John? Or maybe a Jacob? Did he dare start dialing numbers, systematically waking people until he found the right Jack Tyrell?

Of course he dared. He was in love, and this was an adventure.

The first Tyrell he telephoned had a few overripe words for him. The second had obviously already been awake; the screaming infant in the background was so raucous, Noah considered it a miracle that the baby's mother had even heard the phone ringing. The third Tyrell didn't answer. The fourth had an answering machine with a woman's voice on it.

The fifth was Maggie's brother Jack. "Who is this?" he asked gruffly.

"Noah Davis. I'm trying to find Maggie."

"Noah?" He heard a threat in Jack's tone, and then he heard it in Jack's words. "I'm going to kill you."

Noah sighed. "Maggie said you'd only castrate me."

"Well, I'm toying with both options," Jack conceded.

"I love her," Noah said. It was so liberating to say it aloud, so liberating to admit it. "Where is she?"

"She's on her way to Sandy's. So am I. We're having breakfast there."

"Sandy? The brother with the marriage problems?"

"My brother's marriage problems are none of your business," Jack growled.

"They will be, once I marry Maggie. As a matter of fact, she's already my wife, sort of. Give me Sandy's address. I'll meet her there."

"You will not!"

"If you want to castrate me," Noah argued, "you're going to have to find me. If you tell me where Sandy lives, finding me will be a hell of a lot easier."

Reluctantly, Jack laughed. "I don't know," he muttered. "If I tell you, *she* might castrate *me*." He thought for a minute, then recited an address across the bay in Berkeley.

"I'll see you there," Noah said, hanging up before Jack could order him to stay away from Maggie.

The Bay Bridge, like the streets of the city, was nearly empty. Noah wondered whether one of the few cars sharing the roadway with him might be Jack's, whether Jack was going to arrive at Sandy's house ahead of him and warn Maggie. He wondered whether Maggie would flee before Noah could see her, or whether she'd set to work sharpening carving knives for the surgical procedure Jack wanted to perform on him. Noah would bet on the latter. Maggie wasn't the sort to run away.

He knew the city of Berkeley well after having spent four years as a student at the university, and he didn't have much difficulty locating the stucco ranch house that bore Sandy's address in a cozy middle-class neighborhood. Two cars were parked on the long driveway; a third stood by the curb directly in front of the house. Were all Maggie's brothers here? Were they all sharpening knives?

Noah could be in big trouble. But he'd be in worse trouble if he didn't find Maggie.

He parked behind the car in front of the house, locked his suitcase in the trunk and marched up the front walk to the porch. Through an open window he heard men's voices. Perhaps Maggie wasn't there yet. Maybe the brothers would fall upon Noah before he had a chance to see her.

Let them try, he thought, jamming the doorbell with his thumb. Love made him strong. He would prevail.

A man who looked like a younger, thinner version of Jack answered the door. He eyed Noah up and down. "Is Maggie here?" Noah asked.

The man glanced over his shoulder. "Let him in, Sandy," Noah heard Jack call from inside the house. "If he steps out of line, we'll take care of him." Noah hoped he wasn't imagining the undertone of laughter in Jack's voice.

He entered the house, following Sandy down a hall into the dining room. He had expected to see the table spread with breakfast, but instead it was spread with papers. A laptop sat open at one end of the table. An enormous bouquet of flowers occupied the window-sill, and Tyrell siblings filled the chairs.

Noah zeroed in on the sibling he loved. "Maggie," he said. "Marry me."

Four pairs of hazel eyes aimed at him. Then a pair of brown eyes joined them as a woman—Sandy's wife, Noah guessed—materialized in the arched door-way to the kitchen, a full pot of coffee in her hand.

Noah felt like a missionary stumbling upon an an-cient tribe. They stared at him as if he were an alien species. They didn't seem to comprehend his state-ment, and they clearly didn't trust him.

Slowly, Maggie rose from her chair. Her hair rip-pled around her face; her cheeks blushed a delicate pink. Her lips were pursed, her hands on her hips, her brow furrowed. He had never seen a more beautiful sight.

Well, yes he had: Maggie naked, enveloping him, coming. That was just a bit more beautiful.

"I believe 'happily ever after' is possible," he said, figuring he'd better talk fast, before the natives jumped on him and carried him off to be sacrificed to the god of overprotective brothers. "I believe in destiny. I believe I hired you to find the woman I was destined to make my wife, and you did, and you're her. You're she," he corrected himself. "I love you. Marry me."

The woman with the coffeepot turned on Sandy. "Did you hear that? *That's* romantic."

"Are you kidding?" the third brother—Neil, who

looked a bit more like Maggie than like Jack and Sandy—blurted out. "It's the ravings of a madman."

"We're in the middle of a business meeting here," Maggie said. Noah wondered whether anyone besides him could hear the quiver in her voice.

"Go right ahead," he said generously, waving at the table. "Just say yes and get back to your business."

"Noah, I'm not going to—"

"Oh, I think you should," the other woman said. She placed the coffeepot on a trivet on the sideboard between two other lavish arrangements of fresh flowers and circled the table to Noah, her right hand extended. "I'm Maggie's sister-in-law, Karen," she said, shaking Noah's hand. "And I'll tell you what I think. Maggie's so busy making sure everyone else solves their romantic dilemmas, she's overlooked her own. I think you and she should straighten this out right now. It's more important than how to merge Finders, Keepers with Tyrell Investigative. That's my opinion. And now, if you'll excuse me, I'm going to vomit." She turned and dashed out of the room.

"She's pregnant," Sandy explained.

Noah nodded cautiously. Karen's condition ranked with Maggie's business in Noah's mind—important, but not as important as solving their romantic dilemma. He would rather not do it in front of her brothers, but if he had to, he would.

"I love you," he said again. Every time he said it, he felt stronger, happier.

"How do you know?"

"I went to New York and saw what my life had

been like, what it was like without love in it. I wanted an adventure—and I realized that love is the greatest adventure of all. I wanted to make the world a better place, but the best way to do that is with love.'' This was coming out all wrong. He sounded like a corny greeting card.

And she was still standing there on the other side of the table, staring at him.

The hell with it. He stormed around the table, swooped Maggie into his arms and sighed in satisfaction as she relaxed against him. "I know I love you, because when I left, nothing made sense anymore. Nothing made sense but coming back to you.''

Maggie sighed, too. It sounded a little like a sob, a little like a purr of contentment. "Okay,'' she said.

"You'll marry me?''

"I'll ask you to check these contracts. Jack wants to make Finders, Keepers a subsidiary of the family firm, and I don't understand all the small print.''

"It's not small print,'' Jack insisted. "It's standard contract stuff. Do you think I'm ripping you off, here? We're family, Maggie.''

She leaned back and peered up at Noah. "I want you to go through these contracts the way you went through Delaney's release form. Will you do that for me?''

Noah chuckled. "I'll do anything for you, Maggie. Even that.''

She smiled. It was a golden smile, an easy-to-read smile, a smile that said yes. "I'll tell my brothers to sheath their swords,'' she murmured. "I love you, Noah. And maybe someday they will, too.''

"Are you kidding?" Jack called across the table. "I already love him better than you. What do you think, Neil? Is Maggie good enough for him?"

"I think she should marry him," Neil suggested, "and then stay home and keep house for him while we milk her company for all it's worth. What do you think, Sandy?"

"Huh?" Sandy mumbled. "I don't get it. How is this romantic? He didn't even bring her flowers."

"Meet your brothers-in-law," Maggie whispered to Noah. "They're part of the 'happily ever after' deal."

"It's a good deal," he whispered back. "I don't even have to read the small print to know this is as good as it gets."

She wrapped her arms around him, and there, in front of all her brothers, she sealed the deal with a kiss.

HARLEQUIN SUPERROMANCE®

9 MONTHS LATER

DEBORAH'S SON

by award-winning author
Rebecca Winters

Deborah's pregnant. The man she loves—the baby's
father—doesn't know. He's withdrawn from her for reasons
she doesn't understand. But she has to tell him. *Wants* to tell
him. She wants them to be a family.

Available in October
wherever Harlequin books are sold.

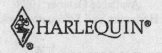

HARLEQUIN®

HSR9ML

SEXY, POWERFUL MEN NEED
EXTRAORDINARY WOMEN WHEN THEY'RE

Destined for Love

Take a walk on the wild side this October
when three bestselling authors weave wondrous stories
about heroines who use their extraspecial abilities to
achieve the magic and wonder of love!

HATFIELD AND McCOY
by HEATHER GRAHAM POZZESSERE

LIGHTNING STRIKES
by KATHLEEN KORBEL

MYSTERY LOVER
by ANNETTE BROADRICK

Available October 1998
wherever Harlequin and Silhouette books are sold.

HARLEQUIN®
Makes any time special ™

Silhouette®

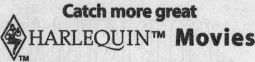

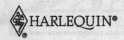

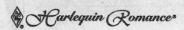

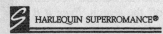

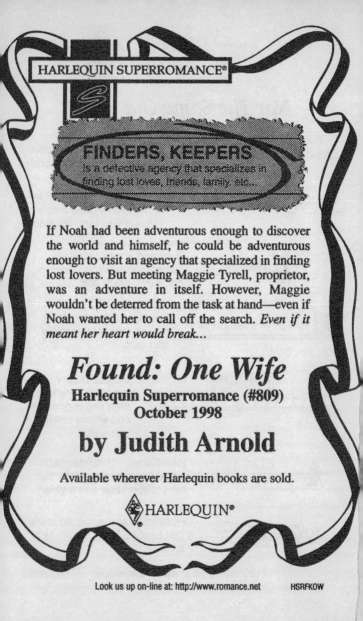

HARLEQUIN SUPERROMANCE®

FINDERS, KEEPERS

Is a detective agency that specializes in
finding lost loves, friends, family, etc...

If Noah had been adventurous enough to discover
the world and himself, he could be adventurous
enough to visit an agency that specialized in finding
lost lovers. But meeting Maggie Tyrell, proprietor,
was an adventure in itself. However, Maggie
wouldn't be deterred from the task at hand—even if
Noah wanted her to call off the search. *Even if it
meant her heart would break...*

Found: One Wife

**Harlequin Superromance (#809)
October 1998**

by Judith Arnold

Available wherever Harlequin books are sold.

HARLEQUIN®

MEN at WORK

All work and no play?
Not these men!

October 1998
SOUND OF SUMMER by Annette Broadrick

Secret agent Adam Conroy's seductive gaze could hypnotize a woman's heart. But it was Selena Stanford's body that needed saving—when she stumbled into the middle of an espionage ring and forced Adam out of hiding....

November 1998
GLASS HOUSES by Anne Stuart

Billionaire Michael Dubrovnik never lost a negotiation—until Laura de Kelsey Winston changed the boardroom rules. He might acquire her business...but a kiss would cost him his heart....

December 1998
FIT TO BE TIED by Joan Johnston

Matthew Benson had a way with words and women—but he refused to be tied down. Could Jennifer Smith get him to retract his scathing review of her art by trying another tactic: tying him *up?*

Available at your favorite retail outlet!

MEN AT WORK™

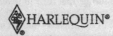 

COMING NEXT MONTH

#810 BUFFALO GAL • Lisa McAllister
Home on the Ranch
When Dr. Andrea Moore awakes on her wedding day, the last
thing she expects is to end up—still single—stranded with a
rock band on her new buffalo ranch in North Dakota. True,
she is a vet, but a *buffalo* vet? More surprising still is her
attraction to the foreman, Mike Winterhawk. He wants her
ranch, and she seems to want...*him!*

#811 BEFORE THANKSGIVING COMES • Marisa Carroll
Family Man
Widower Jake Walthers is a hardworking man who's busy
taking care of his three young children. He doesn't have time
for anything else—certainly not love. Then an accident leaves
him in need of help, and his neighbor Allison Martin is the
only one he can turn to. He doesn't mean to fall for Allison—
she's too "big city" for his liking—but when he does, he
learns she has her own reasons for not getting involved....

#812 IT HAPPENED IN TEXAS • Darlene Graham
Guaranteed Page-Turner
Every morning since her husband's death, Marie Manning
wakes up and reassures herself that her children are fine
and her home is secure. But her world goes from safe to
scary when a neighbor makes a grisly discovery on Marie's
ranch. It doesn't help that Sheriff Jim Whittington thinks
Marie knows more than she's telling. And it *certainly* doesn't
help that her heart beats a little faster every time the sheriff
comes over.

#813 JULIA • Shannon Waverly
Circle of Friends
They'd been friends growing up, living on the small East
Coast island called Harmony. Now one of them is dead,
and Julia Lewis goes home for the first time in seven
years. To a funeral... But coming home is also a chance
to reconnect with her circle of old friends—and to meet
a new man, Ben Grant. A man who causes complications
in Harmony's world...and in Julia's.